PROMETHEUS

Alex Domokos
with
Rita Y. Toews

Hard Shell Word Factory

I would like to acknowledge the help of several people who made this wonderful story come to life—Bonnie, Carol, George, and Lynn. Thanks guys!

ISBN: 0-7599-0567-3
Trade Paperback
Published December 2002
© 2002 Alex Domokos and Rita Y. Toews

eBook ISBN: 0-7599-0566-5
Published November 2002

Hard Shell Word Factory
PO Box 161
Amherst Jct. WI 54407
Books@hardshell.com
http://www.hardshell.com
Cover art ©

"Gather around so that I can tell you what will happen to you in days to come."

- Genesis 49.1

"Prometheus, you are glad that you have outwitted me and stolen fire... but I will give men as the price for fire an evil thing in which they may all be glad of heart while they embrace their own destruction."

- Zeus to Prometheus 1. Hesiod, Works and Days 55

Prologue

BROCK,

Hi old buddy, are we still talking? I'm sorry it took so long to get back to you with the URL for the Nepal site, but with a new baby around the house everything is in turmoil.

When Reg and I joined that trek a couple years back, we were instructed to review this site.

www.lonelyplanet.com/destinations/indian_subcontinent/nepal/

It has some good info and several maps for the region you would be interested in. We heard quite a bit of talk about the Yeti from the locals while we were there, so the ISONS expedition is headed in the right direction.

I got to tell you I'm pretty well green with envy about your trip. Wish I could be going with you but I guess I had my share of adventure before I settled down.

Take care and we'll compare notes when you get back. Cheryl sends you her love and wishes you a safe journey.

All the best,
Steve

Chapter 1

Near Future
Zero Time Minus Eight Weeks
China

COWARD! It's easy to take the moral high road when your neck isn't on the line, but when integrity comes at a personal price...

Colonel Yun-Kai paced the cramped area of his office. Four paces forward, four back. Midway along the route, his gaze was drawn to the black video-phone on his desk, equipped with a direct scrambled line to his superior officer in Beijing. Although reluctant to make the call, he considered himself a man of integrity, and as such, he felt compelled to express his concerns.

The invisible fist that had gripped his intestines the previous evening gave another squeeze and he gasped as an explosion of pain rocked his body. From past experience, he knew the problem would disappear after he stopped wrestling with his conscience. As the agony subsided, he ran a trembling hand through his hair and wedged his bulk into the chair behind his desk. It was time to make the call.

He reached for the phone, and then paused. A conversation about security issues should be done face to face, but his isolated location and the swift advance of the campaign, code named *Avalanche*, made a meeting impossible. And to question his superiors' decision could prove disastrous if they felt he was criticizing *Avalanche*. Yet, the consequences if the strategy went bad were too horrific to contemplate.

Frustrated with his own cowardice, Yun-Kai slammed his fist on the desktop.

It's madness! It will never work. My instincts, and this cursed gut, haven't failed me yet.

The small communications room, part of a massive bunker complex located forty feet beneath the ground of Kashgar, was cold, yet Yun-Kai wiped his sweaty palms on the front of his uniform. After a struggle that pitted his sense of moral obligation against both his job security and his family's honor, he activated the call to the capital.

Honorable ancestors, forgive this foolish man for any shame he may bring to your name, he prayed as the connection was made.

The lean face of General Huan Piao appeared on the screen. "Have the scanners picked up something interesting, Colonel?" Piao asked in a friendly manner. It was a false friendliness, a thin veneer that covered a legendary explosive temper.

"Nothing unusual, General. But it's not the Kashgar station I'm calling about. I feel..." As he hesitated his gut gave another squeeze and the pain forced him to try again. "I feel that it's my duty to discuss the potential danger of campaign *Avalanche* with you, sir." He was now committed to having his concerns heard.

"Danger? What danger?"

"Once *Avalanche* is implemented, in the event of a Red Alert—"

"What the devil are you talking about?" The slow pace and careful enunciation of General Piao's words underscored the anger in his voice.

Yun-Kai groaned inwardly. His worst fears were realized. Once again he cursed the day he had been made privy to the knowledge that China's rocket delivery system was, within certain parameters, a self-launching automatic respond system.

The accusing finger that Piao stabbed at the screen loomed large in Yun-Kai's sight, blocking out the face of his superior.

"I don't remember when you were given the authority to comment on decisions made by your superiors! Need I remind you why you're at Kashgar, Colonel? You're to keep an eye on The Soviet Nation's underground weapons testing. Nothing more!"

For decades after the break-up of the Soviet Union, corrupt officials and others with power had joined together to form the Russian Mafia. This criminal organization stripped whatever flesh was left on the carcass of the country. Finally, the people demanded order, and welcomed a right wing nationalistic dictator who consolidated power by whipping up resentment against the West. The former Russia was now forcibly restored to her previous power under the name The Soviet Nation, complete with a nuclear arsenal and a fanatic at the helm.

Despite the rebuke from his superior, Yun-Kai forged ahead. "Nervousness, stress, unforeseeable miscalculation...General, the retaliatory systems on both sides are automatic and irrevocable."

"You're talking nonsense! You know very well that there'll be no atomic explosion that could trigger an automatic reaction."

"I realize that *we* won't trigger a nuclear explosion, General. But a third party—"

Piao opened his mouth to interrupt but Yun-Kai pressed on. "Iraq, Pakistan or even Korea! Intelligence indicates that Korea's new dictator has surrounded himself with hard-line military advisers." Yun-Kai was relieved to express the nub of his concern.

"It's not my habit to discuss intelligence issues on the phone, Colonel! Even on a scrambled line. But I can assure you that there's not the slightest sign that Iraq is prepared to test again at this time. The international outcry last year has put—"

"But a risk still exists!"

"Enough, Colonel!" Piao thundered. His face was dark with anger and he leaned closer to the screen. "Europeans and Westerners alike have abused us for centuries and now we have Korea breathing down our necks. It's time we regain the position we deserve in the world! This is a nuclear age, and we have no alternative but to obtain nuclear capability on a par with the Super Powers. Look what happened when we took back Taiwan! There's a certain risk involved, *that* I will concede. But without risk we remain a ridiculous giant with feet of clay. Do I make myself clear?"

"Of course, General." Yun-Kai slumped in his chair, defeated.

"Good. We'll have to discuss your posting in Kashgar at our next meeting, Colonel." A blank screen signaled the end of the conversation.

DOES THIS upstart dare to question his superiors' decision? Piao fumed as he severed the connection. *Everything is on target and now this fat buffoon, sitting in a hole in the ground, is going to tell the best strategic minds in the Republic of China that they're making a mistake? The necessary connections in New Delhi have been made and Campaign Avalanche will go ahead as scheduled!*

Piao was never in favor of Yun-Kai being included in the select few who were aware of the true nature of *Campaign Avalanche* and in fact, had even voted against it at the decisive meeting. The phone call was proof that his initial misgivings were justified.

In his opinion, campaign *Avalanche* was brilliant. China needed as much data as possible regarding East-West nuclear strength to plan the strategic location of its own rocket delivery system. To this end, Chinese covert agents passed information to both America and The Soviet Nation, implying that the other was on the verge of developing a satellite paralyzing system. The mere possibility that such a system existed would force both countries to take steps that the Chinese could use to evaluate the nuclear capabilities of the two nations. Such an international "war game" would give China the edge needed for correct evaluation, or further modification, to her own nuclear arsenal.

THE CALL was a disaster. Yun-Kai stared at the blank screen. He had questioned his superior and would pay dearly for it. If *Avalanche* proved a stunning success, Piao would see to it that he was dismissed in disgrace.

Earlier in the day the latest coded report from Beijing had arrived. "The seeds have been sown," it stated. To force the hand of the Americans and The Soviet Nation, the Chinese were using an expedition in Nepal organized under the auspices of the International Society of Natural Sciences, or ISONS, as bait. Insinuations were made to convince each country that the other had an agent among the members of the expedition. The report now in Yun-Kai's hand stated that both sides had reacted to the intelligence with a flurry of coded exchanges to their field officers.

With a weariness that owed nothing to his years, he pressed a signal button to summon his duty officer, Tsong Mei. The young lieutenant responded immediately and snapped to attention in front of the narrow desk. Not for the first time Yun-Kai envied the man both his youth and his slim physique.

"Lieutenant, bring me up to date on the ISONS expedition."

"Sir, a chain of patrols has been established to observe the expedition. Our agent in Kathmandu, a local named Loanche, has ensured that the baggage train and the yak drivers required by the ISONS will be hired from him. He's also been hired as the group's guide."

"What information did Loanche get regarding the expedition?"

"He's been advised that information we've received causes us to question if the expedition is a genuine scientific venture. There's a possibility it's a cover for a covert mission. He's to observe whether any member of the expedition shows an unusual interest in the radio transmitter, or whether anybody makes an attempt to get in contact with suspected Soviet or Western agents in the area. Basically, he's to report any activity not compatible with scientific observation."

With a grunt, Yun-Kai rose from his seat and again paced the small area in front of his desk. "How will he pass his information on to us?"

"Through some of our patrols who are linked by radio with us here at the Center. They've been instructed to mingle with legitimate caravans that will come into contact with the expedition group. That way there'll be plenty of opportunities to pass messages back and forth. They've always been very discreet when contacting us in the past."

"Excellent, Lieutenant. The less Loanche knows, the less danger there is of information being leaked."

"Thank you, Colonel."

In the harsh glare of the overhead fixture Yun-Kai saw a faint smile of hidden pleasure on the lieutenant's face. He dismissed the man, allowing him the impression that he was party to a state secret.

So, our young lieutenant is also under the impression that there's something special about that radio transmitter, and that an agent is attached to the expedition. We create the situation we want by letting Loanche's clumsy intrusion arouse their suspicion. Then, as is inevitable, suspicion breeds suspicion and observers on both sides will report some unusual activity. Danger? Yes. But perhaps the General is right. A country can't gain anything without risk.

Chapter 2

Zero Time Minus Seven Weeks
USA

BROCK LOWDEN sat in the airport lounge rotating a glass of Chivas between his palms. One of the planes on the tarmac beyond the plate glass window was undoubtedly his, and he would give anything to be seated on it now, rather than confined to this lounge with his companion.

Earlier in the day Major Colin Podlanski had reached him by telephone at his home. Brock thought he'd made it quite clear during that conversation that he had no interest in the urgent matter his former senior officer wanted to speak to him about, yet, Podlanski had tracked him down at the airport. He was annoyed with the man's persistence; Brock had too many things on his mind to be bothered with saying no. Again.

"Major, please...just hold it right there." Brock held up his hands to halt the flow of words. "I've been out of the Marine Corps for quite a few years now, and you're no longer my commanding officer, so I'm going to tell it to you straight. You're attached to the Special Intelligence Branch now, so I don't know why you'd want to have this conversation with me." He felt his annoyance ratchet up a notch as he spoke. "I told you on the phone—I've no interest in being part of any spy game your agency is involved in. As a matter of fact, I'm on my way out of the country. If my flight hadn't been delayed, I would've been long gone an hour ago."

Podlanski crossed his legs, taking the time to rest one ankle on the opposite knee. He examined the cuff of his dress pants before he brought the full force of his dark eyes to bear on Brock. "The years haven't mellowed you, Brock. You always did lay it on the line. The agency knows you're on your way to Nepal as part of the advance team for an expedition. And this flight of yours will remain delayed until you and I finish our conversation. You might as well hear me out. The quicker I have my say, the quicker the flight is cleared."

The hand with the glass on its way to Brock's lips made a slow descent to the table. Clear gray eyes beneath unruly eyebrows burned with anger. The corners of his generous mouth, normally curved in a friendly manner, were now taut, sharply defining the lines that ran upward to a finely molded nose. "You son-of-a-bitch! You've been prying into my personal life. You're responsible for my plane being delayed? What the hell's going on here!"

It struck him then that the lounge was unusually quiet. No soft murmuring of couples saying good-bye, no nervous laughter as white-knuckle flyers drank the edge off their dread. A quick look around the room confirmed his suspicion. They were alone. Just inside the door a burly individual in a dark suit stood guard.

"To put it bluntly, Brock, we need your help. I won't waste your time by talking about duty, loyalty, or patriotism. You were open about those sentiments when you left the Marine Corps after that debacle in the Middle East. I can't command you to cooperate, of course, but once you've heard me out I'm hoping you'll agree to our request—willingly."

"The little game of chess that governments around the world have been playing with flesh-and-blood pawns has gone into check, has it? What happened? Used up all your armies and now you have to turn to civilians for help?"

Brock's term in the Marines had given him a hard dose of reality. In his opinion, inflexible governments around the world found it easier to march armies into slaughter than to back off and find a peaceful solution to their problems. Consequently, humanity traveled on a powder keg in space. After the break-up of the Soviet Union in the last century, enough nuclear material had fallen into the wrong hands to blow up the earth five times over. Somewhere, at any given time, a terrorist group could make demands using the weight of their bombs as leverage. Unstable minds with enough power to destroy the entire globe—the perfect recipe for annihilation.

Podlanski squared his shoulders at the rebuke. "Oh, come on, Brock. I'd hardly characterize the world's problems as a game. India and Pakistan are at each other's throats again, and both have their fingers on a nuclear button. That's not what I'd call a game."

"What do you call 'my bomb is bigger than your bomb'? A game. We've both been part of that behavior on the playground when we had pissing contests as kids.

Podlanski's thin lips tightened. "So, in your view, the professional soldiers, or rather their governments, see the world and its problems through the simplistic mind of a—for lack of a better word—bully?"

"Colonel, it's the constant preparation for war in the name of peace that's too simplistic. Not only simplistic, but also outdated and insanely dangerous. Remember old Teddy Roosevelt's concept of 'speak softly but carry a big stick'? That was already outdated when he quoted it from Proverbs."

"A harsh judgment, and an unfair one," Podlanski shot back. "It's been more than sixty years since there's been a major war! Call it whatever you like, I don't care. Why we have peace is irrelevant," his hand slashed the air to emphasize his point, "as long as we have it. Maybe fear holds a better assurance of peace than the wishful aspirations of the idealists. Brock, you weren't even born yet when the horror of the Second World War ended. You know the past only through books written by men with big prejudices, and the perfect vision of hindsight."

"Say what you will, I know about the horror of Hiroshima, Auschwitz, Afghanistan...should I continue? No prejudice can alter the facts. And the facts sicken me." As angry as he was, Brock was relieved to air his grievances.

"All right," conceded Podlanski as he leaned forward in his seat. "You know the facts of yesterday's wars. But we live in a new reality. Today, peace is based on the assumption that no country can achieve absolute superiority over another. If, by some chance, one country could destroy another's atomic arsenal, then and only then would the road to a new worldwide conflict be open. In that case, the one in the superior position would be able to dictate its terms to the other."

"And that's the true aim of all nuclear powers, isn't it—to be in a superior position? Yet each claims that its aim is the prevention of the superiority of the other. This type of thinking creates a snowball that grows bigger and bigger and the danger of destruction grows with it."

"We're very aware of that." The major's tone had become more conciliatory. "Despite what you may think, we're not stupid. Brock, you served under my command in Lebanon. We've buried comrades together and that's a strong bond. If it weren't for that bond between us, I wouldn't be here talking to you today."

"Save your breath, Major." Brock jerked his thumb in the direction of the tarmac beyond the window where aircraft shimmered in the afternoon sun. "Just clear my plane for take-off so I can get on with my business. You'll be pleased to know that life does continue peacefully, despite the nasty cloak and dagger dealings of governments."

As though to mock his words, one of the automatic announcements from the public address system broke into their conversation: "Passengers are reminded not to leave their bags unattended. Any unattended baggage will be confiscated by security personnel."

A thin smile split Podlanski's narrow face and his shoulders rode out a silent chuckle as the weight of the words settled on them. "Let's try this conversation again, shall we? I'm interested in your views about the building tension between China and The Soviet Nation."

Brock sighed and settled into the padded comfort of the lounge chair. It looked like the quickest way to get out of here was to go along with the chat. "I don't see the rivalry as the core of the problem. It's the growing complexity of their technology that's causing the real danger. The more complex a machine is, the greater the potential for failure. And what's more complex today than defense technology? I don't think Doomsday will be the result of a deliberate action. I think it'll be caused by a stupid high-tech failure."

He looked around for the waitress to order another drink. Since Podlanski had asked for his opinion he was going to get it, even if it took a while. The waitress stood with the barman, both trying not to appear too curious. When he waved her over she glanced at the guard near the door, and only moved in Brock's direction when the sentry gave her a nod.

She reminded him of Kate. Maybe it was the hairstyle, or the set of her shoulders. Damn! Why had he let that memory out of its box? It had been almost a year since they parted company. It was actually a good thing he was uninvolved right now. The trip to Nepal was open-ended, but he figured he'd be gone close to four months. The last thing he wanted to do was divide his attention between his job on the trek and any commitments he had in the States.

He ordered a drink and she hurried off.

Once she was out of earshot, he picked up the conversation again. "Given the complexity of computers and programs, we've developed computers that have the capability to practically think for themselves. If we were put in a certain situation today, I think retaliation could result from mechanical judgment overriding human reasoning. Nobody can anticipate every scenario leading up to an aggressive act. What's to prevent a fault in a program that allows the creature to completely destroy its creator?"

Brock took a certain satisfaction in seeing Podlanski stir uneasily in his seat. Obviously this conversation was slipping down paths that the Major hadn't considered when he'd forced the meeting.

"I'll concede that that's a possibility," the older man admitted grudgingly. "But the extinction-of-humanity scenario is impossible, Brock. Some humans would survive on the uplands of the Pamir, in the remote valleys of the Cordilleras, or in the Arctic wastes."

"Oh yeah, what a consolation!" Brock barked. "A few isolated groups of hunters and gatherers who can't possibly recreate civilization. You're talking of a return to the Stone Age! That's not much of an encouragement, my friend."

"And what's the alternative? Would you find it acceptable to live life controlled by some hyped up demigod who somehow managed to get his hands on secondhand nuclear material that was sold off the back of a truck? Is that a more appealing civilization to you? I dread the thought of mind control more than the hardships of the Stone Age."

"I don't want to be dragged into the quagmire of politics."

"I agree." Podlanski heaved a sigh of relief. "Look, what I'm asking for is a few minutes of your time. I don't think I would be wrong to say that under this facade of indifference there's a Brock who cares about his country. I'd like to talk to him."

"All right, all right. Let's get it over with." He might as well listen to what the old bastard had to say. It didn't look like there was any way out of it. He resigned himself to the spiel.

"Look, I'm not trying to twist your arm here. The decision as to whether or not you'll cooperate is yours. In a few days you'll be in Nepal... where we can't force you to act. If you agree to help us it will be of your own free will."

The waitress returned and set Brock's drink on the small table. Before he could fish into his pocket for the proper change to pay for the drink, Podlanski handed the girl a bill and waved away the change. With a smile of thanks she palmed the money and took her leave.

Brock raised the drink in a silent salute and continued. "This is in connection with the expedition, is it?"

"It is. Without getting into details that would compromise national security, the Central Asia desk received some disturbing information about a Soviet Nation breakthrough in laser technology. According to these sources they've reached the experimental stage of a satellite-paralyzing system. Do I have to explain what that means?"

"No." Brock sucked in his breath in surprise. All his former bravado had just been talk in response to a hypothetical situation. It was no longer hypothetical. "If our satellites are out of operation, then we're vulnerable to an attack from whoever decides to take a shot at us. Even technological illiterates like me can see that."

Podlanski nodded. "And it's a real danger. No Nation can tolerate being at the mercy of its rival. Fortunately, we also know that the system is only in the experimental stage. Unfortunately, there's a possibility that they're ready to conduct a high-altitude experiment. The hint is that this expedition you're on is a cover for that experiment. Since their operational forces are nearby, it would be a convenient opportunity to test the system."

"Why the hell would they do it outside their own territory? It doesn't make sense."

"Don't ask me." Podlanski threw his hands into the air in a helpless gesture. "The whole thing might be a feint to test our reaction. But my top man thinks we can't afford to ignore the possibility. Sometimes the most improbable idea is the way to avoid suspicion."

"And, it may be misinformation."

"True. But we have to pursue it."

"That would be where I come in, right?"

"Right. There's no need for heroic actions or valiant self-sacrifice. All we're asking is that you keep an eye on the members of the expedition—especially those from the Ural bloc. There are two of them; Rudolf Weiner, an archaeologist and Ludec Kabela, a Czech defector. You can be our Government's eyes and ears on the trip. It's imperative we know if anything of an experimental nature regarding a laser takes place on that expedition."

"What do you mean...keep an eye on them?" Brock asked warily. He realized he was going to agree to the request. Podlanski was right. For all his disillusionment as a former Marine, he was still a man who loved his country. Or perhaps it wasn't so much his love for his country that was forcing his hand, as much as it was the horrific consequences of any one country gaining nuclear superiority over another.

He shook his head and suppressed a shudder. *I'm just minutes away from departing for Nepal on a major expedition, and I'm allowing myself to be briefed for a spy mission. The old boy still has the power to bend men to his will.*

As though he sensed the weakening, Major Podlanski pressed forward. "I mean just that. Keep an eye on them. Do they have any unusual equipment or do they behave in a strange way? Watch for anything inconsistent with a legitimate expedition."

"Don't you want me to photograph the equipment or record their conversations—*a lá* James Bond?" teased Brock, raising an eyebrow.

"We don't want you to jeopardize your own position. No records are necessary, Brock. All we want are your observations. The instrument may not even exist. We need to know whether the information is authentic or misinformation."

"So, all you're asking me to do is be a silent observer. And how do you expect me to report back to you?"

"You won't report 'til the expedition is over. We can't maintain an effective link in the remote conditions of Nepal without arousing suspicion. As soon as you're back we'll meet with you again. I have a suspicion that the laser is real. One thing you might keep your eye open for is a Chinese involvement. One way or another the Chinese are bound to show their interest. After all, their primary concern is the balance between The Soviet Nation and ourselves."

"Well," conceded Brock as he slapped his hands on his thighs and rose to his feet, "it doesn't sound like too onerous a task. Now, Major, if you'd be so kind, I think there's about two hundred very impatient travelers who are anxious to get off the ground. How long before that flight can be cleared for take-off?"

Podlanski grinned and removed a transmitter from his pocket. "How long will it take you to get to get that carcass of yours on the plane?"

Chapter 3

Zero Time Minus Six Weeks
Paris

LUDEC READ the letter through a second time, but it still made no sense. To receive a letter from Marica, his sister's daughter, was unusual in itself, but this letter was very puzzling.

For their own protection, after he had defected from Slovakia to the West eight years earlier, Ludec Kabela reduced his contact with his family to a postcard each year at Christmas. In the first few years after his escape, he was sure that even the one communication a year was reason enough for the secret police to harass them for several weeks after its receipt.

The tone of his niece's letter was over-polite and rigid:

"...therefore, I am asking you, dear uncle, that when my friend presents himself to you in Paris, you will be so good as to give him your full cooperation with his requests. It is very important for the family here in Bratislava that my friend receives all the assistance he needs. I am sure you understand the situation. As an immigrant, you have firsthand experience of how lonely a man can be in a foreign country and how dependent he is on those who will help him."

He lowered the letter and massaged the bridge of his nose for a moment as he dealt with his emotions. *Yes, Marica, I know very well how lonely it can be when a man leaves his homeland. But sometimes the loneliness is easier to handle than the sickness that builds inside from living in a country where politics pits neighbor against neighbor.* He took up the letter once more.

"Mother is well, except for her rheumatism which is now chronic. She sends her regards.

"Thank you for the help, which I am sure you are ready to provide. Your loving niece, Marica."

What a strange note. There was no trace of the sarcasm so typical of Marica. There were none of the sharp remarks aimed at him, as the head of the family, who had to be tested time and time again by her developing self-esteem. He could sense the tension between the lines.

Was the mysterious friend a defector? No, if that were the case he would just appear with a note from Marica. No, she would not jeopardize herself, or a defector, by writing this openly.

A more ominous reason for the letter scrabbled at the edge of his mind. Someone might be using Marica and her mother as bait to secure his cooperation. But why?

A flood of bitter memories overwhelmed him: the persecution because of his upper-class background; the Dean of the University where he taught who feared a potential rival and used political clout to have him exiled; the pain of uprooting his sister and her daughter, Marica, who were dependent on his support; the lover who cared more for her career than she did for him, and the agonizing decision to defect so he could pursue his career in anthropology.

It had been eight years since that nightmare journey to Paris, and freedom. Why would they bother him now?

Ludec was still pondering the meaning of the letter the next day when he received a call from someone who blocked the video screen to remain anonymous.

"I am a friend of your niece, Marica. Would it be possible to meet with you in the Luxembourg Gardens this afternoon?"

"But of course. Shall we say at three o'clock, near the calliope?"

Could it be that the word friend meant suitor? The thought was so ridiculous that Ludec suppressed a chuckle. Marica had always resented his authority. Now, as an independent high school teacher, she would not ask for his permission to marry. Impossible.

Two years ago Ludec had asked, with some trepidation, for a visitor's visa to return to his homeland. To his surprise he received the visa with no trouble. It had been a strange feeling to once again walk the cobblestone streets of Bratislava.

It was during that visit that Marica delivered an oration to her uncle about the suppressive institution of marriage. No, Marica would not announce her marriage in this fashion.

Once more the thought of government coercion came to mind.

While on that visit he had also sought out one of his former colleagues, and they had an opportunity to speak confidentially.

"Ludec, don't believe for a minute that anything has changed for us. Since the Soviets elected Pavlow Medvediew as their president he's done a great job of getting them back on their feet. Now the Soviet Nation is more powerful than ever and holds us in a fierce grip. Slovakia is nothing but an extension of the Soviet into the heart of Europe. It's an illusion that we are an independent state. We are a satellite, nothing more, nothing less."

LUDEC STROLLED along the east walkway of the Luxembourg gardens enjoying the warmth of the surprisingly mild day. Off to his right a crowd of excited children gathered around a balloon seller, their high-pitched voices mingling with the music from the calliope. The carefree scene added extra warmth to the afternoon.

"Professor Kabela?"

The flawless pronunciation of his name left no doubt in Ludec's mind that the speaker was a native Czech and he turned to acknowledge the greeting. With a sense of shock he realized that the person who addressed him was not a friend of Marica's; he was what Ludec thought of as a gray person.

Ludec classified gray people as those who were overly common in appearance. They were neither good-looking nor ugly; they were neither charming nor rude; they were well dressed but not stylish. In short, they were insignificant creatures that blended with the masses without being noticed. Without a doubt this man was an envoy from the Czech government.

"Yes, I'm Professor Kabela," he acknowledged coldly, in English, the universal language. Although his English was heavily accented and very formal, he immediately disliked the man and couldn't give him the courtesy of a reply in his native tongue.

"My name is Karl Hrovka. I'm from Brunn. Let's continue our walk in these lovely gardens, shall we?" The happy sound of children's laughter still reached them on the gentle breeze. "As I mentioned on the phone, I know your sister and her daughter, Marica, very well."

"What can I do for you, Mr. Hrovka?" interrupted Ludec, trying to avoid unnecessary small talk. These gray men left in their paths lies, deceit, and heartbreak. He had left Slovakia for freedom, but the government still had a hold on him through his family. He now realized he would never be free.

"Patience, Mr. Kabela," Karl Hrovka soothed. "The situation needs a bit of explaining. I've been entrusted with the task of speaking to you about your invitation to join the ISONS expedition to Nepal."

"Your sources of information are excellent, to say the least, since the invitation was issued just over a week ago and only a handful of people know about it." For Ludec, the invitation from the ISONS to join the expedition was a great honor—recognition by the international community of his many years of research as an anthropologist. His native country had never seen fit to recognize his accomplishments.

"Oh, my dear Professor, we have outstanding connections in the

Slovak Embassy. And, of course, your lovely niece Marica..."

Ludec's heart missed a beat. Undoubtedly they had contacts everywhere. What pressures had they brought on his family to obtain Marica's cooperation with the letter? They had secured *his* cooperation, and Hrovka knew it.

"Mr. Hrovka, there is no need to drag Marica into the conversation. What do you want? If it is possible, I will meet your demands." It was tempting to lash out physically. He hunched his shoulders and jammed his hands into his pockets.

"We have no doubt at all about your cooperation, professor. We also rely upon your discretion, since any breach of confidentiality would have dire consequences, not only for Marica, but also for her mother."

"Stop being melodramatic and tell me what it is you want!" Ludec snapped and immediately regretted his outburst. With great effort he willed his body to relax. Slowly, he willed his face to settle in a neutral expression.

"It is a simple request. We have reason to believe that the expedition might be used by the West to test a prototype of a satellite-paralyzing system that would eventually be used against our ally, the Soviet Nation. It might be a laser device or something based on light wave technology. We don't know at the moment which member, or members, of the expedition are Western agents."

Two young boys churned by on tricycles, followed closely by their father. Hrovka turned to examine the roses until the trio had passed, then continued walking.

"We do not have a description of the device, but it is most likely to be disguised as a high-frequency radio transmitter. We would like confirmation of the existence, or not, of that instrument. Of course we realize that the information we have received may be nothing more than a misinformation campaign. It is on your observation, at close range, that we will base our evaluation."

Hrovka came to an abrupt halt on the path and turned to his companion. His eyes caught and held Ludec's in a gaze that was so cold that it sent chills down Ludec's spine. "We expect the information we receive from you to be accurate, Professor Kabela. Sooner or later information from different sources will arrive pointing in one direction or another, and if we see that you've misled us, it will have very tragic consequences for your loved ones."

"How am I to contact you?" The question was a mere whisper emerging from his numb throat.

"We will contact you. There is no urgency. It's the accuracy of the information that's important. We'll wait for your return. Just be vigilant and observant. The evaluation of the information is our job. Have I made myself clear?"

"In the most convincing way," Ludec replied.

"Excellent. I bid you good day, Professor," he said with a small smile. Within seconds he had melted into the masses of Parisians and tourists who mingled happily in the sunshine of the Luxembourg Gardens.

Chapter 4

Zero Time Minus Five Weeks

LIGHT STRAINS of a string quartet rose above the gentle murmur of voices in the reception hall of the British Consulate in Calcutta. Sloe-eyed women circulated with trays of spicy Indian delicacies while waiters passed wine glasses to the assembled guests. Nicole Holden excused herself from a group of four women and moved to the edge of the room near an open window. The soft evening air carried the scent of jasmine into the room.

The room was hot and she felt claustrophobic. No, that wasn't quite true. Although she'd rather be anywhere but this reception hall, it was the ladies' curious glances that she wanted to escape. The garden beyond the window looked cool enough for a stroll, but the quartet fell silent and the tall figure of Lord Kildare mounted the dais to the podium.

"Ladies and gentlemen..."

Nicole listened with only half an ear as Kildare welcomed the assemblage to the farewell reception. Craning her neck, she could pick out three of the four men who would be part of the ISONS trek. She couldn't find Andrew anywhere in the crowd. A light tap on the shoulder startled her but she smiled when she saw who it was—Andrew McFairlain, the fifth member of their group.

It was obvious to Nicole, and anyone who met him, that Andrew was a man of the outdoors. Constant exposure to the elements had given his features a weathered looked and etched fine lines around the corners of his eyes. They were confident eyes, eyes that were used to assessing his surroundings and those who occupied it. His voice was mellow, with sufficient authority to make a listener aware that he was used to giving orders, without being demanding.

"I didn't take you for a woman who would hide behind a plant, Nicole."

With a start, she realized that she was in fact standing next to a potted palm. "You're right, it's not where you'd normally find me. I'd like to get my hands on the person who contacted me at the hotel and told me to come down here for a press conference." Her hand directed his gaze down to her tough climbing pants and hiking boots.

He was about to laugh but she placed her finger against her lips and whispered a soft "*shhh*" to silence him. With a smile, she pointed to the podium.

"The aim of this International Society of Natural Sciences expedition is to find a definitive answer to a question which has fascinated mankind for so many years: Does the Abominable Snowman exist? A resolution was passed at an executive meeting of the Society mandating that conclusive evidence be found either to confirm the existence of the creature, or to finally lay the legend to rest.

"We challenge the members of this multi-national expedition to not return empty-handed." He searched the crowd of faces to pick out each member of the group. "Miss Holden and gentlemen of the expedition, you have been commissioned on behalf of the ISONS, and the scientific communities of the world, to find at least one irrefutable piece of evidence regarding the Abominable Snowman. It is immaterial whether that evidence proves the existence of the Yeti, as the natives in the Himalayas call the animal, or proves that there is no such creature. Your mandate is to lay the matter to rest. To this end, there will be no time constraints placed on the length of the expedition."

A polite clapping of hands rippled through the crowd. Women who had previously stared at Nicole's rather odd choice of clothing now smiled broadly and nodded at her. She was special; she didn't have to conform, their looks said.

"The five members of the expedition were carefully selected by the ISONS for their accomplishments in their respective fields. And it's time we introduced them. We'll do this traditionally. Nicole, if you would step up here beside me, please."

Andrew gave her a little push and she picked her way over the tangle of electrical cables to the podium. This was the part she hated—introductions. She pasted a smile on her face and turned towards the crowd and glare of television cameras.

"Nicole Holden is the only female member of the expedition. She doesn't need any special introduction to the North American public. Her frequent appearances on national television networks, as well as her articles in prominent periodicals, have made her a household name in the West. Nicole will be the recorder for the expedition. We look forward to some very entertaining up-dates as your trek progresses."

She returned frank stares with a quick wave.

"The well-known anthropologist, Ludec Kabela."

Nicole watched Ludec detach himself from a small group to come forward. In his late forties, his dark hair had begun to gray at the temples, which gave him a distinguished look. The flutter of applause brought a smile to his lips and softened the sternness of his tense features. The smile did not totally dispel the sadness in his troubled brown eyes.

"Ludec is known internationally for his research work at the Sorbonne in France and was nominated for a Nobel Prize last year for his study on improving isotope dating of fossils. We're honored that he accepted our invitation to join the team.

"Next—Rudolf Weiner, another international figure with a similar background. An East German, Rudi came to the West several years ago and is an accomplished archaeologist, although only forty-one years old. His latest book, which challenges the translation of older Etruscan scripts, has stirred controversy and made his name well-known internationally in archaeological circles."

Rudi bounded onto the dais and shook hands with Ludec and Nicole while the newspaper cameras flashed and TV lenses focused on them.

"Brock Lowden, an American, served in the United States Marine Corps. During his tour of duty with the Middle East Peace-keeping Forces he became interested in historical languages and today he is not only an authority on Early Semitic and Aryan languages, but is also famous for his nonverbal communication studies."

Brock weaved through the mass of people from the far side of the room. Nicole had met the other American member of the team the previous evening at an informal gathering. She'd thought he seemed distracted, as though the prep work for the expedition weighed heavily on his mind.

"The last member of the group, ladies and gentlemen, is Andrew McFairlain. Andrew has made a name for himself as an outstanding mountaineer. His Scottish background is no doubt responsible for his adventurous spirit. Mr. McFairlain has climbed the most inaccessible peaks around the world and is the youngest person to have climbed the famous, or rather infamous, Matterhorn. He is now a veteran of the Himalayas and his presence is an assurance that no terrain will be a barrier in the expedition's climb to success."

Andrew mounted the dais and took his place beside Brock.

"Human imagination has long been intrigued with speculation on the existence of the elusive Abominable Snowman, and it's time to put an end to the suspense. As for accomplishing their goal, all we can do is to wish them every success."

Cheers and thunderous applause followed the end of Lord Kildare's speech.

The reception hall buzzed with excited conversation as the members of the expedition left the dais and circulated among the well-heeled guests. Nicole was aware that the costs of the trek were astronomical, and relied heavily on private donations from generous philanthropists. She did her part in answering what questions she could, but the majority of people wanted to know about their chances of finding the Yeti. These she directed to Ludec.

LUDEC KEPT a close eye on Brock Lowden as he moved among the various groups. Surely the Americans were smarter than to entrust a former Marine Sergeant with intelligence work. "Ex-soldier" was written all over the man. The other American, the woman journalist, would be a far more sophisticated choice.

Several times he saw Nicole steer guests in his direction. Her smile was warm, and when her eyes met his they lacked any trace of guile. This was not the face of a spy.

He knew Brock had joined the organizational group in Calcutta several weeks earlier to help with the preliminary work for the team. He would have had plenty of opportunity to meet with American covert agents while he collected the appropriate supplies and documentation for the expedition.

Ludec took comfort in the fact that his instructions were to merely observe his fellow team members.

MINDFUL OF his promise to Major Podlanski, Brock had watched the members of the expedition arrive at the hotel. Each was accompanied by a crate, or in some cases, crates, of personal equipment.

He was aware that for any group effort to succeed, especially those of a long duration, it was extremely important that the members form a bond of camaraderie. It would be difficult to work in uncertain, and possibly dangerous, circumstances, unless they had confidence and respect for each other.

He tried hard to overcome the uneasiness he felt in the presence of Rudolf Weiner. For all his efforts, the seeds of suspicion sown in his meeting with Major Podlanski had come into full flower.

He watched as the fair-haired German talked with a wealthy British couple. His speech was animated and he seemed over-friendly. Was this a facade behind which the real Rudolf Weiner observed everyone and everything? He knew his feelings had no logical basis, but gut feelings didn't yield easily to the sober warnings from the mind.

It was interesting that he had no such feelings about Ludec Kabela. Despite only a brief meeting the previous evening, Brock got the impression the man was simply not an adventurer at heart. In fact, he found himself drawn to the Slovak scientist in spite of all his intellectual objections. He sensed a deep strength of character there. The trip would be a long and grueling one; he hoped he could come to depend on Ludec when the going got rough.

Chapter 5

Zero Time Minus Four Weeks
Pakistan

"THE RUMOR is ridiculous," Nanda Banerjee declared as he continued with his oral report. "Utterly ridiculous. The opponents know everything about each other that is worth knowing. This shared information is what keeps the equilibrium, so to speak. It's like a stalemate on a chessboard. No one can make a decisive move without losing the game, so only insignificant moves are made, back and forth, endlessly." Nanda accompanied the last portion of his report with the graceful waving of his slender hand.

Bahadur Khan, President of Pakistan, noted with disgust that his visitor's nails were covered with a coat of lacquer. Everything about Nanda Banerjee bothered him, right down to his Indian speech pattern. Words weren't spoken; they flowed out, like water bubbling in a brook.

As Khan lounged in an intricately carved chair behind the wide mahogany desk, he made a conscious effort to hide his contempt for the Hindu. Nanda was, after all, one of his best informers. Khan had found the contents of the intelligence file on Banerjee a fascinating read, but it gave him even more reason to loathe the man.

A wealthy merchant, Nanda had been in the employ of Pakistan's secret service for many years. It was an easy task. The corrupt officials in New Delhi were not too inquisitive about the source of Nanda's wealth, nor were they interested in the origin of the gifts that Nanda used as bribes in return for choice pieces of gossip. These gifts were his key to almost any secret.

Nanda, not content with his connections in both the Pakistan and Indian government circles, had extended his network into the diplomatic corps. And, as a spider carefully spins its web, his silken strands stretched into several other countries.

Diplomats and embassy officials were eager to keep up their connections with the generous merchant, for he gave lavish gifts and lavish parties.

Nanda Banerjee was welcomed in places where Bahadur Khan was only tolerated.

As Khan considered the merchant's information he toyed with the end of a letter-opener, running the smooth pommel over the intricate inlaid design of the desktop. "As things stand now, there's an assurance of peace between the Super Powers since there are no surprises on either side," he mused out loud. "But it would be an extremely unstable world if either the Americans or The Soviet Nation were able to come up with a weapon such as you describe. Then we'd all be walking a tightrope above a bottomless abyss."

"How right you are, Mr. President," Nanda agreed with a slight smile. "That we do not live in such a nightmare of surprises is due to the fact we are able to peek at each other's cards. One might say that my work is to prevent any unpleasant surprises."

Khan ignored this bit of self-praise. "Speaking of surprises, what do you know about this upcoming ISONS expedition by the Royal Geographic Society? I hear from other sources that all is not what it appears. What's behind this smoke screen?"

"I was not able to get much out of New Delhi. But I did learn that the information might come from a kibitzer, a third party standing on the sidelines of this game between East and West. And, as the saying goes, 'for the kibitzer, there is nothing to lose.'"

"Are you talking about China?" This was startling news indeed.

"Yes, Mr. President.

"How the hell can China influence both great powers simultaneously?"

"With a few choice tidbits given to both sides at the same time. You must know, Mr. President, that The Soviet Nation has no monopoly on misinformation."

Nanda's last comment was accompanied with a slight smile of superiority, which struck a raw nerve in the President. Although he had reached supreme power through a swift and bloody coup, he nevertheless battled with an insidious inferiority complex.

Born to an impoverished mountain family, Bahadur Khan had enrolled in the army at an early age to escape the cycle of poverty. In the army, he had been rewarded for what was essentially the bully in him. They labeled it bravery, determination, and ruthlessness. He had advanced steadily up the ladder of power until he was high enough to grab the top position. Despite his current position, he suspected that he was being used, not respected. Officials from The Soviet Nation treated him as an upstart suppressor of his own people; the West seemed to have an even more derogatory and less well-disguised opinion. He could do nothing about their opinion of him, but he would not tolerate someone like Banerjee showing open contempt.

How I'd like to slap the supercilious smile off this effeminate toad's face. Unfortunately, he's very good at what he does. One day though...one day I'll take great pleasure in destroying him. And he'll know who was behind it too. I'll make sure of it.

"Do you have any information as to what the rumors say?"

"My source in Tokyo says there is talk of a laser breakthrough with satellite destroying potential. Naturally, each party is afraid that the other will get ahead of them in that field."

"That information lacks logic. Why would the Americans choose this corner of the world for their experiment? How can anyone sell that nonsense to The Soviet Nation? On the other hand, why should the Americans buy into the idea of the possibility of a Soviet experiment outside their own borders?"

To the dictator's great annoyance, the superior smile broadened on the merchant's face.

"Mr. President, the mistrust between the two powers has reached enormous proportions. The Soviets still blame the Americans for the economic collapse of the last century, from which they have only recently managed to recover. They feel they can no longer afford to ignore any possibilities when it concerns the West. So they are easily convinced that the expedition was chosen for the experiment." Nanda's slim brown hands danced and scribed arcs in the air to emphasize his words.

The shining fingernails and smug expression on the merchant's face were too distracting. Bahadur Khan rose from his desk and made a circuit of the lavish room, straightening pictures on the wall and aligning the edges of books on shelves as he went. From the west window of the Presidential office he watched a line of fighter jets streak by, on their way to patrol challenged air space. How many generations had lived and died while India and Pakistan snarled and snapped at each other over the territory of Kashmir?

Nanda grew edgy in his chair and Khan smiled with pleasure at his discomfort. Finally, he turned to address the merchant. "And the Chinese? What would they gain from all this?"

"That is anybody's guess. But let us suppose that the Chinese were to emit a laser beam of their own and then watch both the Soviet and the American reaction. They would gain valuable information on both countries' ability to detect the transmission and to gauge the speed of their response. It would be information of incalculable value for their future nuclear build-up."

The mid-day sun shot arrows of light through a narrow gap in the curtains. It fell in dappled pools amid the host of gadgets on the desk. Khan parked a hip on the edge of the warm surface. It gave him great satisfaction to be able to look down at the seated man. "I assume, my dear Banerjee, that this is sheer speculation on your part?"

Forming a steeple with his fingers the merchant hesitated before conceding the point. "Yes, it is speculation, but it is logical speculation."

Despite the dictator's calm face, his cunning brain was now in high gear. For decades Pakistan and India had been in a race to develop their own nuclear devices. India was the first to demonstrate her nuclear power and Pakistan followed with a rather weak display ten years later. The enormous outcry from around the world, coupled with threats of trade sanctions, were enough to deter any further tests by Pakistan, but perhaps circumstances were now falling into place that would allow another test.

For a moment the irksome presence of Nanda Banerjee was forgotten as scenarios and the consequences flashed through the president's mind.

Now that China has created this tense situation, each of the parties will point a finger at the other. We would possibly escape detection.

The Soviets will read it as a Chinese experiment, and the New Delhi government can easily be bribed to accept that explanation. The Americans though...hmm, they will be more suspicious of Pakistan, but not too eager to condemn her. We're an important roadblock in the Soviet Nation's new push toward the Arabian Sea.

The Israelis now...yes, they will be the most alarmed. They fear any Islamic state with an atomic arsenal. But I'm sure the United States will be able to control their outcry.

If the site of the explosion is chosen carefully, it will be difficult to lay responsibility for the blast at Pakistan's doorstep.

Eager to get rid of the Hindu, Khan rose and extended his hand with a superficial smile.

"Thank you, Mr. Banerjee, for your valuable information. What can I do in return to express my thanks?"

"If it is not too much trouble, your Excellency, I have an urgent shipment due for France. Would you be kind enough to instruct the harbor authorities at Karachi to get a fast release on it? In commerce, time is money."

Bahadur grunted at the ridiculous explanation. "You mean you don't want to have your ship searched, if I read you correctly." *The man truly thinks I'm an idiot!*

"Yes. A search would delay departure. That, I assure you, is the only reason."

As soon as the merchant left the presidential office, Bahadur pushed the intercom button connecting him to his adjutant.

"I want to speak to the Commander of the Air Force—immediately!"

Chapter 6

Zero Time Minus Four Weeks

BROCK BRACED against the seat in front of him. The chartered plane bucked and shuddered as it labored over the snow-covered peaks of southern Nepal. The metal frame of the aircraft creaked and groaned, conjuring visions of twisted debris buried in an endless stretch of snow, his body torn and frozen in the wreckage.

Partnered by a powerful air current, the plane did a neat side step. His queasy stomach threatened to give up the meager breakfast they had grabbed at the airport. No wonder the flight attendant hadn't offered snacks or drinks.

"Shit!" Rudi, who was seated across the narrow aisle, clenched his armrests in a white-knuckled grip. "Give me solid ground under my feet any day." His normally cheerful countenance was drawn, drained of color.

Nicole peered around from the seat directly ahead of Rudi. With a mock grin on her face she asked in an over-innocent voice, "Would either of you be interested in a sandwich? I brought a few along in my carry-on bag."

The two men answered with weak groans. The plane hit another air pocket that slammed them against their seat belts, and then mercifully entered smoother air.

Brock dug for reading material in the seat pocket in front of him. No in-flight magazine, but intermingled with a number of air-sickness bags he found a few brochures on Nepal. Anything would do, as long as it offered a diversion from the rough flight.

One item in a brochure caught him by surprise. "Would you believe it?" he commented to no one in particular. "It says here that Kathmandu didn't get electricity until the 1960s."

Andrew, who was seated directly behind him, leaned forward and chimed in. "I've been here on a couple of climbs. Apparently, once they got electricity the population in the valley just exploded. I'm sure it was a beautiful place at one time, but now, well..." he left the rest to their imagination.

As the aircraft descended into the smog of the Kathmandu Valley, the trekkers pressed their faces against the small windows for their first view of the capital. Seen from above, the entire twelve by fifteen mile valley was one mass of low buildings, with the spectacular Himalayan peaks as a backdrop. Brock heard the click of Nicole's camera as she framed several aerial shots to accompany the reports for the Society.

"WELCOME! Welcome to our beautiful country." The enthusiastic greeting came from the man who met the trekkers as they exited the immigration hall at the airport. "I am Mr. Jungal, representative of the Ministry of Tourism, and I will be your escort to your hotel. Come. Madam, I will carry that case," he stated as he plucked a bag from Nicole's hand. "Your private bus is just here, outside the door. Come, please."

The little man's energy and beaming round face were in sharp contrast to the greeting of the immigration officers. For an hour they had investigated the crates and personal luggage of the group, then demanded that a trek report be filled out on three separate forms.

En route to the hotel Jungal provided a cheerful running commentary of the sites along the way, interspersed with a brief history of the country.

"Kathmandu is an ancient city that sits at the crossroads of major trade routes linking the empires of India, Nepal, Tibet, and China. Ah...here, you see the Swayambhunath Stupa. Sir, it is beautiful, yes? And there is the all seeing eye of Buddha. There is no nose, just the Nepali number one, indicating there is but one way to enlightenment, and that is through the Buddhist path."

The Stupa was indeed beautiful, but sadly, Brock realized the city was even more congested than was evident from the air. Their bus was forced to crawl through streets clogged with traffic, animals, vendors, worshipers, and trekkers. Advertisements screamed from lofty positions on rooftops, pagodas, and curbsides, exhorting him to purchase computers, satellite systems, pizza, liquor, or hothouse vegetables. Cigarette ads covered entire sides of houses. Evidence of rampant consumerism was everywhere he looked. Stench from the humid cluttered capital oozed onto the bus and hung in his nostrils.

Jungal's voice continued to flow over him. "Because of the tremendous number of visitors to our beautiful country, we have wisely formed guide unions. There would be chaos here if the government of Nepal did not organize the Sherpa guides into groups and unionize them, like the taxi drivers in the West." His chatter was punctuated with broad smiles, which showed a great number of gold teeth.

"When Lord Kildare informed our Minister of Tourism of your esteemed expedition, he entrusted me with the job of looking after you. Your porters have been hired under our best guide, Loanche, who is not only familiar with the land but also speaks English. You see, I have thought of everything."

When he had finished this speech of self-praise the little man gave a small bow from his position at the front of the motor coach, and seemed to wait for applause. Brock fought to conceal his smile.

It was Ludec who thanked the tourism representative for his invaluable assistance. Jungal continued to stand at the front of the bus, beaming at them. To avoid what might become an embarrassing silence, Ludec asked, "Do you know if the crates that were forwarded from Calcutta on Tuesday have arrived? We have a lot of equipment in those boxes. I believe our Society had prearranged with government representatives to clear everything through the red tape."

"Ah, of course! I have the list here," Jungal replied and quickly produced a hand-held computer. With an air of great efficiency and drama he brought the list to the screen and began to read off the contents of the crates: "medical kit, radio in sealed unit—seals intact, antheroscope..."

The mention of the radio peaked Brock's interest. From his seat, where he appeared to be absorbed in the tourism material, he strained to overhear the conversation without drawing attention to himself.

His keen interest was reinforced when Rudi asked Ludec, "Who'll be assigned as the radio operator?"

Ludec seemed uncomfortable with the question, and in his accented English replied, "Why don't we wait until we get together at supper before making any decisions? I know I'm tired from the trip and I'm sure you all feel the same."

Further conversation was cut short as the bus drew to a bone-rattling halt at a small hotel in the Thimi district.

A DINNER gong summoned the group to the private dining room the hotel had assigned to them.

Ludec arrived first, followed by Brock, Rudi, and Andrew. Travel posters, trapped behind scuffed Plexiglas, were interspersed with photos of famous climbing groups to add color to the bland walls. A single table stood in the center of the room

"Hey, Andrew, is this you?" Brock asked as he stabbed a finger at one of the photos.

Ludec wandered over and peered over his shoulder. Andrew and

Rudi crowded in. With a sense of shock that stirred his suspicion, Ludec realized that the group in the photo was identified as a Soviet expedition.

Andrew grinned. "I'll be damned! I'd forgotten about that picture."

Several minutes later Nicole entered the room. Her presence drove all other thoughts from Ludec's mind.

She had changed from the slacks and khaki blouse she wore on the flight to a practical, yet colorful, dress. A touch of make-up highlighted her face and her dark hair was twisted up and clasped in a simple knot. This change was not wasted on Ludec or the other men in the room.

She was about thirty years old, in the prime of her life and comfortable with the circumstances she found herself in. Wide-set, dark eyes peered out from behind the fringe of her eyelashes with complete confidence. As the men greeted her, a smile hovered on her well-defined, full mouth. High cheekbones and a strong chin were saved from masculinity by a softness that was all female.

Once again Ludec looked for signs she might be a mole planted on the expedition. He found none.

"Ah, Nicole, there you are!" Andrew McFairlain cried in delight as she approached the table. "I've saved a chair for you here, beside me. We've taken the liberty of ordering the house wine. All except Rudi here, who prefers his beer." With a flourish he drew a chair back from the table and guided her into it.

"I tried to convince everyone to try one of the local drinks—Raksi, or *chang*, their rice beer, but no one felt very daring this evening."

Rudi held up his hands in surrender. "If it's not made from hops, then it's not beer."

As he spoke, the waiter arrived with two bottles of wine and his beer. The conversation turned to the expedition.

"Are we going to set a point in the climb when we start looking into Yeti sightings?" Rudi asked.

Startled, Ludec realized the question was directed at him. Since they were all internationally recognized personalities, Lord Kildare had avoided imposing a hierarchy on the group, knowing that a natural order would emerge. Ludec had noted several times when the group's members had stepped back to allow him to take charge, tacit acknowledgement of his leadership, or perhaps the deference was due to his age.

He wasn't entirely comfortable with the role. But then, whom would they turn to if he declined the position? Brock. He had the leadership capabilities and the confidence to lead the group. Given the alternative, Ludec decided to accept the role as leader. It would be easier to keep his eye on the American this way.

"I think we should start investigating as soon as the supposed sighting is one the locals actually believe, as opposed to one that they use to get tourists excited. Does everyone agree?"

Everyone agreed to Ludec's suggestion and the conversation continued to flow around the table as they waited for their supper. Ludec tensed when Rudi asked, for the second time that day, about the radio.

"Can someone tell me about our new radio transmitter? I've heard that it's the most sophisticated instrument the ISONS could get their hands on."

"Yes," Andrew replied. "Lord Kildare told me that the Society didn't want breakdowns in communication because of atmospheric disturbances in the higher regions. They've very generously provided us with the latest in satellite radio technology."

"Great, but who's going to handle it?"

At the mention of the radio, Ludec glanced to where Brock was seated. Had he tensed? And why was the German so interested in the radio?

Again Andrew spoke. "I am. On each of my major climbs I've been the radio operator. Plus, I have a background in electronics. The equipment was purchased on my advice and I'll be in charge of it."

This was an interesting piece of news to Ludec. He hadn't realized that Andrew had supervised the purchase of the equipment.

"Ah, here's our supper." Nicole said as two waitresses entered the room carrying large trays. A third followed, rolling a server with carafes and a soup tureen.

After a short silence while they busied themselves with their food, Nicole asked, "So Rudi, what are your thoughts on this Yeti business? You know, we've been so busy with the trek preparations that we haven't had much time to talk about the creature."

"I'm almost embarrassed to admit this," began the German as he took another sip from his beer, "but, even though the story of the Snowmen have been around for years, I haven't heard much about them until recently. I gather that speculation about the Yeti used to be a hot topic, and it's become something to talk about again, I suppose. As a scientist I'll keep an open mind. It's not our job to form opinions, we're here to find facts."

Ludec nodded. "I do not care whether or not the creature exists. What I care about is proving the supposition beyond a reasonable doubt one way or the other." The wine and the meal were enjoyable as was the company. He resolved to relax and put thoughts of conspiracy from his mind until some overt action confirmed Hrovka's suspicions. If he continued to analyze every move each member of the group made, he could build a case against anyone, strictly from speculation.

"Do you think," asked Brock, "that if we were to disprove the legend, and published our findings in scientific journals, that the stories would die out?"

"Not overnight," answered Ludec. "Remember, it took centuries to convince people that the earth was round, so it might need a considerable amount of time to lay the legend to rest—especially among the natives in the mountains. Legends of this sort become so woven into the fabric of their folk tales that it really doesn't matter whether they are believed or not. What really matters is that the story is passed from generation to generation—it's tradition."

They finished the meal, then Ludec rose from his seat, "I don't know about you, my friends, but I'm almost ready to call it a day. Tomorrow we meet our guide and organize the porters. Is there anything more we should discuss tonight?"

"Just one more question, please, before we break up," began Nicole. "Are we walking from the first staging area, or are we going to use trucks? If I understand correctly, only the first portion of the track is accessible by truck."

All attention turned to Andrew. "You've all been preparing for this expedition for some time, but only slow acclimatization can prevent altitude sickness. I suggest we start walking from the staging area to the east of Bhaktapur. It will be a fairly easy climb for the first few days and when we do reach the more rugged regions we'll be more or less accustomed to the altitude and the rigors of the terrain. Any other thoughts on this? Any objections?"

It seemed like a reasonable plan to Ludec and he bid the group good night.

Chapter 7

Zero Time Minus Three Weeks
Near Moscow

FJODOR GILBRECHT, head of Electronic Research, and Vladimir Karanski, chief of Equipment and Security Development, lounged in front of the fireplace in Gilbrecht's *dacha*, enjoying a glass of brandy. The night was chilly and the crackling fire warmed not only the air but their spirits as well.

"A fine dinner, Fjodor. I would like to ask where you got your hands on beef of that quality, but I'm afraid you'll tell me it came from the genetic modification division." Karanski had enjoyed his dinner and was sprawled in his chair, chin resting on his chest. His long legs extended before him, crossed at the ankles.

Gilbrecht nodded his thanks for the compliment. Karanski had an appreciation for fine food so Gilbrecht had put a good deal of thought and effort into tonight's menu. He figured he had one shot at eliciting Karanski's help, and the fact that he had indeed paid a bribe to the head of the genetics division for the modified beef caused him no remorse whatsoever. The gourmet meal and fine brandy appeared to be paying off.

He drew a small plastic case from his pocket then leaned forward in his chair. "It's time to get down to business," he began as he turned the case end over end in his hands. "This little device might be the most important invention in many years. If the actual tests go as planned, it will super-charge the capacity of a conventional laser chip many times over. It's the fourth generation of the super chip. Our entire research group has pushed themselves to the wall in aid of our great homeland."

"You can spare me a propaganda speech, Fjodor. If anybody recognizes the value of your work, I do." Vladimir's voice rumbled up from his massive chest.

Sap from a log on the fire exploded, blasting a shower of fragrant sparks against the brass screen. From the dining room, the sound of dishes and glassware being cleared from the table lent a comfortable air to the setting. Gilbrecht felt some of the tension leave his body. The evening was going very well indeed.

"Perhaps I'm too enthusiastic in my desire to free our great country from dependence on Western technology," he conceded with a smile.

"On the contrary, it would be very nice to rid ourselves of that dependence. But before you continue, do you have any more of this wonderful brandy? I'm guessing that it's Danish."

"Does any other country produce brandy of this quality?" Fjodor asked with a chuckle. "I'm afraid we won't be liberated from the superiority of this Western drink for quite some time." He rose and refilled the proffered glass. "*Na Zdarovje!* To your health."

They touched glasses and sampled the amber liquid, savoring the fiery glow of its passage.

"Now tell me, Fjodor, what's the practical application of this little invention of yours? I'm not a technological person you know."

"You're contradicting yourself, Vladimir. The intelligence branch of your department has been breathing down our necks for more than a year, demanding that we develop a device, or program, to improve our current missile technology. This is the result." He passed the case to Vladimir. There was nothing remarkable about the unit and he wasn't surprised when it was returned without comment.

"With the addition of this little device and accompanying computer program, our anti-nuclear defense system will be greatly updated, maybe even to the point of ninety-five percent accuracy. One of our priorities was that it be free from human interaction. That's the only way we can be sure that someone with itchy fingers doesn't get control of the button."

His words captured his guest's attention.

"This box is an example of precision and sensitivity. It can detect the minutest particle of radiation and analyze it in microseconds. And then, depending on its reading, it will give the command to launch our retaliatory missiles. Our laboratory tests have confirmed that it's so sophisticated nothing but a thermonuclear explosion can activate it. It is foolproof, accurate, and fast. Moreover, it doesn't need the human evaluation that in the past has slowed down our decisions. The computer program that assists the chip is nothing short of genius. In short," Fjodor pronounced with great pride, "when installed, our nuclear protection shield will be far superior to anything the West has."

"Are you implying that with this invention we could achieve nuclear superiority? Fjodor, when you invited me here this evening you promised the best of news, but this news is far better than I dared hoped for." He was on the edge of his seat now, his eyes wide with astonishment.

"My friend, I can say with certainty that about ninety to ninety-five percent of the attacking missiles would be destroyed. Which, of course, surpasses America's destruction capability.

"You realize of course," he continued, "that we need to get this tested and made operational as soon as possible. News of its development will eventually leak out. As much as we hate to admit it, we have to assume that the Americans have their eyes and ears inside this facility. Nothing is secure anymore, even here at Selo 14."

The brain center of the new Soviet Armament Program, Village 14 (Selo 14), was situated near Moscow and was home for select members of a scientific community. Security was tight, and Fjodor's wife often complained that it came at the expense of personal freedom, but he had come of age during the decade after the turn of the millennium and viewed it as a welcome form of protection.

"Does it give us any edge on attack, or only on defense?" His brandy forgotten now, Vladimir rose and warmed his back against the heat of the fire. Outside, on the perimeter road, a car passed the heavily guarded compound. For a moment, headlights probed the darker recesses of the room, and moved on.

"The precious minutes we gain in evaluation will allow us to launch a retaliatory attack almost instantaneously. That gives us a valuable edge on the counter-attack."

"You sound very confident, Fjodor. There's no room for error or malfunction?"

"We did thousands of tests under laboratory conditions. Now we need field tests to see if it functions under actual conditions with ambient values. This means that we need access to the defense network to add the device. Just for a couple of hours."

Karanski reached for the case and examined the contents once more. "There's been talk that your group was looking smug these days. This would explain it. What do you call this miracle device of yours?"

Fjodor was ecstatic. The evening was having its intended effect. "We've given it the code name Phoenix. The Soviet Nation has risen from the ashes. With this device added to our defense system, Vladja, we're going to outshine every nuclear nation out there." It was time to attack the final hurdle. "You're on friendly terms with Big Shot, aren't you?"

Big Shot was the nickname of the District Nachalnik, Anton Petrov, director of the entire research installation. He was also one of the most influential members of the government Central Committee.

"What are you asking, Fjodor? The last thing I want to do is mix friendship with duty."

"I understand that, Vladja. But think of how grateful Big Shot would be if this invention was put into effect under his personal sponsorship."

"True...true," mused the security chief. Deep in thought, he returned to his seat and took up his glass of brandy. "It would help his political advancement."

To say nothing of your own. You're sadly mistaken if you think your aspirations have gone unnoticed.

"Let me tell you what I'm proposing, then you can judge for yourself if it's worth approaching Big Shot.

"We organize simulated war games near the border of the Alliance of Southern States. There's been some nationalist action there so it wouldn't seem out of line if we activate the troops at Tashkent. We've already got several contingents along the northern border of Afghanistan. With India and Pakistan exchanging missiles, it's the best replication of an actual war situation. Perfect to give us the ambient readings we need."

"You've given this a lot of thought. I like what I'm hearing."

"We could insert Phoenix anywhere along our defensive line, in Moscow, Vladivostok, or Irkustk, add the program, then launch missiles of differing calibers just north of the Afghanistan border. If the evaluation of Phoenix confirms our laboratory findings, then Big Shot can be the first to make the announcement in the Party Congress. It would add a little sparkle to his rising star, right?"

"It would mean a lot to him," confirmed Vladimir, nodding. "Imagine the title he might get," he continued, obviously warming to the idea. "Father of the Soviet Nation Anti-Nuclear Defense System, perhaps. It would be a great help in rallying the majority of the Central Committee behind him when the position of First Secretary becomes vacant.

"I think you're right, Fjodor," Vladimir said, clapping his hands together as he came to a decision. "You know what? I have an appointment with him tomorrow morning about eleven o'clock. I'll mention it to him in an offhand way. If he seems enthusiastic I'll call you. Be in your office with all your data prepared in case I ask you to join us. I can't press him, mind you, and I can't promise anything, but be prepared."

Fjodor had difficulty containing his exhilaration and his relief. He had worked hard to develop Phoenix, but his efforts were not solely on behalf of his country. The greater motivation lay in the small second bedroom of the *dacha*.

Fjodor's daughter, Polina, had been born with a heart deformity. She was now in her teens, and if the operation she required wasn't performed within the next two years there was very little chance she would survive into her twenties. If this device and operational program proved successful, Fjodor would be a strong contender for the development bonus awarded each year. The bonus, plus his savings would just cover the cost of the operation.

The men rose from their chairs and Vladimir made ready to take his leave. They shook hands at the door. As he left he called over his shoulder to Fjodor, "In your office, tomorrow morning."

With a small wave of acknowledgment Fjodor closed the door. His whoop of delight brought his wife from the kitchen where she found him capering around the room like a madman.

Chapter 8

Zero Time Minus 48 Hours

IN THE code room at Kashgar station, Colonel Yun-Kai smiled as he read the communiqué from Nepal: "Expedition now on its way to Komcha Bazaar. If they ask for permission to enter our territory, what instructions should we give to the commander of the border guard? How much should we reveal concerning the nature of our surveillance?" Tsong Mei, the same young lieutenant who had served him so faithfully in Kashgar, had signed the encrypted message.

What a stroke of luck, Yun-Kai mused as he re-read the message. *The young fool had acually asked to be transferred. He was far too ambitious to have around the tracking station. Better that he be my eyes and ears in Nepal, than Beijing's eyes and ears here at Kashgar.*

With a flick of his finger he set the communiqué tablet on "encrypt" and sent back an answer, "Maintain high security. Give guards information on need-to-know basis only. Allow to assume that close observation is only normal suspicion extended to all foreigners in region."

As he finalized the forwarding procedure for the message, a tone indicated an incoming call from Beijing. Yun-Kai groaned. Huan Piao was on the other end.

"Colonel, we've been informed of some disturbing news regarding Pakistan. Have you picked up anything there at Kashgar?"

Was there a hint of nervousness in Piao's deep-set eyes? "No, nothing, General." Yun-Kai slid a handkerchief from his pocket and mopped the folds of fat at the back of his neck.

"The news came out of New Delhi, via our Singapore agent. It seems the Pakistani Air Force has been put on alert. I'm surprised you have no information."

"No, nothing has come through here." *Damn the man! He knows that information wouldn't be routed through Kashgar station unless it was picked up in The Soviet Nation. He's out to break me!* Taking a deep breath to steady his voice, Yun-Kai continued, "It could have something to do with the latest uprising in Afghanistan. If the United Islamic government in Kabul falls, then there's not much to stop the

Soviet Nation from moving their troops in. From there, Pakistan is the only obstacle in the way of the Soviets getting that outlet to the Arabian Sea"

"True...Khan has his hands full. Pushed by the Soviets from the north, and by India from the south. He's come whining to us again, asking us to give more support to the Afghan resistance." Piao stretched and cracked a huge yawn. "What's your take on his latest show of force?"

On his end of the videophone, Yun-Kai marveled that the man gave little thought to what was visible to the viewer on the other end of the call. Well, never mind. It was better to watch him clean an ear with his little finger, or pick his uneven teeth, than it was to listen to one of his tirades.

"Pakistan is under constant pressure from the Soviets to make sure they don't aid Afghanistan. Since this is just an alert, I think they're rattling their sabers to show The Soviet Nation that they're not taking the pressure lying down." He merely mouthed what he was sure the General wished to hear.

Pursing his thin lips, the General nodded. "I agree with that assessment. I wasn't worried, but in light of *Avalanche*... some of the others were acting like old women." He finished his statement with a high-pitched snicker that grated at Yun-Kai's nerves.

Piao's cordial attitude was a welcome sign to Yun-Kai. Some of the tension he had felt since the disastrous conversation regarding *Avalanche* began to lift. "I'll report to you immediately, General, if I receive word of unusual developments in Pakistan."

As the connection was severed, he fought back the demon of doubt that capered in the back of his mind. Could Pakistan's action have anything at all to do with campaign *Avalanche?*

Chapter 9

Zero Time Minus 48 Hours
Israel

THE HEAT of the sun was relentless. When he asked for the most private table in the courtyard restaurant, Colin Podlanski hadn't realized that it was also the most exposed. He inched his chair further into the shade of the table's colorful umbrella and welcomed the return of the waitress with his iced tea.

In Israel he was known as Peter Anderson, an American businessman from Massachusetts. To those who cared to inquire, Peter had a wife, Marlene, and two children—Matt, age twelve, and Sonja, age nine. He had a house facing Plymouth Bay, enjoyed both fishing and hunting, and had a net worth of about a million dollars. Some of his cover story was close to the truth.

As he waited for his contact, he silently ran through the important details of his cover story. Recently in Israel there had been a rash of kidnappings of wealthy Americans, and he toyed with the idea of downgrading his wealth a bit. It might make him a less desirable target. Yes, it was time Mr. Anderson had a severe financial reversal.

Christ, it was hot. Where was Malcolm?

Malcolm Singer, his Israeli counterpart, had arranged the meeting, although he'd given no hint of what it was he wanted to discuss. It had been several years since they'd met face-to-face, and, business aside, it would be good to see his old friend again.

Through the noon hour crowd of diners a tall man approached. It was Malcolm. Dressed in tennis garb, he clutched a tennis racket under one arm. Malcolm's features, which could have been either Arabic or Hebrew, had aged gracefully over the years. As he approached, Podlanski noted that a wound he received in Lebanon had left a crescent-shaped scar near the base of his chin. He greeted Podlanski with a broad grin and extended his hand, "Shalom, Peter."

"Shalom, Malcolm," Podlanski replied as he rose and clasped the proffered hand in a warm grip of friendship. "Tell me, is it always so hot this time of year?"

"Usually. The Dead Sea region is one of the hottest on earth."

"Yes, but we're far from the Dead Sea."

"Not far enough."

The conversation was a code. If the Dead Sea was mentioned, the speaker felt it safe to talk freely.

A waitress appeared at the table and Malcolm dispatched her immediately for a glass of ice tea—heavy on the ice. When she returned, both men placed their orders, then settled back and discussed generalities until their lunch arrived.

Malcolm leaned over his plate and asked Podlanski, "Have you received any recent intelligence on Pakistan?"

"Pakistan? Not that I'm aware of. What have you heard?"

"A report of an upcoming Pakistani Air Force exercise. With Pakistan and Afghanistan sharing a border, anything they plan has an impact on the tense situation there."

Podlanski realized he would take no pleasure from this conversation with his friend. He would have to walk a very fine line. "You understand our policy towards Pakistan, Malcolm. We know that Khan is a bastard, but despite his tacit support of the Desert Wind rebels, he isn't a puppet of Islam." With a sinking heart he watched as Malcolm laid aside his fork and shook his head. Podlanski plowed on. "He's stayed the hard line against the fundamentalist Islamic movement implemented by previous..."

"Does it matter what they call themselves? Al-Qaida, Desert Wind...it's all the same. Does a name change make a difference?"

"Of course not! The best thing for both our countries would be to put a lid on the Soviets, let the Pakistanis and Indians exhaust each other and keep all the Arabs separated. Our end goals aren't that far apart."

Malcolm nodded. When he spoke it was with some degree of resignation. "The feeling in our department is that we shouldn't be concerned with the Pakistani move just yet. The Soviets have a keen interest in containing any movement that would indicate support for Afghanistan. We've decided to take a wait-and-see attitude."

Podlanski heaved a quiet sigh of relief. While they were on the subject of Pakistan he decided to do a bit of digging in another area. "By chance, have you heard of any new developments in Pakistan's nuclear program? Any rumblings that they may be preparing for another test?"

"The information we have is from very low-level sources, so low as to be almost speculation. But Pakistan must realize that it would be a foolish move on their part. If they do test, they risk retaliation from several fronts. Any aid from Canada, and of course the U.S., would be terminated. The Soviets might use it as an excuse for a new thrust, but they'd provoke China and India as well. In our opinion—they simply can't afford it."

"So your sources are low-level, eh? I don't want to alarm Washington."

"Don't even bother your embassy about it. It doesn't do any good to cry wolf."

"True. You know where I'm staying. If you hear anything within the next few days, you can reach me there."

The two enjoyed the remainder of their lunch, recounting stories of shared times when both were younger and less burdened with the fallout of angry nations.

A half-hour later they said their good-byes. "Shalom," Malcolm said as he rose from the table. He left, whistling a popular Israeli tune.

The sky had clouded over as they ate, dampening the effect of the heat. Podlanski settled back, content for a moment to enjoy the sights of the good-looking girls lunching in their beach attire.

As Malcolm threaded his way through the press of tables towards the street exit, Podlanski followed his progress. A fair-skinned young woman seated by herself caught his eye and his instincts as a trained intelligence agent stirred.

He had noticed her earlier, when Malcolm arrived. She had come onto the patio and asked for a table in the sun. He'd thought it odd that a person with such light skin would deliberately ask to be seated in the sun.

As Malcolm passed her table she removed her music headphones and tracked him with her eyes. He stepped through the arched doorway onto Ben Yahuda Street. As he cleared the doorway she gathered her possessions and left the restaurant along the same route.

Could Malcolm have been mistaken? Perhaps he was followed to the restaurant.

Chapter 10

Zero Time Minus 48 Hours
Near Moscow Selo 14

THE STRIDENT buzz of the videophone jolted Fjodor Gilbrecht from a deep sleep. His wife, Olga, stirred beside him on the bed but made no effort to answer the instrument. It was a firm rule in the house that she answered the machine only if her husband was not at home.

"Hello," barked Fjodor in a dry voice still choked with sleep.

"I realize the hour is late for a call, Frodja, but I'm sure you won't mind. We've been able to move the tests on Phoenix up by several weeks. Your new device has made quite the impression on the boss and others very high up in the government."

"On whom?" Still groggy, he rubbed his eyes and struggled to focus.

"You're still asleep." Vladimir chuckled. "I'm talking about *Big Shot.* He believes in Phoenix so strongly that he's been lobbying at the highest level. He's already chosen his title: *Founder of the Soviet Nation's Rocket Defense System.* He applied a lot of pressure, and pulled some strings, especially in military circles." The excitement in Vladimir Karanski's voice grew as he talked. "He's obtained permission from Marshal Grutchkoff, of Air Defense, to test your little invention, Fjodor!"

Gilbrecht heaved the blankets from his body and sat on the edge of the bed. With a trembling hand he smoothed limp strands of hair from his face. Finally, they were taking more than a passing interest in Phoenix!

"When, Vladja? When will they want to test it? And where? It must be soon."

"They understand that now, and they're acting on it immediately. It's to be done under your supervision near the Afghan conflict zone. That's right where you wanted the tests done to get the most realistic combat conditions. And here's the really exciting news. It has to be done in the next thirty six hours—so get up and let's go!"

Gilbrecht was already on his feet, reaching for his clothes. A vision of his daughter as a healthy young woman flashed through his mind. Polina, laughing as she danced with young men at the Selo disco. Polina, beaming with pride as he cradled his newborn grandson in his arms. If the test went well...no, the test *would* go well. It must!

"This is short notice," he protested mildly as he cradled the phone between his chin and shoulder to stuff his feet into his socks.

"The military wants to act quickly in order to avoid the possibility of a security leak. A fast, unexpected test stands less chance of interception. They'll give you twelve hours of complete control to link up your instrument to the nationwide defense system. Is that enough time to measure the speed and accuracy of your invention's response?"

"The area is perfect for the tests. It should be enough time."

"The plane leaves from the military airport, and I have a car on the way for you."

"Vladja, you are a devil!" Fjodor Gilbrecht replied in glee and slammed down the phone. His wife received a playful slap on her fleshy hindquarters as he made his way towards the bathroom.

Chapter 11

Zero Time Minus 48 Hours
Pakistan

UNDER PRESSURE from President Bahadur Khan, Pakistani Intelligence had become quite effective over the past several years. Agents were drawn not only from Pakistani nationals, but also from the new, for-hire Janissary groups that were springing up around the world. The Janissaries were only used when it was impossible for a national with distinct Indian features to mingle with locals of other countries.

Bahadur Khan accepted the report from his aide and waited until the man had left the room before he broke the seal. *This is interesting news.* An agent had been able to eavesdrop on a meeting between an Israeli and American agent in Jaffa. The report stated: "Although the conversation was difficult to hear, the name of Pakistan came up several times."

As usual, the Israelis run to the Americans and the Americans side with the Israelis. What is it that they plot now? The day couldn't come soon enough when the Arabs scattered the children of Abraham to the four winds.

Khan thumbed the button on the intercom to his adjutant: "Make arrangements for a meeting this evening between Commander Mirphor and myself at my country estate. Two helicopters. We'll return in the morning."

The Palace had more security leaks than a sieve and he needed to speak freely with the commander of the Air Force.

One of the happiest days of his life had been the day his daughter married Mohammed Ali Mirphor, a young fighter pilot. He had an over-serious nature perhaps, but he was extremely capable. Khan made sure the young man rose swiftly through the ranks. A year ago he had been placed in charge of Pakistan's air force.

It would be good to get away from the prying eyes in the Palace, even if just for a few hours. The country estate was situated in one of the few pristine locations left in Pakistan, and accessible only by air. They would be assured of absolute privacy there.

THE HELICOPTER hovered near the edge of the estate until the pilot received the all clear to descend to the landing pad. From this height, Khan was able to pick out elements of the ring of security drawn around the area. An army of guards, and the latest electronic surveillance gadgets, ensured the confidentiality of any conversation.

Mohammed was waiting for Khan on the patio at the rear of the house. It was only at this country estate that Bahadur could afford to ignore the strict no alcohol laws of his Islamic religion.

His son-in-law, however, who was a dedicated follower of the Prophet, would not touch alcohol.

"A grapefruit juice for you, Mohammed? Some figs perhaps?"

"Just the juice, please."

Bahadur Khan decided to abstain from his customary drink and ordered grapefruit juice for the two of them. When they were free from the presence of the servant he asked his Air Force chief, "Have the details of the mission been worked out?"

Here, in the country, the air was pure and filled with the perfume of pine and acacias, a welcome relief from the stench of the over-populated city. Khan rested his elbows on the carved balustrade of the veranda and looked out over the forested ravine below. A beautiful sight, so different from the rock and scrub of his childhood.

"Yes," the younger man answered, "all personnel have been briefed. Four squadrons will take off. One will fly close to the border to divert the Indian radar system, one close to the Afghan border, one close to the Khyber Pass—about twenty kilometers to the northeast, and one into the valley itself. That's the least inhabited corner of the country."

Mirphor downed his juice in a swallow and abandoned the glass on a small table. He prowled the veranda as he talked, an aimless wandering that Khan found distracting.

"The fourth plane will be the one that releases the bomb—very close to the border," his son-in-law continued. "It will be dropped so close to the demarcation line that if there's an international investigation we can argue quite convincingly that the Soviets did it to intimidate Pakistan. The Chinese will blame the Soviets as well, since they sympathize with the Jihad movement of the Afghans. India will undoubtedly blame us, but there won't be any solid evidence—just their word against ours."

As he spoke, the President nodded his approval of the details. But something was wrong with his son-in-law. The set of his shoulders, his wandering of the terrace, the lack of eye contact. This was a man with something on his mind. Did he disapprove of the test?

The young commander continued, "The bomb has been set with a delayed timer; it's not impact explosive. We'll have plenty of time to clear the area since we'll be flying at about Mach two, twice the speed of sound."

"And none of the pilots are aware of the true nature of the flights?" He sought out a chair and settled in. Hopefully his example would prompt Mohammed to sit down and cease his pacing.

"None, Generalissimo," Mohammed replied, using his father-in-law's formal title.

Finally, the young commander turned to Khan and looked him in the eye. "And as added protection, I'm flying the plane that drops the bomb."

"You? Are you mad?" Khan shot from his chair. As he strode up and down the veranda he ran his fingers through his thick head of hair. "No Air Force commander should participate in a mission, especially not a mission of this nature!" The old peasant's eyes flashed with concern. The young officer weathered the storm calmly.

"Look, Father," Mohammed dropped all formality. "It's for added security. If another pilot has to release the bomb he needs to be briefed. Word might get out before the flight. Plus, I'll be able to report the effects first hand. I also feel that it's my duty to do this." He paused, and turned to observe the tranquility of the scene below the veranda. "The squadron thinks the flight is another demonstration of strength to proclaim our territorial rights. It wouldn't be unusual for me to fly on this type of mission."

Everything he said had merit. Somewhat mollified, the President conceded the point. "I don't like it, Mohammed. I just don't like it. But...I'll go along with it."

"*Inshallah*...if Allah wishes," replied Mohammed.

MOHAMMED wasn't surprised by his father-in-law's reaction to his announcement. What the old man didn't know was his real reason for flying the plane with the bomb was more important than he had let on. The Generalissimo would have been greatly alarmed had he been able to read his thoughts.

An ardent believer of the Koran, Mohammed Ali Mirphor, was deeply disturbed by the suffering of his Islamic brothers in Afghanistan. He'd recently heard of a new atrocity perpetrated by The Soviet Nation. The Soviets had used helicopters equipped with anthrax to attack unarmed villagers. After a period of careful soul searching, Mohammed had come to a decision.

While still a youth he had developed a passion for flying. To satisfy this passion, he watched videos of memorable flights from around the world. Some were made during World War II and showed the Japanese Kamikaze pilot attacks on American naval forces. When their ammunition was spent, they had given up their lives by flying their aircraft into the ships.

Another video that never failed to stir his blood was the attack on the World Trade Center in 2001. Here was an action he could personally relate to, young Muslim men willing to sacrifice themselves for their beliefs rather than their country. The memory of the heroic efforts of those suicide bombers seemed to mock him, silent accusations of his own inaction. The time to act had arrived.

He recalled his latest conversation with a Jihad member: "Mohammed," Therez had said sadly, "I've just come from a refugee camp near the Tajikistan-Afghanistan border. Our brothers in the camp have seen a sizable Soviet troop built-up near there. We're sure their aim is to destroy our guerilla bases close to the border. Of course that means any civilians in the way will be targeted too."

He, Mohammed Ali Mirphor, would be the angel of destruction and the deliverer of his brothers.

Inshallah...if Allah wishes.

Chapter 12

Zero Time Minus 48 Hours
The Expedition's Journey in Northern Nepal

NAMCHE BAZAAR was a delight to Ludec's senses. Perched at 12,000 feet above sea level on the edge of a deep gorge, the town fanned across the side of a steeply terraced hill in a U-shape, reminiscent of a Roman amphitheater. The view of the surrounding peaks, including Everest and Lhotse, was breathtaking. Many of the buildings within the town were capped by sky-blue roofs, with wide borders of blue painted around the windows and door. Poles, festooned with white prayer flags, fluttered everywhere.

At this level the air was so clear and thin that he felt he could reach out and touch the distant mountain peaks. Even the sun felt closer, and its hot rays quickly burned unprotected skin.

Their guide, Loanche, suggested they book rooms at a hotel and take a day to acclimatize. The group had gained a lot of elevation during the day's climb so he knew the recommendation was a good one, yet he battled with a feeling of unease with the suggestion. The guide seemed to hover too close to their conversations, and his eyes were just a bit too watchful for Ludec's comfort.

"You go on ahead," he told the rest of the group. "I want to check the crate that got knocked around today. It contains some of my most sensitive instruments."

The Sherpas guided the burdened yaks to a meadow near the outskirts of town where they began to set up camp for the night. Ludec was halfway through the contents of the crate when a cheer erupted around him. A heavily laden rock-salt caravan came down the track from Tengboche and joined the group in the meadow.

Namaste, a Nepali greeting expressing respect for one's soul, was called back and forth around him as old acquaintances were renewed within the two groups. It struck Ludec that life here was so simple; a meaningful job, personal security, and good friends. It really didn't take much to be happy. The West had lost something very precious in their pursuit of wealth, and their incessant desire to dominate one another.

He watched as the taller figure of Loanche wove in and out of the colorful crowd. He seemed to be looking for someone. A brightly decorated yak crowded in and blocked Ludec's view and he lost sight of the guide in the mass of activity.

LUDEC HAD a restless night due to a headache, and overslept the next morning. When he entered the restaurant an hour later, it was empty. After a breakfast of chapatti, Nepal's form of unleavened bread, and an omelet, he set out to explore the sites of Namche Bazaar, the last large center they would see for several weeks.

It was Saturday, so the bazaar was chaotic. Goods of every conceivable type, from pots and pans, to woven slippers and clothes were for sale. Foreign, exotic smells mixed with the familiar aroma of fruits and vegetables. It staggered his imagination to realize that every item not created by hand in the community had been brought to market on either the back of a yak or the back of a human.

A group of Tibetans occupied one corner of the market. Faces made dark by years of sun and layers of dirt broke into broad smiles when he passed. They were not looked on favorably by the Nepalese, but their goods were first-rate so the trade was brisk at their tables.

The vendors were clad in tattered sheepskin jackets and pants, or ragged shirts and sweaters. Colorful scraps of ribbon or bits of cloth were woven into long braids, and earrings made of beads and stones adorned their ears. The scene was a photographer's dream.

"Oh! Hi, Ludec." The comment was accompanied by a light laugh. "Fancy meeting you here!"

He was startled by the greeting and tugged off the knitted cap he had been trying on. He saw Nicole and returned her smile.

"It's nice to see a bazaar that still sells traditional handicrafts." He passed the brightly patterned cap to her for inspection. "I'm considering buying this one as a souvenir. Who knows, I may even end up wearing it? What do you think?"

Where had she been? Whom had she spoken to? Last night she commented that she was going to a satellite up-link office to file a report with her newspaper and ISONS. Namche Bazaar had the last up-link to the outside world. Had she used the time to contact someone else? There was nothing in her manner to suggest she was covering up any guilt. Ludec hated the suspicion that kept him from completely enjoying her company.

"It would be an excellent memento, Ludec. And the color suits you, too." She handed the cap to him. He completed his purchase with the vendor and they began to make their way through the crowded market together.

The tilt of her head, the touch of her hand, her independent nature—she reminded him of Adelka. The thought of his former lover brought back bitter memories.

When the dean at the University in Prague began to feel threatened by Ludec's growing reputation, he started a smear campaign to rid himself of a rival. Using Ludec's political leanings and background as leverage, he orchestrated his transfer to Bratislava, a dead-end backwater for anyone with aspirations.

Adelka, the light of Ludec's life, had a capable, self-reliant nature, part of the reason he was so attracted to her, but she was determined to make her own decisions and be the master of her own future.

"There is no way, Ludec, that your career, or mine for that matter, will survive being banished to such a hinterland. I'm so sorry, my sweet, but I must stay in Prague."

When he made the decision to defect to France two years later, Adelka had already married. His hurt was so deep that he had steered clear of anything closer than a pleasant acquaintance ever since.

Although Namche Bazaar was a town of fair size, it still retained a traditional flavor, with none of the consumer-driven influences of the West. The air was cool and clean, and the streets free from the overwhelming stench and advertising that had cluttered the thoroughfares of Kathmandu. Ludec pushed all other thoughts from his mind as he and Nicole explored the cultural center, and then the temple. They worked their way through the warren of narrow streets peering into first this shop, and then that, just for the pleasure of the experience. By late afternoon dark clouds bullied their way in, threatening rain. Although reluctant to end the pleasant afternoon, he suggested they return to the hotel where the evening meal waited, as well as a welcoming soft bed.

ALTHOUGH THE weather had threatened rain last night, today it had cleared and was perfect for their climb. Brock turned his face into a mild breeze that carried the combined scent of meadow grass, incense, and the earthier smell of the cantankerous yaks. He had earned a healthy respect for the moody beasts.

The final scrutiny of their trek papers as they left the town provided a light-hearted start to the day. In an effort to hide his amusement, Brock turned his back on the scene at the security check. Loanche had been forced to go in search of the official and had obviously found him at his breakfast. Shoeless, chapatti in hand, and not yet in his uniform, the official gave the trek papers a cursory glance and slammed the stamp on the forms. It was a far cry from the checkpoints Brock had endured in Lebanon.

On the edge of the group he noticed Nicole watching the scene unfold with an amused look on her face. If there was laughter on the trail the group was sure to include their female member. He had spent more than one pleasant afternoon walking in her company.

Government technicalities taken care of, he noticed Loanche slip a few rupees to a Red Sect ascetic and the group left Namche Bazaar accompanied by prayers for the safety of the expedition. Seated on the ground in the traditional lotus position, the priest used his right hand to beat a *damarue*, a small magic drum, while he rang a bell with the left. Brock figured it was as good a method as any other, provided the group met with no mishap. Chanting in an incense-filled cathedral or banging a drum on a stony trail, the prayers seemed to rise to the same entity.

As interesting as Namche Bazaar had been, he was happy to be on the move again. Huge rhododendrons in full bloom clung to the scant soil along the trail and draped their blossoms over rock walls adorned with drying yak dung. Although smelly when fresh, once dried, the disks were almost odorless and were used as fuel to heat homes and to cook food.

He put his linguistic skills to use to decipher text on a long, beautifully rendered *mani* wall that skirted a sprouting barley field. The flat stones of the wall were carved over the centuries, depicting gods and goddesses, *mandalas*, and Buddhist prayers that were complex. This wall carried the words *Om Mani Padme Hum*—hail to the jewel in the lotus—repeated over and over again.

They were not under any time pressure and the journey to this point had been an enjoyable one. Brock was thankful the relaxed pace allowed their bodies to become accustomed to the thin air that brought on altitude sickness. So far, other than an occasional headache or bout of loose bowels, they had all escaped the sometimes fatal phenomenon.

Any problems or differences between porters and beasts had been worked out, and overall he felt the group members were now comfortable with each other.

Benefactors of the Society had been generous with their gifts so the expedition organizers had left the duration of the trek, and the final destination, open. That meant they were free to follow any leads they received regarding Yeti sightings, no matter where those leads may take them. Now that they had left the last community behind them, he knew the radio became a crucial link with either Calcutta or

Kathmandu. As needed, supplies would to ferried to them via hired helicopters.

The question of leadership had been resolved without any formal announcement. It was clear that initially Ludec had felt uncomfortable in the role, but as the days passed he became resigned to the position. Brock still felt a shade of suspicion about the man, but realized the feelings had come out of his meeting with Podlanski, rather than from any actions on Ludec's part. As long as Ludec's leadership did not hinder his observations he had no reason to object to it.

His thoughts were interrupted as Rudy dropped back on the trail to walk alongside him. Several times over the last few weeks Brock's suspicion had lingered on Rudolf Weiner. His desire to please or be of assistance had become obvious to the entire group. The tall German's strangely subservient attitude seemed a little out of character for a member of the Aryan nation.

"Are you going to keep a complete record of all the translations you do of the *mani* stones and *stupas?*" Rudi asked.

They moved to the edge of the trail to allow a group of Sherpas, each burdened with a load of lumber, to pass.

"No. Most of them are far too complex to interpret at one reading. It's good to have something to do, though. We haven't met anyone yet who doesn't understand English." As the expedition's linguist, there had been little call for his skills to this point. For practice, he deciphered scripts or prayers carved on rocks on the many monuments they found along the trail. These more often than not detailed the ancient history of Nepal. There were also numerous memorial inscriptions carved on *chorten*, a cupola set on a square base and topped with a number of round discs. He was philosophical about his limitations as he remarked, "We're after the Abominable Snowman and there's very little chance of any verbal communication with the creature."

THE FORMIDABLE peaks of the Annapara loomed ever closer. As they climbed, the track narrowed to the point that the group was forced walk in single file. Rocks formed a wall on one side of the trail; on the other, a deep abyss fell away to a rushing watercourse on the valley floor. Brock's head spun when he peered over the edge. Tropical vegetation flourished down in the valley along the river.

They continued to climb. At this altitude the Europeans and Americans suffered from lack of oxygen. Andrew suggested frequent halts in order to give everyone a chance to catch their breath. The use of oxygen was not anticipated on the trek, although they had brought along the equipment.

They approached the region from where Yeti sightings were the most consistent. At one stop they were shown what was believed to be a Yeti skull. Brock had his reservations. The object looked like nothing more than a large hairy coconut. An old woman was the keeper of this treasure, and as she unlocked the box containing the skull she assured them that there were several types of Yeti. This skull was from a smaller Yeti that lived closer to Tibet. The small Yeti was very intelligent she pointed out, and although they didn't speak, they could communicate with a high-pitched whistle.

"You will know when you are near a Yeti lair," she informed them solemnly, "because of the foul odor. It is very offensive."

AS BROCK made his way along the trail he was submerged in his own thoughts. How would they ever prove the Yeti did not exist? To acquire negative proof was an almost impossible task. They needed positive proof—a specimen—living or dead. Then they would only be faced with the problem of getting the animal out of the mountains.

A spine-chilling cry ripped the air. In front of Brock, Nicole uttered a gasp of surprise and stood rooted to the trail. In the ensuing silence the gushing sound of the river below was heard. The winding, narrow track blocked any view of the place from which the cry had come.

"Let me go ahead," Brock ordered as he pressed Nicole against the rock face and hurried forward. Further along the path he caught up with Andrew who was also elbowing his way towards the source of the scream. Rounding a sharp turn in the path they came upon a scene of chaos. Rudi Weiner, with a harness around his waist and shoulders, was about to be lowered into the abyss by frantic Sherpas.

"What's happened?" the duo demanded, almost in chorus.

"One of the porters fell! It was the damnedest thing. A little moan and he was over the edge."

"He was carrying our radio," Ludec added. "By some piece of extraordinary luck it's entangled in the harness and caught on a tree. Rudi is going down to see if he can save the man and retrieve the radio."

"This is my responsibility," Andrew stated with such firm authority that no one objected. "I'm responsible for the radio and I'm the most experienced climber."

With well-practiced hands Andrew removed the harness from

Rudi and buckled himself into it. He began the descent.

Brock watched Rudi for his reaction to Andrew's assumption of authority. His swift submission seemed to indicate he had no ulterior motive for retrieving the radio.

Nicole had now joined the group and watched with horror as Andrew descended on the harness.

"What happened to the porter?" she demanded.

"We don't know yet. He's hanging in his harness. It doesn't look good, but he may be only unconscious.

Andrew's voice rose from the abyss, "Okay...I've cut him loose. I don't think he's breathing. Start pulling...careful...stop...okay, go ahead..."

When the Sherpa was pulled up over the edge it was obvious that he was dead, but they had no time for mourning. The commanding voice of Andrew rose once again from the abyss, "The radio is on the rope now. Start pulling...slowly...slowly...good!"

The tension within the group was electric.

The cumbersome box nudged its way over the edge of the cliff.

"Thank God Kildare had the radio packed in Styrofoam! That precaution has paid off," Ludec commented as the box was manhandled onto the pathway.

Brock was alert. They hadn't used the radio up to this point. *How does he know how it's packaged?* Rudi's next remark drew Brock's suspicion back to the German.

"We'd better test it. Without the radio, we're in big trouble."

Nicole edged her way to the radio box and joined the conversation. "My God, what a setback if it's been damaged! Andrew, are you trained in radio repair?"

Andrew opened the case, removed the instrument and turned it on.

"Hello...Snowman calling Calcutta...Snowman calling Calcutta..." No answer. Again he sent the call out. "Snowman, come in please. Snowman calling Calcutta..."

Even the Sherpas seemed to catch the tension. Everyone held their breath and leaned in closer, waiting.

Then... "Snowman, this is Calcutta. Calcutta speaking. Snowman, do you read me?"

"Loud and clear," Andrew replied with a grin. "Loud and clear."

Chapter 13

Zero Time Minus 4 Hours
Soviet Military Base Near the Afghan Border

THE OLD veteran sucked angrily on his cigarette then cleared his throat with a phlegm-rattling cough. Rain drummed on the roof of the car and coated the road with a white froth.

General Ostrowski, hero of the Great Patriotic War, recipient of the Order of Cutusow, the Red Star of Valor and many other medals, fumed. A *civilian*—a nobody—was being permitted to conduct an experiment on the defense system! A decade ago, such an insult would never have been allowed. No one would dare go over the head of the military.

But those days were gone. In today's political climate it was the civilians, sitting in their comfortable *dachas*, who held the upper hand. And the orders had come from Marshal Grutchkoff, a shrewd rival who held enormous power in the Supreme Soviet.

Yes, he would have to be very careful today to keep a guard on his tongue. Let those fools play with their gadgets for twelve hours. It wouldn't be the end of the world.

He comforted himself with the fact that he was still the commander of all forces operating in the ASSTA, the Alliance of Southern States Theater of Action. He had a compliant mistress, a good cook, and access to a chauffeured limousine. And generally he was free to make his own decisions. Except for today....

IN THE FRONT seat next to the driver, Aljosa Zaburin, General Ostrowski's adjutant, gauged his superior's foul humor. When the old man chain-smoked he wasn't in the mood for conversation.

"Aljosa," Ostrowski barked, "when does this asinine experiment begin?"

"At noon, Commandant," the young man replied as he contemplated the ineffective action of the windshield wipers. The rain now fell in a torrent. The old man was cranky, and it was storming, not a good start to the day.

"Is everything in order?"

"Yes, sir. We've done all the prep work and are waiting for the arrival of the principals with the computer chip. Once the system is installed, all the recorded data will be sent directly to Central Defense Headquarters for analysis."

"I know all that! I was present at the briefing, if you care to remember," Ostrowski snapped.

Aljosa's anger flared. The rebuke was unfair. First the old fool asked for details of the preparations then snarled at him for giving the information. He was like a bear in the spring. Nothing made him happy today.

"You're from the engineering corps, Aljosa. Do you understand the technicalities of the experiment? I confess that my computer knowledge does not extend to defense systems."

Aha! Here's the real reason for the old goat's fractiousness. He has to admit he doesn't understand what's going on.

"A true soldier doesn't require a computer to dispatch tank units or fire rocket launchers," continued Ostrowki. "Will we be forced to depend on the accuracy of that damned experiment for half a day?"

"The old system remains intact, General. If the new invention is as good as the inventor claims, for twelve hours we'll have a faster, more accurate defense system than before. I believe the new system runs parallel to the old, so we'll never lose the capacity to retaliate in the event of an attack."

Ostrowski grunted in reply.

The car came to an abrupt halt at the airport, terminating the conversation.

The driving rain had slowed their arrival somewhat and they were barely on time.

"Oh, shit, they're already here." Ostrowski complained as they pulled onto the airport tarmac. The military plane was nosed in at the drab terminal and comrades Gradoznij and Gilbrecht were in the process of disembarking. One of the airport staff had met the visitors with an umbrella but the colorful shield was brusquely turned aside by Gradoznij.

"Greetings, Comrades." Ostrowski's broad smile hid the annoyance Aljosa knew was simmering below the surface. Undoubtedly the old man would have welcomed the umbrella, but if Gradoznij refused the comfort, then he must refuse it, also.

Ostrowski stretched out his enormous arms for the traditional bear hug. "You are most welcome to this small corner of our great country. And you're in good time. All is in place for the experiment to begin at twelve noon, exactly." He was now the picture of a General in full command of his troops.

"So, you were able to get a direct link to Central Defense while we do the testing?" enquired Fjodor Gilbrecht. He shifted his briefcase from one hand to another and wiped the rain from his face.

"All is arranged. Come, gentlemen. The car is warm and dry." He stepped aside to allow the men to precede him. "Our chief interest, of course, is in your invention, but before we establish the linkup I propose we have a glass of vodka in my office for good luck and success."

The old bear would have made a superb actor, thought Aljosa, as he trailed behind the group. He did his best to avoid the large puddles that had formed on the tarmac but his boots leaked and the cold water quickly soaked his socks. It would be a miserable day.

Chapter 14

Zero Time Minus 2 Hours

THE MORNING dawned with a beauty that brought an ache to Mohammed Ali Mirphor's heart. Was it a reproach for the cataclysmic devastation he would drop on the earth from his position high above the clouds?

He lingered at home to spend extra time with his family and took special delight in the innocence of his young children. He loved his wife, two energetic sons, and beautiful baby daughter, but managed to say farewell to them without sharing his inner torment over the mission he was about to fly.

The previous day he had received news from Iran through his network of Islamic fundamentalists. The phone call strengthened his resolve.

"Mohammed," the contact said, "it was a massacre! A Soviet expeditionary force came upon a group of Afghan Jihad members and slaughtered them."

"And you're certain it was a Soviet force?"

"Not totally Soviet. The reports said it was a coalition of Soviet Nation forces and members from the Alliance of Southern States. There're also reports of a Soviet paratrooper concentration in the vicinity of Shir Sherif. It looks like a final thrust is being made to wipe out the tribes that escaped into the mountains."

Mohammed Ali Mirphor felt that destiny was calling him to play out his role in the struggle of his brothers. A slight shift in the fighter jet's flight path would suffice to free the Islamic fighters from the scourge of their oppressors.

In the tiny mirror of his barracks washroom, he made a final adjustment to his well-tailored uniform and checked his appearance. Everything had to be perfect for this special day.

Outside, noise from the military airport increased as activity escalated. It wasn't often that so many planes took to the air in one exercise. A signal light flashed on the secure video-phone line to Karachi. He suspected the call was from his father-in-law and was tempted to ignore the signal. The older man treated him well enough, but always there was the reminder that without his influence, Mohammed would never be Commander of the Air Force.

Before thumbing the 'receive' button he touched the white scarf in his pocket. The white headband was a symbol of the Kamikaze fliers of World War II. He would have preferred a symbol of the martyrs at the World Trade Center but knew of none. No matter, the white scarf strengthened his resolve for this mission.

"Mohammed," he heard the familiar voice of his father-in-law. "I just want a few words with you before you leave."

"Yes, sir." Once again Mohammed wished he had ignored the call.

"There's no need to be formal at this time. Mohammed, I know you understand the significance of this test. It's vital that we know our retaliatory capacity in the event of an Indian nuclear attack."

"Yes. Of course, I understand."

"I'm afraid I have to make one other thing quite clear. Under no circumstances are we, I mean the official government of Pakistan, prepared to admit any responsibility for the test and its consequences."

Mohammed tightened his grip on the scarf and fought to keep his expression neutral. "The location of the drop has been well chosen, Sir. As you say, nothing will prove one way or the other as to whom was responsible. We might be accused, especially by India, but the others have more reason to point fingers at each other than at us."

A range of emotions crossed his father-in-law's face before he continued. "When are you taking off?"

"At noon."

"Short of making it an order in my capacity as President of Pakistan, is there any way I can dissuade you from your decision to pilot the plane?"

"Would you rather have that nuclear power entrusted to a pilot who secretly harbors some desire for revenge against...let's say, India? Flying at Mach two, with a few seconds of evasive action he could be over Bengal, or even New Delhi, and could have dropped the bomb before I could regain control of him. I should be in total control so I must pilot the plane."

They said their goodbyes, then Mohammed touched the scarf in his pocket once more and left the barracks for the airfield. When he was seated in the aircraft, he would fasten the scarf around his head, as the Kamikaze pilots had done. The only way to absolve Pakistan of bombing the Soviet coalition forces was to follow the bomb to its target. No evidence would be found to determine who had used the destructive force.

Chapter 15

Zero Time Minus One-Half Hour

FJODOR GILBRECHT fought to contain the tremble in his hands as he removed the small box from his briefcase and raised the lid. The computer chip lay clipped to the bottom, an insignificant square of silicon, aluminum, and copper.

This was the defining moment in his career. A failure at this point would be the end of him, a success...he didn't allow his thoughts to go any further than Polina's new heart.

He passed the box to General Ostrowski. The big man grunted as he pushed away from the wall where he was leaning for support, arms crossed over his barrel chest. Fjodor was amazed at the amount of vodka the old veteran could consume. Once the alcohol had loosened his tongue he made it plain what he thought about the role of computers in the army.

The General's opinion wasn't a surprise. The Soviet Nation's aging military leaders were, as a whole, still firmly rooted in the technology of decades passed. They refused to see that in today's reality tanks and armed foot soldiers were no longer used in foreign wars; they were used to subjugate rebellious nationals.

"So this is the miracle device that is going to give The Soviet Nation nuclear superiority? I wish you good luck with it." He handed the box back and turned away, but not before Fjodor caught the sour look on his face.

A technician stood ready to receive the chip and the operating program. Fjodor handed the program disk to him and stood back as the code was read into the system. Then, together, they watched the digital clock mark the minutes...then the seconds until noon. As the numbers turned over, Fjodor handed the chip to the technician.

His fate now rested on the tiny lump of silicon and the programming of the system.

MOHAMMED Ali Mirphor watched the first planes break away from formation and head toward the border with India. Several seconds later the formation dissolved as one group disappeared in the direction of

Afghanistan and the other up the Khyber Pass.

He was alone.

The mountainous landscape slid away beneath him as he knotted the white scarf around his head with firm hands. There! The target was directly ahead. He beat back a wave of doubt that threatened to overwhelm him.

What were the words to that prayer he had learned as a child at his father's knee? The words were a reminder that the loss of life was only part of a Divine scheme. He was almost at the target! What were the words?

Inna li-llahi wa inna ilaihi raji'un.

Surely we belong to Allah, and to Him we shall return.

He cleared his mind of all thought and edged the controls into a dive. As the ground rose up to meet him he became one with his aircraft and its lethal payload. He was an instrument of Allah, the deliverer of his people.

IT WAS TIME to take a break from work and indulge in a light snack. Colonel Yun-Kai patted his substantial stomach. He had lost five pounds this week. It would do no harm to treat himself as an incentive to continue his weight-loss program.

As he stood to leave for the canteen, the line on the video-phone from the tracking room lit up. *Damn! Not now.* He jabbed at the button.

"What is it?"

It took a minute to cut through the hysteria in the voice and decipher the message. His brain took in only part of the words "...all-out nuclear exchange...multiple missiles..."

Yun-Kai doubled over as an explosion of pain tore through his stomach. *Avalanche!* They had sown the seeds of war.

Chapter 16

Zero Time
Northern Nepal

THE NARROW path the group had been following finally expanded into a small plateau above a rushing river. The site provided an ideal place for the expedition to halt for the day.

Nicole slid her pack from her shoulders and took a moment to savor the beauty around her.

The valley they had entered tapered off in a V-shape to the north, and its narrow end led the eye to the stunning mountain vistas beyond. Below them, dense, jungle-like vegetation grew along the riverbank, evidence that the effects of global warming had reached even this altitude. Seen from this height the growth appeared lush, a potential hiding place for the savage marauding mountain cats that preyed on *tahr*, a type of mountain goat plentiful in the area.

The members of the expedition were grateful for the rest. The tragic mishap of the previous day had affected the morale of the entire group. Nicole was especially pleased with the stop, since the proximity of the clear flowing water below was an invitation to have a bath and hand-wash a few items of clothing. The river was actually a swift-flowing creek, but spring run-off had swollen its volume to the point that the foaming turbulence flowed with a roar. Further down, fed by the tributaries, it became a real river, but at this point it only announced the promise of its size.

She collected her laundry and all the necessities for bathing and was about to start down the embankment when Ludec's voice stopped her.

"For heaven's sake Nicole, you're not planning to go down to the bottom of the valley by yourself, are you?"

"Why not? It's not far. If I crisscross the slope it's only about two hundred meters."

"I'm talking about what might be hiding in the jungle. It could be dangerous."

"You forget, Ludec, that I was a foreign correspondent in the Balkans and several other war zones. I know what danger is."

With a stern shake of his gray head he replied, "You don't want to push your luck too far, Nicole, and what's more, I'm responsible for you here. I'll escort you." He collected a rifle from the equipment and prepared to leave with her.

"You're not treating me as an equal partner," she protested, hoping that he would allow her to go on her own. If he persisted she would have to forego the anticipated bath.

"I would say the same thing to a man. Loanche has warned us against going into the jungle unarmed."

She was exasperated but smiled in spite of herself. "You sound exactly like my father." She started down the slope with Ludec in tow. "I have to warn you, Ludec, I'm a rebel. I became a rebel before I hit my teens. Show me something conventional and I feel I have to protest against it." The incline was steeper than she had anticipated, forcing them to maneuver carefully. Loose stones broke free and clattered down the slope, leaving dust trails in their wake.

"And I suppose your parents felt the brunt of it."

"Perhaps. But it wasn't just my parent's authority that I protested against; it was authority in general. I hated all the laws and regulations forced on me by society. I was at war with good manners, sweet talk, and politeness; the things my teenage judgment considered were masks that covered a person's true feelings. At that age I think we all want to be honest to the point of rudeness, don't you agree?" As she spoke of her external struggles during her teen years, she remembered the struggles that raged within her—the desperate need to feel protected and loved by the very people she lashed out at.

"Say no more." Ludec chuckled. "I know the syndrome. My niece, Marica, was exactly the same way when she was a teenager. And, I'm afraid, she's still a rebel today."

He stopped for a moment and stared out at the horizon, as though looking into the past. Was there something there he remembered with regret, or was it just the musings of a man who could now look back and see the total picture?

"Fortunately, or unfortunately, depending on whose point of view you look at," he continued, "a suppressive government such as the one that she lives under is a good target for her hostility."

"Are you close to your niece?" She wanted to learn something about this quiet individual.

"She was a child when her father died so I became a substitute father. I never married, but Marica was like a daughter to me. We fought the inevitable battles of youthful rebellion."

They concentrated on maintaining their footing as they picked their way down the remainder of the steep decline.

As they neared the bottom they were met by the noise of the jungle. The occasionally sharp cries of the colorful birds, the rustle of the foliage as a troop of monkeys moved overhead, and the incessant rush of the water filled their ears. Nicole relished the cooler temperature and greenery that sharply contrasted the hot rocky trail they had followed for so many days.

To her delight, several *dape*, the national bird of Nepal, took flight. The males were as stunning as any peacock she had seen. Their bodies were an iridescent deep royal blue, their head feathers rich, bright green with touches of red and yellow.

She let Ludec break a trail to the water then they followed the bank to a small bay where the flow was calm. A large flat stone set on the edge of a deep pool made the perfect spot to wash her clothes. She rolled up her pant legs and waded into the chilly water while Ludec settled himself on the shore with the rifle close at hand.

Nicole picked up the conversation where they had left off. "So, even without being a father, you had to go through the agony of child rearing." She removed underwear and T-shirts from her pack, added washing powder, and went to work on the garments. It was a task that she had done many times during her career as a foreign correspondent.

"Yes, and it was a bittersweet duty. Behind the verbal scrimmages there was always a hidden expression of love." The memory brought a smile to his face. "I tried to remember that rebellion is a maturing child's attempt to cut the umbilical cord. And of course, there's a difference between the feelings of a teenager to a parent and those of a teenager to an uncle. The parent might be hurt by their child's need to escape from what is perceived as family bondage, whereas an uncle...well perhaps he finds it easier to accept this urge for equality with a smile." He held up one hand, then the other, as a balance for his statement.

Nicole raised her head from her task and cocked an eyebrow as she asked, "Were you this understanding when Marica rebelled—or is this the wisdom of hindsight?"

"That's a hard question to answer. I guess I realized that she needed to rebel against something so she could measure her growing strength. A battle of words seemed to be the best way to defuse anger."

Laughing, and with a touch of impishness in her eyes, she said, "You'll be pleased to know that on that point I agree with you totally."

"That's comforting. But is it any assurance that in the future we are not going to have another clash of wills?"

"Of course not! And, I'll have you know, I'm the type who expresses rebellion not in words, but in actions." With a few quick twists she rang the water from her clothes.

"Is that a threat?"

"A warning. Rebellions are necessary and invigorating. They're an expression of human existence. You might say they're a release of boredom and stagnation."

"You mean they're a part of progress?" He seemed pleased that the conversation had become an intellectual exchange.

Her laundry complete, Nicole emerged from the water and draped the wet clothing across the warm rocks where they would dry in the sun. She wiped her damp hands on the front of her shirt and joined Ludec on the bank. The day was warm and the grass was an inviting place to sit and exchange ideas while the clothes dried.

"Certainly, conflict is a part of progress. If Einstein hadn't rebelled against the old concepts of classical physics, relativity would never have been discovered."

"But neither would the atomic bomb."

"Ah," she held a finger in the air to emphasize her point, "but that was a byproduct of man's destructive nature. The Theory of Relativity opened up new visions for man. One might say it was the antidote to dogmatic thinking."

"And the source of uncertainty. All the ideas that people had held and protected for so long were thrown into chaos."

"Isn't it better to doubt than to base one's conviction on falsehood and error?" It was easy to imagine this man seated in an overstuffed chair smoking a pipe. She felt comfortable here with him and was glad he had insisted that he escort her to the water. Once again she had rebelled against something needlessly.

"Perhaps. It's very difficult to know whether people are being firm for the sake of a belief that is held to be true, or whether they're just being stubborn for the sake of refusing to admit they may have been wrong."

They sat in easy silence for a moment, enjoying each other's company. Insects buzzed softly as they went about their business. Nicole flopped onto her back to watch the clouds scud across the sky. It was a moment of pure pleasure that passed far too quickly.

"You know," she teased as she sat up and brushed off the bottoms of her feet to put her socks and boots back on, "I came here for a bath as well as to wash my clothes, but I think I'll have to give up on that idea. I'm not prudish but I'm also not used to having a guard in my bathroom."

"I'm sorry," he flustered in obvious embarrassment. "I don't want to be an obstacle to you. I promise not to look if you want to go behind the rock and..."

Laughing, Nicole shook her head. "Forget it! I wouldn't feel comfortable. But now we'll have to wait until my clothes dry out before we can leave."

Ludec's reply was cut short when an urgent call rose above the rushing sound of the river. It was Brock's voice, "Nicoolle... Ludeeeec..."

Nicole rose from the ground, flushed with guilt. *What's wrong with me? I'm acting like a schoolgirl caught in an embarrassing situation.* She fought to suppress a grin as she called out, "Here, Brock. We're over here."

Ludec grabbed the rifle and scrambled to his feet beside her. Brock was closer now and they heard the thud of his feet as he tore through the foliage in their direction. Disturbed birds shrieked their agitation and monkeys screamed.

"Nicole! Ludec! Where are you?" She heard a tone of desperation in the call.

He emerged from the greenery, sweating from his charge through the forest, his shirt torn and one arm bleeding. Bending over he rested his hands on his knees, inhaling deeply to catch his breath in the thin air.

Panic welled in her, a dreadful foreboding. She moved to his side and grasped one of his arms. "What's wrong? What's going on?"

"What's wrong?" he echoed as he sucked air into his lungs. "We had the radio on...its nuclear war...an all-out exchange! We're destroying ourselves!" He sank to his knees, exhausted, but with enough energy to pound his fists into the soft earth.

Chapter 17

Zero Time
In Northern Nepal

STUNNED silence greeted his words. Nicole's hands flew to her mouth and she whispered, "No! No, that isn't possible! What are you saying?"

Brock raised his head and took in the serenity of the small glade. Perhaps he was suffering from the high altitude. Here, beside the cool river, with the fresh smell of juniper and jungle greenery surrounding him, the news he carried seemed surreal. For an instant he had a sensation of floating out of his body, an observer as three men frantically tuned a radio into first one channel and then other. No, he'd heard the news, all right. Rudy and Andrew had heard it, too. It was the world that had gone mad, not him.

It took a huge amount of effort to get to his feet. "Impossible? No. It's been possible for a long time. But we believed the politicians who fed us the lies. It was inevitable. Both sides never stopped building up their arsenals."

"Where did this news come from?" Ludec demanded. "Perhaps the reports are a mistake or a sick joke."

"First from Karachi. Then confirmation from Calcutta, New Delhi, Lassa, Kabul...from all over. There's no other news. Lots of confusion...One report contradicts the next, but on one fact they all agree—a total annihilation is in progress."

Nicole's expression turned from disbelief to horror. She snatched up her wet clothes and stuffed them into her bag.

Brock had taken a tumble down a portion of the slope to the riverbed, and his arm ached, as well as the right side of his jaw. He probed at his teeth with his tongue. Thankfully, they all felt solid.

They worked their way back through the trees as quickly as they could and began the steep climb back to camp. His lungs were still raw and they burned when he drew a deep breath, but his breathing had slowed to a near normal rate.

"Did you hear anything from Europe?" Ludec asked with a grim voice. He had slung the rifle across his back from the strap and was using both hands to claw his way up the steep grade.

Brock shook his head. "Andrew was at the receiver when I left. He said there were already signs of order breaking down. I doubt we'll get organized programming for much longer. Everybody will be on their own." They continued their scramble up the slope in silence.

Brock's head spun with images of home. His mother, father, the farm. Inexplicably, the old swing hanging from the oak tree at the side of the house flashed across his mind. It swung, empty, pushed by a warm breeze.

When they reached the camp they found Andrew at the radio, which had been set up on a small, folding table. Rudi paced frantically in front of the table—his face twisted in anguish, white lines of tension around his lips. Of the group of porters, Brock noted that only Loanche, the guide, showed any interest in the dramatic turn of events. The women busied themselves preparing the evening meal while many of the men had begun their daily gambling games.

The overwhelming majority of the Sherpas were Buddhist and their world was more solid, more indestructible, and more static than the world of the Caucasians. For Buddhists, the eternity of nature was an unchangeable fact, and human existence only a transitory step on their journey. During his time with the natives, Brock had come to sense an enormous gap between the uncertainty of many of his beliefs and the Sherpas' calm confidence in theirs. For the porters, being alive imposed only one obligation—that they continue life. Not the life of an individual, but life in general. It was their only duty.

He joined the other Westerners crowding around the radio, their minds, like his, undoubtedly filled with thoughts of the outside world— homes, faces, melodies, feelings, landscapes, human bonds that connected an individual to life. If the reports were true, everything they had known was in the process of disintegration.

Try as he might, Andrew's fevered efforts to gain a station turned up static, broken by a few disjointed phrases. "Come on! Come on, please," he pleaded to the non-responsive instrument. "Give us some news. Any news...just give us some news! Talk to me, someone, anyone..."

In the gut-wrenching agony of the wait, Brock remembered his conversation at the airport with Colonel Podlanski. He had mocked the man, compared politics and nuclear armament to a pissing contest, or a game of chess. Now that game of chess had gone into checkmate and the contest had ended.

Consumed with bitter rage he turned to the others and spat out through clenched teeth: "Okay, it's over! Finished! Let's get this out in the open—now! Who is it? Who's the agent here?"

He rounded the small table and grabbed Rudi by the front of his shirt. "Rudi, it's you, isn't it?" Without waiting for an answer he released the startled man and turned on Ludec. "Who is it? Were you the agent, Ludec?"

There was confusion in everyone's eyes except Ludec's. "Ah, Brock. I'm the only one who understands your question."

"You! So it *was* you. I should have known."

"Yes, I am, or rather, was, the spy. You surprised me. I suspected Nicole for a while. But there really was nothing to spy on, was there? I was told only to watch for a *suspected* spy."

"You suspected me?" asked Nicole incredulously. "Of what?"

A sense of disappointment worked it way through Brock. He had come to like Ludec. "What do you mean there was nothing to spy on? I was told..."

Then the older man's words registered. Ludec had been told only to watch for a suspected spy. Those were the same instructions he had received from Podlanski. *There was no spy!* It had been a misinformation campaign after all. Without meeting Ludec's gaze he addressed him.

"I thought it might be Rudi. But what does it matter now? There's no one to report to. And there was no spy, just suspicion."

"What the hell are you two talking about? Have you lost your minds?" Andrew continued to turn the dial of the radio as he spoke over his shoulder still trying to find a broadcast.

His hands clenched at his sides, Brock threw his head back to contemplate the serenity of the sky. A harsh laugh escaped him. "Lost our minds? Yes...maybe we have. Ludec and I were both victims of misinformation. Somewhere a seed of suspicion was planted and it grew. Suspicion—it eats at you from the inside. And it grows. It consumes you so you can't think for yourself. You can't get rid of it." A huge weariness weighed him down and he moved to a camp chair where he took a seat. "This...this holocaust that's happening down there," he shot his arm out to indicate the trail leading down to Kathmandu, "it was probably set off by the same type of misinformation. A horrendous game, and look at the cost. Just look at the cost." The last came out as a whisper. He covered his face with his hands to hide the pain etched there.

"We've all played games of some sort or another," Nicole agreed as she stared in disbelief, eyes wide and glazed, at the crackling radio.

"But nothing that could possibly lead to this."

They concentrated their attention on the radio, desperately hoping to pick out messages from the static. Andrew turned the dial but only crackling and whistles came from the speaker. Then suddenly the panic-stricken voice of an announcer came through.

"...and we can't establish contact with either Europe or the United States. The destruction in Asia has been concentrated in the industrial parts of Siberia; in China, along the coastal area and in many isolated spots where rocket-launching stations were suspected to be located. There are unconfirmed reports of raging forest fires in the Taiga. The destruction is massive. There are reports of radiation clouds. We have no means of predicting the formation of a total blanket of dust—the so-called nuclear winter. Whether this will be a universal phenomenon or something affecting only certain parts of the globe is open to speculation."

Suddenly the broadcast was cut off as if a power failure had shut down the station.

"Could it be possible that we had anything to do with this?" Brock asked Ludec.

"There's no use speculating," Andrew cut in. He had given up on the radio. There was nothing to pick up. "There's no history anymore to record your stupid cloak-and-dagger games. Let's face it. There is no future—period!"

The harsh words rang in the empty air.

Rudi broke the silence. "From now on, for as long as we live, we start a new history. Today is day *Zero*."

Nicole, who had slumped to the ground beside the radio, turned her face to the group. "The question then begs to be asked," she said softly, "how long is this new history going to last?"

One thing was clear to all of them. There would be no place to go back to. They had no choice but to move forward.

Chapter 18

**Zero Time Plus A Day
In Northern Nepal**

RUDI FOUGHT the beginnings of a headache. Was it tension or was it
the altitude? He'd followed the medical instructions religiously: small
meals and plenty of water. Until yesterday they had taken their time on
the climb so their bodies had adjusted well to the altitude. Today,
however, they were on a forced march and the cold thin air no longer
seemed to satisfy his need for oxygen.

"Do you feel a change in the air?" he gasped to Brock, who
preceded him on the trail.

"Yeah," Brock answered curtly, indicating he was in no mood for
conversation or his own oxygen-starved lungs made him incapable of a
longer answer.

Towards the head of the line, Rudi saw Andrew and Ludec
walking side by side on the rocky pathway.

Far off in the distance the sparkling peaks of the Makalu and Tesi
Lapcha glittered like cut diamonds. Would their beauty soon be
obscured by the pending nuclear winter? The Sherpa porters behind
him chattered amongst themselves, their occasional laughter seemed
jarring compared to the morose silence of the Europeans.

From his vantage point near the end of the line of trekkers, Rudi
occasionally caught a glimpse of Nicole as she followed close behind a
group of Sherpa women, each carrying enormous loads. For a moment
her profile stood out, sunburned from their time spent in the high
altitudes. He realized with a start that somewhere in her past a native
American Indian might have been part of her family tree. His
suspicions would remain unvoiced. Long ago he had learned that a
German should never have an opinion on matters that touched on
ethnicity. Such a remark might label him a racist, even so many years
after Hitler.

He had known no war, but he knew the ice-cold feeling of fear
that war gives birth to. His father, who was declared unfit for duty in
World War II, had served as an air-raid warden; he'd been a failure in
Grandpa's eyes.

For several weeks before his father's death, his parents had spoken in whispers of the *Stasi*, the security police. One day the dreaded *Stasi* came and took his father for interrogation. When he came home he was pale and agitated, and refused to talk to Rudi about the incident. The next morning they found him dead in the attic. Rather than inform on his friends, he'd hung himself, just months before the fall of the Berlin wall, when they would have been free of the *Stasi's* grip. His father was a hero in Rudi's eyes.

Now, at age forty-one, his own life was about to end before he could taste the glory of fame. After years of archaeological study and finally being accepted as an equal by respected older archaeologists...what was left? He'd been too busy for a wife and family. Somehow there always seemed like there would be time later for domestic things. Now...? Perhaps that had been a good thing. Who was there for him to mourn?

And no matter what he discovered here in these beautiful mountains, no one was left with whom to share his find. Everyone the world over had heard the warnings of nuclear armament and not taken them seriously. Rudi was like the others...he had failed to see that when there is power, sooner or later the power would be used.

THE CLATTER of falling rock drew Brock from his reverie. He turned to find Rudi pressed against the rock face as a small slide of scree tumbled onto the trail. A mountain goat, or some other animal must have dislodged the rock above the track. After making sure his fellow trekker wasn't injured, Brock returned to his troubled thoughts.

Suddenly, when the future was so uncertain, it seemed important to review the past.

His siren call to adventure came in the form of a recruitment advertisement on television. The Marine Corps was his ticket out of North Dakota's sea of wheat. One tour of duty in Lebanon, however, was enough to shatter his illusion that the Marines were the guardians of peace.

Testing showed he had an aptitude for languages so he was shipped stateside to attend school in Virginia. He became a Middle Eastern specialist, able to carry on conversations in languages from modern Arabic to classic Hebrew and everything in between. When he returned to Lebanon, his outlook was different...he was different. He no longer felt connected to his fellow Marines, and often found himself engaged in conversations with world travelers in Lebanon on business. After his discharge, he enrolled in the graduate program of Oriental Studies at Milwaukee University. Diploma in hand, he was invited to an ongoing excavation in Turkey where he gained the reputation of a skilled professional with outstanding physical endurance

And now what? What had become of those institutions to which they should have been reporting their findings? They probably lay in smoldering ruins. The outstanding scholars, if alive, would be desperately searching for food like animals. And the potential for radiation sickness lingered. If the missiles carried biological warheads, sickness would have been released into the atmosphere—anthrax, ebola, hemorrhagic fever and other unthinkable horrors would spread sickly devastation on the populations of the world. Millions were dying horrific deaths without treatment or the possibility of a merciful overdose that would shorten their misery. He had seen the movie classic *On the Beach*, yet had never dreamed that one day he would be reenacting the role of Fred Astaire.

He sighed and drew himself out of his thoughts.

Nicole preceded him on the trail. *What a body.* Her long stride accentuated the sway of her hips. She seemed to enjoy walking with Ludec, but today she was alone. Perhaps, like him, she was lost in her past.

IT DIDN'T escape Nicole that recalling the past was part of the dying process, and dying was surely what the world was doing.

They had given up on the radio when they could no longer get in touch with any of the radio transmitters. The atmosphere was so charged with electronic particles that all that came through was the sound of crackling disturbance.

Brock speculated that some of the ordinance dropped might have been graphite cluster bombs, which incapacitated the electrical grids within a huge radius of the bomb's epicenter. This was the explanation she chose to believe. To admit there was simply no longer any radio stations capable of transmitting was too difficult. Communication was her field, her life, although she had chosen print as opposed to broadcast journalism.

Growing up in Portland, Oregon, she didn't know what she wanted to do with her life. But her rebellious nature and social consciousness attracted her to Berkeley. From there, she spent a year with CARE in Bangladesh before returning to finish her degree in journalism. After a brief stint with the *San Francisco Star*, *Press International* snapped her up and sent her globe hopping. Calcutta,

Afghanistan, Moscow, and then she was sent to Seoul to report on a cluster of kidnappings. Kidnapped herself by the group of terrorists, she used the opportunity to burrow so deeply into her captors' minds that her later articles on terrorism had become source materials on the subject and had earned her a Pulitzer Prize.

Lately, however, she had come to realize that the plum assignments were going to the fresh faces, those with cutting-edge writing styles. Was she becoming too complacent for her audience, or was it simply a matter of youth galloping over the backs of those who were entering middle age?

The invitation from ISONS was a welcome one, offering time to reevaluate her future. The assignment also fit her interest. To discover the substance behind the legend of the Abominable Snowman was not the most important of issues, but as an ardent seeker of truth she had been eager to find that truth, one way or another, not only for herself but also for her millions of readers.

She realized now just how insignificant the Yeti issue was—actually, how insignificant life in general was. And still they were pressing on...why?

Chapter 19

AT NOON they stopped for a silent meal of Sherpa stew, a soupy mixture of potatoes and vegetables. The meal was unappetizing, or perhaps Nicole simply had no appetite, and she was glad when the group moved on.

Climbing through the rough terrain she became aware of Brock's outstretched hand reaching out to assist her around a particularly narrow corner. Normally she resented any gestures that suggested female helplessness but today the touch of another human being was comforting. Was her touch a comfort to him as well?

"Is this just a nightmare, or is it real? Maybe it's just a group delusion...some unknown effect of altitude sickness." For a moment she was no longer the independent woman, the battle-hardened journalist. She was simply Nicole, and she wanted someone to take her in his arms and console her, stroke her hair and tell her he would battle all her demons and take away her fears. The moment passed and she was grateful that she hadn't given in to her weakness.

"I wish it was. But no, unfortunately, I think it's real." He paused as a wave of sorrow washed across his face. Then he shook his head; perhaps to clear out the mental images that were too horrific to be allowed to take root. He swallowed hard and gave voice to his own dark thoughts. "I don't know what to hope for. Total devastation? Survivors scattered in some corners of the earth? Maybe there're more people like us—isolated people out of reach of the radiation."

"There *has* to be some people. Even after Hiroshima there were survivors."

"Survivors with deadly burns, radiation sickness...if you call those poor souls survivors then yes, there were. But don't forget, now we're dealing with biological weapons. The horror that's happening out there...Christ..." He shook his head again. "It's hard even to think about it."

"How can I forget?" Nicole bit down hard on her lip. "The big cities—Tokyo, Los Angeles, Sydney, Jakarta...they wouldn't be primary targets. There must be some people left in those regions."

"Alive, maybe, but no longer part of an organized society." It was obvious to Nicole that Brock was overcome with the magnitude of the devastation he envisioned. "There would be panic everywhere. A total breakdown of authority. How could civilized life be possible anymore? It would be impossible to keep anyone with guns—the police, the military—from disintegrating into renegade bands when the future is so uncertain. I'm sure it's every man for himself."

The calm surrounding them was in sharp contrast to the scenario that Brock painted.

"No! I refuse to believe that. We're not animals. We're people...people with morals and ethics. Man has a charitable soul. It's what separates us from the animals. There must be groups out there who're ready to help the victims, even if the situation looks hopeless."

"Maybe. But I don't hold out hope for many people surviving. No, I think the floodgates of bestiality have opened wide. We've both been in a war zone, Nicole, so you know what happens to man when his survival is threatened—instinct takes over."

She concentrated on placing one foot in front of the other. It didn't take much thought and it grounded her in reality. "And our chances up here? Give me your honest opinion." Was she really ready to hear it? No, she wasn't, but it was better to face the demon than to run from it.

"I'm not a prophet, or a clairvoyant, so I'm just guessing here. But judging from what we've learned from nuclear tests, an all-out atomic exchange would probably destroy most of the biosphere—the layer that sustains life. It's as thin as the peel of an apple, and it's very fragile. Being up here at this altitude gives us a pretty good chance of surviving. It's probably the best place on earth to be."

The soft wind was a caress on her cheeks. But was it already a deadly touch, contaminated with radiation? She remained silent as Brock continued to speak.

"The nuclear winter this madness might trigger, though, is something else. We might still get some sunshine, since the sun up here can penetrate the dust cover easier than in the lowlands. But, in my opinion, as far as civilized life is concerned, we're back to the Stone Age. It's not a pretty picture, but you asked."

It was the first time any of them had articulated what they thought, and Nicole felt reality slip away a few degrees. She fought the sensation, knowing that if she gave into it she would become hysterical.

Brock smiled bitterly. "For our Sherpas now, the transition won't be so drastic. Few of them have ever experienced the benefits of modern technology, and they already live close to a self-sustaining level of existence. You watch them." He jutted his chin in the direction of a group of Sherpas just in front of them. "They're going about their daily business as though nothing has happened. They sing their songs just like they did yesterday. The rhythm of their walk is the same. If you ask them what's happened to upset the white men they'll probably grin and say that something very bad has happened. But then they'll sit down to one of their games and soon they'll be laughing."

"And Loanche, the interpreter, what's your take on him?" She had noticed that Loanche took far more interest in the reaction of the Westerners than the other porters. He tended to hang around the edge of their group, always busy with one thing or another, yet always aware of their conversations.

"Nicole, if we, with all our schooling and Western training are confused, then what can you expect from a simple man like Loanche? He's probably just as unconcerned as the other porters. To them, we've been living in an illusionary world. To us, they're hiding their heads in the sand like ostriches."

"An illusionary world." She echoed his words. "That's a good way to describe it. How any of us sees reality is subjective. As a matter of fact, right now I feel as though I exist in two distinct spheres. One part of my mind refuses to acknowledge what I've been told has happened. I find myself thinking of my family and friends as they were when I left them. Then, the other *reality* kicks in, and I'm overwhelmed by the prospect that everything that's important to me is gone, so I close off that part of my mind. In a way, we choose the reality we're most comfortable with. But blessed are the ignorant, because they have hope."

Brock chuckled as he noted, "You've just invented a new beatitude."

They fell silent and concentrated on the rocky trail.

THEY CROSSED another of the interminable ridges. The yaks, the beasts of burden of choice, dutifully followed their drivers. Far ahead a group of Sherpas led the way, following each other in single file. The pace of their steps was in such harmony with the undulating terrain that Nicole stopped for a moment to watch. She realized the Westerners fought nature with their nervous and hurried strides, while the natives adjusted their movements to the rhythm of nature.

Being a mountain climber, Andrew McFairlain was an exception to that observation. If it weren't for his height, Nicole would have taken him for one of the natives. His rugged face, weathered by years of outdoor activity was now a rich shade of brown. The network of fine wrinkles surrounding his dark eyes was interrupted by full eyebrows, a shade darker than the unruly growth on his head. Like the natives, Andrew had developed his shoulders into powerful lifting machines that were capable of carrying massive loads or hauling crates of supplies up sheer mountain walls. Perhaps being attuned to the harmony of the land was in his genes, since he said he'd come from a highland family whose ancestors had had to survive in the rugged Scottish landscape.

She had often walked alongside Andrew over the past few weeks, and had learned only a little about his background. He seemed to be a loner by nature, perhaps a consequence of his profession. Or was it the other way around? Perhaps his profession had come about as a result of his nature.

Andrew's father was an accountant and he had not been keen to follow in his footsteps. He used the first opportunity that presented itself to sever his ties with the cloudy British Island. By lying about his age he'd been accepted as a deckhand on a windjammer. The vessel deposited him in New Zealand where the irresistible peaks of Mount Ruapehu had been the first testing grounds for his climbing skill.

She was worried about Andrew. He had given up on the radio, and now he seemed to have withdrawn from the group. She was glad to see Ludec walking alongside him on the trail. Ludec's quiet nature hid a deep wisdom that she had come to appreciate. Perhaps he could share some of that wisdom with Andrew.

LUDEC contemplated the troubled profile of his companion. His face was dark, his features tense. "You've been very quiet, my friend. Would you like to share some of your thoughts with me?"

For a moment Andrew didn't acknowledge his attempt at conversation. Perhaps he resented the fact that someone would intrude on his personal suffering while he was trying to sort out his thoughts on the cataclysmic events. Then, just when his silence could be interpreted as a rebuff, he said, "It's beyond belief that the entire population of any country has been annihilated! A've got tae think some folk have survived."

Ludec was surprised to hear that the stress had brought out the occasional soft burr of his Scottish heritage.

"Perhaps. Pockets here and there. But even if small groups such as ours survived, we have to ask ourselves: Is there any future left for mankind?"

"Your question's too dramatic, Ludec. Man doesna' live for

mankind as a whole. And A'm sure the survivors down there are demonstrating that right now! Man lives for himself. What's really at issue here is can *we* survive? Not the people of Europe or the people of North America. No. Only we—or perhaps only maself. Can I survive? That's the question."

The question seemed more a plea for reassurance than a quest for an answer. Ludec's impression of this Highlander was that he was a survivor, a man with a gift for working with his hands and mechanical devices. He would be a valuable teammate if the group required technical knowledge to survive. But he also sensed Andrew would not be comfortable in a philosophical or theoretical discussion.

"The first time the question of survival arose for me was when the police broke into our home one night and took my father away. He never returned. He had been a liberal in his political beliefs— something that was not tolerated by the government of Bratislava.

"I was a young man at the time, and life became meaningless for me. Yet, life continued to go on. In my pain and desperation to understand how I could continue to live when I had no desire to live, I turned to one of my professors. This man had been a prisoner in the Gulag during the war so I was sure he would understand how I felt. He said to me, 'To live, my son, is not necessarily noble but it is always a duty.' Now I say the same to you, Andrew. We have no choice. We have to live."

"Why...why? Live...for what?" For the first time he turned his face to Ludec, who was shocked at the agony etched there.

"Your gun is in your backpack, isn't it? If you're so sure that there's no future, why don't you use it? What are you waiting for? Do you want me to convince you of the senselessness of staying alive? You see, by inaction you have already made your choice. Ultimately we all have absolute authority over our lives. By the fact, Andrew McFairlain, that you are still alive, you've already demonstrated that you've found some reason to continue living."

"The last message we received came from Lassa," Andrew said, evading a direct reply. "That's proof that there might still be some safe areas."

"I've no doubt about that. What's irreparably broken is the global network of communication: radio, air flight, international diplomacy, and worldwide services. They're gone forever. We're on an island here," he waved his arms to encompass the panorama around them. "The new Robinson Crusoes."

Their conversation was interrupted by the shout of the headman,

Loanche, signaling from the top of the hill. The monastery of Panchen-Bo, their destination for the day, was in sight.

Chapter 20

Zero Time Plus A Day
Evening

NICOLE stopped to admire the stunning beauty of the scene. The monastery of Panchen-Bo stood guard on the other side of an evergreen-and-rhododendron-studded chasm. In the gathering twilight the monastery's massive walls were sharply etched against the white peaks still illuminated on the horizon beyond. With watchtowers on each of the four corners, Panchen-Bo resembled a fortress more than a religious establishment, yet it still managed to convey a sense of strength and dignity.

Her stomach did a flip-flop when she saw their route across the deep chasm to the foot of the monastery wall. The dizzying void was spanned by a *jhalunga,* a flimsy suspension bridge. The yak drivers made the crossing first, experiencing little difficulty handling the beasts. The porters followed without incident. For the Westerners, however, the crossing was not so simple.

To Nicole's horror, the abyss below seemed to beckon. From somewhere in a dark corner of her mind a voice whispered that she should jump now and avoid the agony that would soon be her fate. A siren call to embrace the inevitable. Her fear sucked the strength from her legs until she trembled, but it also caused her to grip so tightly to the ropes that she could barely move forward.

Human beings are strange creatures, she thought as she forced her reluctant legs to carry her across the seemingly insubstantial structure. *Although the world is dying all around me, I still fear death.* Intellectually she knew their chance of survival was nonexistent, yet she still fought the thought of dying.

Brock preceded her on the bridge and as they waited for the rest of the party she shared her fear with him.

"That's one experience I don't want to repeat any time soon. How about you?"

"Well," he admitted with a wry grin as he watched his companions slowly inch their way across the gap, "I wasn't what you would call comfortable."

"Why is it, I wonder, that we fear death when death would very likely be a blessing?"

"You and I could never be existentialists, Nicole." In answer to the unspoken question on her face he continued, "When I was studying languages I did a minor program in world religions. It wasn't all that interesting at the time, but it's sure helping me understand the reaction of our Sherpa porters.

"They're existentialists?"

"Oh no. Far from it. Existentialists believe that they're in this world for a specific, limited time and there are urgent decisions to be made before that time runs out. They claim that there's no predetermined universal right choice for anything and they're free to make choices based on whatever information is at hand."

"That sounds like a good philosophy to me right now. Why did you say I could never be an existentialist?"

"Because they also believe that man's greatest freedom is the ability to choose his own death. Could you do that? Make a conscious decision to take your life at any one point in time?"

There it was, the very question she had been asking herself since hearing the news. Was there any use in going on if what lay ahead was sickness and horror and a slow death? Obviously it was a question that was on Brock's mind, too. She didn't believe for a minute that the topic was a coincidence. Had he experienced the same urge to end his life with a topple over the side of the bridge?

She was sure that for all of them, every move, every thought, every action in the next few days would be enacted with the future in mind.

"Would I do it? I don't know. Would I be capable of making the decision? Given my fear on the bridge just now—I'm not sure. I wanted to live at the very moment I was tempted to end it all."

"And I reacted the same way. So I wonder whether man has the ability to suppress his instinct for survival to the point where he has the freedom to make the choice to end his life."

"But people do it all the time."

"True, but are they making that choice with a clear mind? Usually a person who commits suicide is ill or depressed. If any of us here are totally free of the instinct to survive, then this is the time and place to put that theory to the test. Obviously you and I want to live, in spite of what's happened, so our survival instinct is intact and strong."

The last of the group stepped off the swaying bridge so they turned and continued along the trail. From the frown of concentration on Brock's forehead it was obvious to Nicole that he was still mulling their conversation over in his mind. She remained silent, allowing him to work it out. "If our existence is no more than instinct, or compulsory behavior, then we're not living our lives freely, are we?" asked Brock. "And if that's the case, then we're nothing more than robots and can't be held responsible for our actions. Can you accept that? I know I can't."

"No, I can't either. I have the ability to make the ultimate decision about my own life—or death. Maybe the time for that decision just hasn't arrived yet, but...well, it might not be far in the future."

The shiver that ran up her spine as she spoke the words had nothing to do with the chill of the mountain sunset.

During their conversation Rudi moved up behind them and caught the tail end of their exchange.

"What about you, Rudi?" she asked. "How do you feel about this instinct business? Are we prisoners to our survival instinct?"

She sensed a keen mind behind Rudi's agreeable facade.

"I agree with Nicole. I'd say I have the ability to act against the command of instinct. I'd even say that being able to act outside of instinct is what separates us from the beasts. Sure, instinct might guide me in suggesting the easiest way to survive, but I think I have values that go beyond instinct."

She stopped on the trail and looked him directly in the eye as she asked, "And would you be able to take your own life, Rudi?"

Rudi avoided eye contact as he replied: "Ask me next week, if we're still alive."

The trio continued in silence, each lost in their own thoughts.

From their position at the end of the cavalcade, Ludec and Andrew paused to examine the imposing monastery towering above them. It was a powerful symbol of another life and another culture. Although constructed of stone, plaster, and wood, Ludec sensed a spiritual dimension to the structure.

"Do you feel another presence here, Andrew? A mystic presence from a different world?"

"You bet. What I don't get is a sense of whether this *mystic presence*, as you put it, is good or evil."

"We can not know that because we have never been a part of it. The culture of the East has a passive element that has somehow endured through the centuries. And it lacks impatience, which I think was the chief ingredient of our Western lifestyle. In my opinion, that impatience was the driving element of our desire to obtain everything at once. Not later, but right now. It led us into the nuclear age before we were ready for it."

Andrew shook his head as he replied. "I disagree with you, Ludec. I think rivalry is the moving force of life. As long as we live we'll compete. It's what drives man forward."

Ludec was both pleased and surprised with his companion's reply. He seemed to have lifted himself from his earlier depression, but more than that, Ludec realized that Andrew was a deep thinker.

"You may be right," he agreed, as he adjusted his pack for the last bit of the walk. With the fading of the light the air had become cold and his muscles were tensing. It would be good to get rid of the weight on his back. "But the competitiveness of the West ran out of control. China, for instance, believed in the philosophy of Confucius and produced the most tolerant and obedient social order on earth. They were also one of the least belligerent and least expansionist powers on earth."

"I see a flaw in your theory. Look at Japan, South Korea, Hong Kong. They followed the example of the West."

"On the other hand, there's Nepal and some other Eastern regions. In these countries the peaceful oil lamp of mysticism shines more brilliantly than all the neon signs of the Western big cities. Man is so complex," he concluded with a discouraged shake of his head.

There was a touch of sadness in Andrew's voice when he replied. "If only we'd been content to live with those oil lamps. Even the nostalgia for the *good old times* wasn't enough to lessen our appetite for progress. I guess we just weren't prepared to live with the oil lamp, or for that matter the horse and buggy, or sailing ships."

"And look where it led us—to destruction! If there is to be a future for man, I would like to see it develop in the Eastern pattern."

Ludec looked once more at the structure above them. A movement in the sky caught his eye. In the gathering gloom a large bird made its way across the heavens. An eagle perhaps, on its way to its nest for the night. Most creatures sought the safety of their nest when darkness descended. It was a very deep darkness that now approached, and their small group was far from home.

"Somewhere along the line we did seem to lose the ability to differentiate between what was good for us and what simply met our wants rather than our needs," Andrew conceded.

"That is exactly what I meant. So for a better society to succeed in the future we need to develop a universal desire to be tolerant and patient, as I said—in the Eastern fashion. Perhaps if we had developed a universal spirit of peace the soldier in charge at the North Dakota silo, or his counterpart in Kazakhstan, would not have pushed the button."

Heads down now, they concentrated on their footing. It was becoming increasingly difficult to discern the path in the failing light.

Andrew challenged him again. "Sorry, Ludec. Not even that would have been enough. Unfortunately, man programmed machines to make those important decisions. And the machines may have been programmed intelligently, but they had no ability for moral feelings. No ability to decide in favor of man—or the extinction of the human race."

Ludec took up the train of thought. "Man's most important decisions, those requiring wisdom and ethics, were given over to preprogrammed data. And morals can't be programmed, they have to be taught."

Their conversation stopped as the line of trekkers reached the monastery grounds.

They came together as a group just as darkness descended. The porters used the broad meadow in front of the monastery to set up camp; cooking fires were lit, pack animals unloaded, baggage piled up, and tents erected.

The campsite was almost complete when a welcoming committee in the form of three lamas carrying yak-butter lamps arrived. Their mission—to convey the greetings of the head lama of Panchen-Bo monastery to the Western visitors. This was a time for diplomacy and tact, and Ludec knew their combined vocabulary wasn't sufficient for a fluent conversation. He summoned Loanche to be their interpreter.

It soon became clear that the lamas had heard of the situation in the world at large and offered long-term hospitality under the protection of the monastery. They were prepared to supply firewood and other necessities for the porters, and invited the Westerners to be their guests inside the compound walls.

"Please tell the lamas that we appreciate their kind offer but we need a few minutes to decide what we're going to do. Explain to them that this unexpected event has completely changed our original plans."

Loanche nodded and spoke for a few moments with the small group. The lamas bowed and drew off several paces to allow the Westerners some privacy.

In the flickering light of a cooking fire Ludec surveyed the faces of his team. Confusion, grief, exhaustion—negative emotions. They no longer had a purpose and drifted easily into despondency. They needed time to mentally regroup and redefine their plans.

"We need to make a decision. What would you like to do?" he posed the question to the group at large. After a short silence Nicole answered tentatively.

"Our mission is over. We're shipwrecked so to speak. We've nowhere to return to. I know I've no desire to go back and see the horror of what's happening down there."

Brock nodded but remained silent.

Rudi toed a portion of dried yak patty that had slipped from the fire. He didn't raise his head as he said, "We're here on an isolated island that might be the last stronghold of what we have come to think of as civilization. I vote that we stay here with the natives and make the best of it. In my opinion, we should accept the offer and use the monastery as a base for our future."

"If there is any future," Andrew added in a low voice.

Feeling that he had a consensus, Ludec conferred with Loanche, who then translated their answer for the lamas.

The five of them shrugged into their backpacks once again and followed the three lamas through the main gate into the compound.

Chapter 21

THE MONASTERY had electricity, which was a great surprise to Nicole. It was, however, used sparingly. Here and there glowing bulbs faintly lit the corridors and revealed narrow passageways decorated with intricate woodcarvings and lifelike ceremonial masks. Shadows dipped and leapt across the walls and floors as the group passed, creating an eerie atmosphere that precluded conversation. Their guide lead them along the route, turning here and there, up and down stairways and around corners until the visitors soon lost all sense of direction.

When they once again stepped into the open on an ornate balcony that connected two wings of the compound, she saw the peak of Pumori Nuptche in the distance lit by the last rays of the dying sun, and realized they were in the western wing of the compound. Individual rooms for special visitors must be in this wing.

She had the privilege of a separate bedroom. The others were given two rooms and it was left to them to choose their roommate; Brock chose to share with Rudi, and Andrew with Ludec.

Stepping over the threshold, she stopped and surveyed her room. She was surprised by the lushness of the lodgings.

The walls were covered with oriental rugs. Some from Bokhara and Mongolia, others had Indian motifs and still others were definitely of Chinese or Tibetan origin. All had one quality in common— exceptional beauty. There was no western furniture in the room. The bed was a *gundri*, or platform, covered with a yak hide. The walls displayed ornamental cupboards with little niches filled with statuettes and ceremonial vessels. In one corner, under an ancient parchment with an inscription that she couldn't decipher, was a prayer stool. The only electric bulb in the room lit this corner, although elsewhere oil lamps dispersed their glow into the darkness. The two windows were covered with silk curtains securing her privacy from the outside corridor. It was a magnificent room.

Her eyes were drawn back to linger on the details of the prayer stool. *How strange, here we are in a situation when there appears to be no future, yet I can still admire and appreciate the artifacts of the past.* The entire situation was surreal. Given the circumstances, it was quite conceivable that within a few years the earth would continue to rotate in space with all these beautiful treasures still intact with no one left to appreciate them. What would happen to the concept of beauty without human appreciation? Would it continue to exist or have value? Was value independent of human perception?

She realized that this was the first time she had been alone to consider the horror that man had perpetrated upon man, and she was surprised by her thoughts. She considered herself a person who lived with her feet firmly planted on the ground and was seldom preoccupied with abstractions. *But then I've never been confronted with the possibility of total annihilation before.*

The door opened and a maidservant came in with a pitcher of warm water on a tray; she also carried a bowl of spicy rice laced with tiny slivers of meat, and a teapot with a fragrant brew. She prepared a basin of water for Nicole to wash with, and then with a warm smile, left the room as silently as she had entered it.

Nicole realized that she was hungry and was grateful for the sparse meal. After finishing the rice she bolted the door before undressing to wash, marveling over her concerns of nudity at a time when the whole world had been denuded of everything that would call attention to modesty.

Why are we so obsessed about bodies and bodily function, she asked herself as she dipped her hands into the warm water. *Why am I so embarrassed over the prospect of using a chamber pot or going to the toilet? It's ridiculous to pretend that we're angels who have no use for chamber pots.* She laughed as she realized that by dwelling on the idea she was contributing to the obsession.

Why, when the whole globe is a naked wound, millions upon millions of people are lying in the streets of the great cities, burned to raw flesh, am I unable to accept the reality of the situation? Her mind could comprehend the fact, but something deep inside kept her from accepting the actuality. *I should be incapacitated or at least suffering from hysteria. Is this mental inertia one of man's coping tools? After all, the process of dying starts at birth. We live in the shadow of death, but we choose to ignore the fact that death is the result of life. I'm being forced to confront that fact now, the totality of death. Not just personal death, but universal death.*

She suddenly realized why it was so difficult to comprehend the enormity of the situation—she had seen no evidence of the horror. *If I was shown just one glimpse...*shuddering, she cut the thought short.

Finishing her toilet she bent to retrieve her comb from her pack near the bed. As she searched for a mirror to comb her hair there was a brisk knock on the door and Ludec called out, "Hello in there, are you ready? We have been summoned by the Abbot."

Startled, she grabbed at clean clothes and quickly dressed. From the discussion going on just outside her door Nicole realized that the four men were waiting for her on the veranda. "In a minute," she called back, and true to her word it was only a few minutes later that she stepped out onto the open corridor and into the cool crisp magic of the mountain evening.

Rudi sensed Nicole's awe as she exited her room.

Stars crowded the black velvet of the night sky. In the thin air they appeared so close it seemed possible to reach out and pluck them from the sky. A three-quarter moon glowed a curious red, but it shed enough light to illuminate the mountain peaks and reflect light from the snowcaps.

"Incredibly beautiful and peaceful, isn't it?" Rudi commented. It wasn't a question that required an answer. "I'm having a hard time imagining that the unspeakable has actually happened out there— everywhere."

Ludec stood with his back to them as he leaned on the balustrade, drinking in the beauty of the night sky. Without turning he replied, "We all are. Anybody who is surrounded by this splendid isolation would find it hard to grasp the gravity or the extent of the destruction. Here, close to the stars, we are a few privileged individuals. But who knows how long we will be protected from the horror now being experienced by the rest of the world."

"And we're closer to heaven than we've ever been before," added Andrew.

Rudi wondered whether the comment was meant literally, or as a light joke.

Reluctantly, he tore himself away from the beautiful scene and the group made their way to the end of the corridor where their guide waited.

Rudi was surprised to see Loanche there, in deep conversation with the Abbot's emissary. He knew that Loanche had been asked to stay in the monastery temporarily in case an interpreter was necessary, but did he have a room at this end of the building? It seemed unlikely, since these rooms appeared to be for guests.

There was something about the man that Rudi disliked. The guide never made direct eye contact with the Westerners, even when they engaged him in conversation. Perhaps it was a cultural habit, but it made him appear sneaky.

"Loanche," Andrew said as the two groups met, "I'm rather concerned for our equipment..."

"No problem, *Sahib*," the native replied before the mountaineer's query was complete. "I have just asked this novice the same thing. He says the equipment is in a storage room. Tomorrow he will take you there so you can see for yourself that it is well stored."

The man's efficiency did little to assuage Rudi's suspicions.

They were led by the guide through winding passageways that ended at the anteroom of the Rinpoche's apartment. A Rinpoche, Loanche explained, was the designation given to the head of a monastery—what the Westerners would call the "Abbot". As they entered the room an attendant struck an enormous brass gong to announce the arrival of visitors.

Rudi had never been inside a Nepalese monastery before so he paused just inside the doorway to take in his surroundings. Two lamas in saffron and red robes were seated behind a highly polished long wooden table at the far side of the room. Four pairs of enormous pillars supported the ceiling; each pillar inlaid with brilliantly colored tiles—green, blue, red and gold—creating the jewel-like appearance found on Thai temples. Colorful paintings on the walls depicted Buddha at different stages of his life, but always searching for enlightenment. Intricately-carved window shutters were closed against the cool night air.

Rudi felt overwhelmed by the exotic grandeur of the room.

He was so absorbed in his scrutiny of his surroundings that he nearly missed the gesture of courtesy made by Loanche towards the seated lamas. With both palms pressed together he bowed deeply from the waist. The lamas returned the greeting with similarly pressed palms but remained seated. The head lama who, to Rudi's surprise, was the younger of the two, indicated to the attendant that cushions were to be provided to the Westerners rather than having them sit in the lotus position which was so unnatural for them.

He was again taken aback when he noted that the older lama was wearing bifocals, and the younger, an expensive wristwatch. These items clearly indicated that they were in the presence of two sophisticated and worldly individuals.

It became clear that although the younger lama had the title of Abbot, courtesy demanded that the highly revered older man should initiate the conversation. He spoke now in heavily accented English.

"Bodhisattva Dzung Tse welcomes you to our modest monastery.

I, Bongen Dadzi, welcome you also. We are well informed of the tragic situation in the world and therefore invite you to stay with us for as long as you wish. The most reverend Abbot offers his help to you as he would to his brothers. The catastrophe which has befallen the world makes us as one family."

The older lama had barely finished his sentence when Andrew, with tactless haste, blurted out, "So you have a radio transmitter?"

"Yes, we do," the younger priest answered in almost flawless English. Rudi wondered if the faint smile on the Abbot's face was in response to Andrew's impatient query. And where had the man learned his English? Were there other foreigners in the monastery? He turned his attention to the Abbot, who was still speaking.

"The capacity of our radio is much weaker than that of the Chinese military; however, the commander of the Chinese forces has told us of the horrors of the firestorms raging in the affected cities. Sadly, the chances of survival below are slim. Our chances, and therefore your chances as well, are better at this high altitude."

Chinese? Of course, Rudi thought, *we're practically on the border of China!*

"Is there any news from America?" Brock asked. His anxious voice and tight expression made it clear that he dreaded the answer.

"Neither from America nor from Europe, I'm sorry to inform you. Not even from Soviet Siberia. Those areas seem to have been hit hard. No doubt there are survivors, but they must be disorganized and in isolated pockets. No contact, no communication. We are now on our own, I'm afraid."

"You said the Chinese have been here? But this is Nepal. When did they come here?" Ludec asked.

"Within hours of the event they passed through in force. They do not make any secret of the fact that they plan to dominate this region. There is, after all, a good chance of survival here. There are no boundaries anymore, or for that matter, any international law. The Chinese will undoubtedly try to occupy all the high land where the radiation danger is least. If they must, I expect they will use force."

"Force? What kind of force? What's the Chinese commander doing to secure the territory?" It was Nicole who asked the question. Rudi realized they were questions that a reporter might ask; her training had obviously overcome her personal concerns. He smiled, despite the gravity of the situation. Then his smile faded.

The older lama folded his hands into his lap and sucked in his breath. A look of complete distaste crossed his brown face before he dropped his gaze to his hands. The younger lama froze; his eyes narrowed and his body language indicated they did not like that Nicole had spoken. It struck Rudi that they had reacted negatively to Nicole because she was a woman. He glanced at the others and saw the same realization cross their faces.

Reluctantly, the younger lama turned his gaze to Nicole to address her. As he opened his mouth to speak the older lama hissed loudly, but the younger man ignored him.

"Madam, we are now in a situation of total war. A war for survival. Colonel Woung Lei's first order was to secure the mountain passes leading from the south in an attempt to bar the entry of the fleeing masses that would overwhelm us. Fortunately for you, you came from the west, evading the Chinese demarcation line. There are limited resources here. He feels these resources must be secured for their own use, and for our small population."

"And do you approve of this exclusivity? You, a follower of Buddha, the peacemaker?" Nicole challenged.

"Where is there peace today? I don't approve but I accept the reality of the situation. It was one of the most revered Christians who prayed for the wisdom to fight against only those evils that we are, in our power, able to change."

"But you could protest..."

"No, Madam. I'm quite aware my protest would be useless. It is time to submit ourselves to fate."

"In that case, it doesn't make sense to offer us asylum. We're only five more mouths to feed," Rudi pointed out.

"You are here now, and on a more practical level, we believe you may be able to help us consolidate our position at the monastery."

This last comment was a surprise to the group and they exchanged glances. Andrew recovered first and commented, "So, it wasn't out of the goodness of your heart that you called us family."

With a faint smile the Abbot conceded, "Perhaps I should have said *useful brothers*."

What's he really after here? Rudi wondered. *A coalition against the Chinese? Yes, that makes sense. The monks have no technical know-how. The Chinese have weapons, but without the support of the locals they can achieve little.*

The Abbot continued speaking. "As members of a family, we need to find harmony in our approach to the situation we find ourselves in. If there is any purpose in our survival it is not to recreate civilization on the system that we had in the past. A new civilization is needed with new qualities and new values."

Brock shifted on his cushion and re-crossed his long legs. There was an unhappy scowl on his face when he spoke. "Forgive me, but I'm a bit surprised that a representative of one of the oldest religions known to mankind would advocate change." Rudi sensed Brock wasn't buying what the Abbot said.

The Abbot seemed undisturbed by the implied challenge of the remark. Before he could reply the faint sound of chanting penetrated the chamber through the shuttered windows. Hundreds of years of culture were imbedded in the droning modulations. The words were unimportant because the strangely harmonious tones spoke of an imperturbable permanency and a harmony with the indestructible essence of life itself.

Nicole nodded towards the sound of the chant, "For those people nothing has changed. They're unaffected by what's happened."

"Exactly, madam." The Abbot's tone was soothing, almost hypnotic. "And therein lies the secret. They have adhered to the original teachings of the ancient masters and have embraced the permanency of their values. How different those teachings are from the nationalistic substitutes that many have tried to replace them with."

The room, the soft voice of the lama, and the chants from the Sherpas had a mesmerizing effect on Rudi. He stated: "Something went wrong for the people of the West."

"Yes, something went very wrong. People were content to be Buddhists, or Christians or followers of any denomination you wish to name but only up to a certain point. They followed only to the point where their faith's demands conflicted with their own selfish interests. It was then that they stopped being followers and began to look for excuses that justified pursuing their own interests. Our simple people out there," he nodded his closely shaved head in the direction of the window, "have not looked for those excuses. They still live in a state of acceptance."

Brock interrupted with an explosion of anger. "This is a petty discussion! Empty talk when there's no assurance that any of us will be alive in six months! Instead of moralizing we should take stock of the situation. If your generator breaks down, even if we know how to fix it, will we have wire, solder, or insulators to do the job?" He ticked the items off on shaking fingers. "It'll be our labor...our initiative that'll save us, not theoretical knowledge!"

Rudi shook his head. The man had a temper that flared under stress. Was this why he'd left the Marine Corps?

Ludec rested his hand on Brock's arm to calm him. His anger expended somewhat; Brock drew a hand across his chin and spoke in a subdued voice.

"Sorry. It's just...I guess I'm a person who needs..." He balled his hands into fists and dropped them into his lap.

When Ludec spoke his voice was soft and he addressed Brock, rather than the lamas.

"You think the future lies in preserving our technology, Brock? Perhaps that will be impossible. The story of Atlantis used to sound so fantastic. They would have needed incredible technology to build up their advanced society. I realize that that myth may have had a solid foundation. But where is Atlantis today?"

"Ludec has a point," Andrew agreed. "Who knows, maybe legends like the fiery chariot of Elijah were born around campfires of people who survived cataclysms like this but weren't able to rebuild their societies. Perhaps our Sherpa friends out there will be the ones to create legends about our vanished western civilization."

When the Abbot replied his voice was calm, his face impassive. There was no acknowledgement of the outburst. "Technology, with all its merits, was never the key to civilization. It has value in physical comfort, but the future, if there is any future, must be built on deeper foundations. We know how shallow, and volatile, a culture founded on technology is."

He raised his hand as a signal and a novice monk arrived with a tray bearing large Western style mugs filled with steaming tea. The trekkers welcomed the break and rose to stretch their cramped legs.

Ludec suspected the interruption was planned to allow the Abbot's idea to take root. Tea in hand, they took their seats once more. The Abbot picked up the conversation again.

"I visualize a simple lifestyle; a way of living close to nature. I do not pretend to be God. I'm nothing more than a seeker of new avenues, since we have all witnessed where the old road has led us. The competitiveness of the past may have been the motor of progress, but its speed rushed us into the abyss."

Ludec saw a flaw in his plan.

"But what man knows he can not unlearn. What you are asking us to do is to forget the past and all we have learned. That is impossible. I agree it would be a better world if we could forget how to produce the bomb, or how to manipulate viruses for bacteriological warfare. Memory is one of man's greatest assets, but it's also our greatest adversary."

The Abbot nodded, acknowledging his statement. "Then perhaps we must find ways to use the past to better serve the future."

"But we're bound by our own nature to recreate the past," Ludec countered. "After all, when man conquered fire he took his first step in meddling with natural order. From that moment on, the making of the bomb was nothing but an accumulative process. How can we reverse that?" Nobody stirred in the room. All eyes were now on the Abbot, but it was the older lama who spoke.

"It is not necessary to reverse our progress, only to harmonize it. The wealth and knowledge used to build an atomic arsenal could have been used to build hospitals or to produce food for the millions of hungry people in the Third World countries.

The young Abbot continued the thought. "We must control science rather than have it control us. We must stop producing more and more even when it is not needed. We must create better standards, which take into consideration the spiritual need of man. But spiritual needs must harmonize with the material necessities..."

"Abbot, forgive me, but what you're describing is Utopia," said Ludec.

"Utopia...yes, perhaps. But consider we are in a unique situation. We have been liberated from the unnecessary burdens of over-civilization. The lethal gas formulas and bank accounts and robotic manufacturing systems have been wiped out. We have the privilege of being the founders of a new world."

The Abbot went silent for a moment and surveyed his audience. Ludec was stunned by the intense power that radiated from the man. He made eye contact with each of them before he continued, "I'm asking for your cooperation in that plan. Are you willing to join with me in creating a new order?"

The room became very quiet.

Ludec eyed the others. None seemed ready to speak on their collective behalf. Did their future depend on their answer? Would he ask them to leave if they decided not to go along with his plan?

Ludec took up his role as their leader and replied on their behalf, "We will cooperate, but we are individuals and maintain our right to disagree, and to express our opinions freely. That is the condition of our cooperation."

Satisfied, the Abbot again addressed them. "In that case you are welcome at Panchen-Bo. We will now provide the necessary leadership to our simple people for a new beginning. From my schooling I faintly remember a quote that seems appropriate to the situation. I may be misquoting, but I believe it said something like this: '*To make an end is to make a new beginning. It is in this beginning that we make a new start.*'

"I feel it is my duty to inform you of the state of affairs here. In a sense, we are the wards of the Chinese forces." Despite the incredible control the man had over his facial expressions, Ludec detected a fleeting shadow of anger, then it was gone.

"What you're really saying is that we're prisoners, aren't we?" Rudi asked in a tense voice.

"Prisoners? That's a matter of point of view. Who is to say whether the bird in the cage is a captive or whether the rest of the world is excluded from her cage in order to preserve her freedom inside? We are either prisoners or wards of the Chinese according to point of view."

"Still amounts to the same thing though, doesn't it?" Andrew stated.

The Abbot continued without acknowledging the comment. "Since the monks of Panchen-Bo represent the most powerful organization in the vicinity and the population is totally loyal to us, the Chinese have to seek our cooperation as well. It is not clear who is captive and who is free.

"You have all had an exhausting day so I suggest that any further conversation about the immediate needs of our little island of survivors be postponed." With that statement, he repeated the traditional gesture of greeting, which in this case was a sign that the meeting was over.

Loanche translated the guide's request for the group to rise and follow him back to their apartments. They exited the room quietly, each contemplating the strange conversation.

Chapter 22

NICOLE WAS only too happy to leave the reception hall. Her anger and humiliation simmered just below the surface and she knew it wouldn't take much more to have it boil over. The tension of the last two days had her nerves drawn as thin as a piano wire.

At the first turn in the hallway she heard Loanche bid them goodnight. Ludec replied, then moved up to walk beside her.

"For some reason I do not trust that man. He seems far too interested in our affairs. He wasn't needed tonight, yet he knows exactly what plans we have in mind for the future. Tomorrow I think I will suggest to the lamas that Loanche's assistance is no longer needed."

She agreed with Ludec, but her anger put a hard edge on her tongue.

"Do whatever you like. My opinion carries no weight around here." Her words seemed to hang in the narrow hallway. They negotiated the remaining corridors in strained silence.

When they reached the living quarters Andrew yawned and raked his fingers through his hair. "I'm bushed, but I'll never sleep."

"I'm with you there," agreed Brock as he kneaded the small of his back.

She didn't want to be alone with only her foul mood for company. And there was so much to talk about. They were guests in the monastery that was true, but that didn't mean the lamas were the only ones who should call the shots.

"In that case," Nicole said as she waved them towards her door, "I invite all of you to my room. I believe it's the most spacious—and it's private. After all, we have the right to a bit of privacy while we plan our own blueprint for the future, don't you think?"

The tone of her voice drew a look of concern from Ludec. She wasn't a superwoman. She was a lone female surrounded by men. She was scared and there was no other woman she could turn to with her fears.

As they entered the room he asked, "Is that sarcasm I hear, Nicole?"

Her anger boiled over. "Yes, this is sarcasm you hear, Ludec. And what's more, I'm damned angry. With all that preaching from the Abbot I feel like I've been dropped into the middle of a cult. And he treated me like I'm a...a third class citizen. Look at us! We're trapped here."

Her anger dissolved and she fought hard to stop the tears that threatened to fall. "What's going to happen to us? Foreign food, foreign language, foreign customs, and foreign deities! A foreign environment all around us with no way out!" Her hands flew to cover her face and block out the shock in their eyes.

Get a grip on yourself. This isn't a pity party. You're letting everyone down.

Being a woman in what was largely a man's world had seldom been a hardship for her. In her view, as long as she pulled her emotional weight she was accepted as part of the group. When her emotions were at odds with the group, she became the token female. She had worked hard at controlling her emotions and was proud of her success. Now she felt she was failing badly. Her treatment by the Abbot, her exhaustion, and the literal end of her world combined to break down her defenses. She was the token female in a man's world.

She sucked in a deep breath and was about to apologize when she felt herself engulfed in gentle arms. It was Brock. Her first instinct was to draw away. But it felt so good to be held, to breathe in the scent of a man and feel his strength. He made her feel so safe.

When he spoke she felt his words rumble up from the depths of his chest. "We're in this together, and we're here for each other. Like a family. Remember what the Abbot said about the bird in the cage? He might be wordy—but he has a point. It's a matter of perspective. Hell, a few days ago I was sure Rudi was a spy!"

"And I must confess," said Ludec with a nod, "that I felt the same way about Brock."

"So here's our first example of how quickly artificial barriers can be broken down," Brock replied.

He stepped back from the embrace and guided her to the *gundri*. Her cheeks burned with shame because of her outburst, but the wave of emotion had crested and was receding. Sheepishly, she looked around the room. There was concern in her friends' faces, but no censure.

"Unfortunately Brock, the barriers you mention weren't artificial," Ludec stated. "I was sought out and blackmailed to play my part in their dirty spy game. That suspicion was placed in our minds for a definite purpose—to divide us. When we are divided we are weak."

"That's putting it mildly," Brock agreed, "considering how few of us there are."

Ludec nodded, then continued. "But now we have the opportunity to develop a feeling of brotherhood—unity if you prefer. We have a common purpose, survival; but we need to develop a consensus on how to go about achieving it. We're sailors shipwrecked on some strange island. Worse than that! We're in a situation where there's no hope of rescue."

"And despite the utter hopelessness of our situation here we are, planning for the future. Tell me, does that make sense?" Andrew asked. He had taken a seat in the corner of the room where he was using the wall as a headrest. The day had been a long one for all of them and he didn't even bother to open his eyes when he spoke.

"That is one of the wonderful things about human nature, Andrew," Ludec replied. "Men can not live without plans, and plans are the ultimate expression of faith in the future. '*As long as we breathe we hope*' says a Latin proverb. I've had reason to remember that quote in the past—and it proved to be true."

"All that talk about the harmony of man with nature. That only existed in the Garden of Eden." Andrew accompanied his comment with a dismissive flip of his hand. His voice held a hint of a scoff. "And by the way, who do you think the Serpent will be this time around?"

"I don't know who the Serpent will be, but there's no doubt as to who Eve will be!" As tired as Rudi was, after equating Eve with Nicole, he seemed to perk up and moved his cushion in to be closer to the group.

Rudi's words sent a cold bolt of shock through Nicole. It was only now that it dawned on her that the men would regard her as the potential fertility goddess of the future.

On most war correspondent assignments she had been the only woman among a group of men. She was far from being promiscuous but she did have a healthy appetite for sex, and in her relationships with her occasional lovers she was sure she gave as much satisfaction as she received.

She was confident in her sexuality, but at the same time she had always protected herself from a deeper involvement. And the demands of her career kept her constantly on the move—not the ideal circumstances for forming long term relationships.

While still in college she had experienced an unplanned pregnancy. Since then, she'd used a contraceptive implant, an invention which, much like its precursor, the pill, had a tidy way of absolving moral consequences for sexual conduct. Her career seemed too important to jeopardize with a pregnancy. Now she was in her thirties and had never had a child. She had not had the implant replaced this year; her intent was to make some definite plan with respect to motherhood.

She had developed genuine platonic feelings towards her companions. Brock was obviously attracted to her and she found that flattering. Andrew, with his masculinity, she found attractive and knew he felt the same way about her. Her feelings towards Rudi were more platonic; he was like an older brother. Even Ludec, with his silver temples was an attractive man. It was strange to sit and scrutinize them so coldly, thinking of them as specimens for mating.

Still, the question was an important one—who would be the new Adam?

Ludec broke the unnerving silence.

"Once again we are looking at another of those artificial barriers. As humans we've been out of harmony with nature when it comes to our sexuality. Perhaps the barrier has been for valid social reasons, to protect the family unit for example, or perhaps it's been a barrier to curb population explosions. But no matter how you look at it, we are the products of educated inhibitions."

"Hey, speak for yourself," Rudi groused. "I've never considered myself inhibited when it comes to sex."

"Okay," Ludec smiled, "Rudi excluded. And you brought up a valid question. Do we want our race, the Caucasian race, to survive? It's not a question we have to deal with immediately, but at some point, if we survive, we will be forced to make a decision."

"Are you suggesting that I sacrifice myself on the altar of fertility for the future of the Caucasian race?" Nicole cried. She was stunned that they could talk about her sexuality in such an easy fashion.

"I hadn't thought about it in those words, but I suppose that is what I'm suggesting. But the answer, and the responsibility, is yours alone. Of course we would never force the role of Eve on you."

"Oh, and isn't that considerate of you," she snorted. "Let's be realistic. Even if I did conceive, it would take nine months before I gave birth. And that's only one child. We need more than one child to secure survival."

"But we are not talking survival. Survival of the Sherpas, if there is any survival at all, is assured. What we're discussing here is the survival of our white race—if the human race survives," he said calmly. "Only we...sorry, only you, can secure the survival of the Caucasian race. At some point you may have to decide if that is a role you are willing to accept."

"It's a terrible responsibility! And moreover, it smacks of racism. I'm sure we'd all like to think we're free from prejudice, but when the question of the extinction of *our* race becomes a possibility, well.... Look at you, Ludec—you called it the *Caucasian* race. You mean the *white race*. Now we'll see just how free from prejudice we really are."

She was tired, and she was angry, and her emotions had re-surfaced. But it was an important question. There was no use putting an end to the conversation because she knew that if they left the room she wouldn't sleep anyway. " I've always wanted a child. I guess, like a lot of other people, I feel that a child is a way of leaving a little bit of ourselves behind when we die." The tension in the room was overwhelming. They seemed to be hanging on her every word. She rose and began to pace, clasping and unclasping her hands. A month ago these would have been very personal thoughts, but so much had changed.

"The possibility of the extinction of the human race just didn't occur to me before." Suddenly it was too much. It was getting hard to breathe. "Oh, please," she cried as she returned to the *gundri* and once again put her trembling hands over her face, "let's stop talking about this for now." Her exhaustion had her on the verge of tears.

RUDI WAS almost sorry he had brought up the topic, but the preservation of the Caucasian race was a compelling subject. It wasn't an easy matter to change the conversation.

He cleared his throat. "The most pressing question, as I see it, is to find a decent substitute for fossil fuel. If they're using oil up here it won't be long before the supply is exhausted." The men turned their attention to this new issue.

On the trek he had come to like each of his companions. It was interesting to watch everyone's reaction to the problems at hand. He was seeing each of them in a new light.

"True. Any ideas on how to do that?" asked Andrew, who appeared to have the most practical sense of all of them.

Rudi turned his attention to the question. "There are two age-old, nonpolluting and ever-present sources of energy my friends—wind and water. This is the perfect chance to give them a try." He found himself getting excited about tackling the problem. Andrew immediately grasped the proposal.

"Of course! That river would be an excellent source of hydro energy. All we have to do is harvest it!"

"I hate to throw cold water on your ideas," Ludec commented, "but I fear the medicine may be more dangerous than the sickness. It will take us more energy to develop a hydro-electric plant than the benefit we would derive from it. But then I also admit, hydro-electric power is far more practical than oil."

"It'll be hard work, but not impossible," Andrew assured them. "I noticed that there's a prayer wheel downriver. If the locals built that, then they can imitate it on a larger scale. What do you think, Rudi?"

"We've got the fast-flowing water in the gorge, and it's obvious from the design and construction of the footbridges that the people of the area are resourceful when it comes to construction. And maybe there's a way to make use of this damned wind that never seems to stop blowing, too."

"And then, in the end, we will very likely end up with assembly lines and surplus productions that contribute to new consumerism and a polluting society," Ludec added with the trace of a smile. "Sorry," he held up his hands as though to avoid a blow. "I was just playing the role of devil's advocate."

"Isn't there a middle ground between the two evils?" Andrew asked.

Ludec shrugged, then said. "Perhaps up to now human history has been nothing but a search for that magic balance between the simplicity of the Stone Age with its uncertainty, famine, and diseases and the sophistication of our modern society with its poisonous air, genetically altered food, and artificially maintained vegetation. Maybe this drastic end is nothing more than a mercy killing. An escape from the horror of a lingering end on a planet which has become exhausted."

"It's an enlightening conversation gentlemen," Nicole said from her place on the *gundri*. Her voice was thick with unshed tears. "You sit here discussing the theoretical ills of humanity while people drag themselves across the ruins of what used to be cities..."

"Nicole, I'm sorry—" Ludec began, but she plowed on, cutting off his words.

"We don't even want to imagine the horror, do we? Can you imagine this then? Can you image what it will mean for me to become a mother at my age? Without hospitals, without the help of a doctor...without love?" Her tears broke and coursed down her pale cheeks.

With some guilt Rudi realized they had overstayed their welcome. He stood and the others followed suit. Quietly, they began to leave. Brock placed his hand on her shoulder as he passed.

Rudi thought it only a consoling gesture and was surprised when Nicole seized it and held him captive. Eve had selected her Adam. He felt a spasm of jealousy, then let it go. Nothing would divide the group quicker than jealousy.

Chapter 23

Zero Time - The Second Day

THE TIME was well past midnight when the Bongen Dadzi and his companion, the Abbot, noiselessly departed the small acoustic compartment. The room existed for the specific purpose of listening to foreign visitors' conversations.

Eastern technology, which had preceded Western knowledge in printmaking, gunpowder, and understanding the significance of the compass, also knew the elementary laws of acoustics. The so-called whispering corners, or chambers for the purpose of gathering information, had been in use for centuries in the east. The monastery of Panchen-Bo was one of the oldest structures in Northern Nepal and it had a wonderful whispering corner.

The lamas remained silent until they reached the sanctuary of the Abbot's apartment.

Bongen Dadzi was the second highest-ranking person in the monastery's hierarchy and tutor, or guru, of the younger man. He turned to his pupil and drew his robes around himself more tightly before he spoke.

"It is very strange to see how difficult it is for these Westerners to adapt to a new situation. Their way of thinking is anchored in the mud of quantity. 'The more the better' seems to be their philosophy."

"I remember the difficulty the Westerners had at the University of Santinikentan," the Abbot answered as he mixed yak butter into the tea he was preparing. "Many of the students and faculty who came to the school were from the West. It was the excellent reputation, and the fame of its founder, Tagore, that drew them there. Ah, how the wise one used to quote the sacred Sanskrit scripture."

He closed his eyes and began to recite: "'When all are liberated from earthly desire, then the mortal becomes immortal!' These words are the foundation of Buddhism, but they were almost incomprehensible to the Western mind."

Bongen Dadzi's heart warmed at the sound of the words. He continued the quotation where the younger man left off, "'When all the knots tying the heart to earthly matters are cut, then the mortal becomes immortal! Thus it is written.' How does the Western mind grasp such a concept, when they consider price over value?"

"As materialistic as they are, my Guru, there is one fact that we have to remember. The capitalist societies have trained their people to be innovative thinkers. For them a problem isn't their fate, it's a challenge they seek to conquer. You heard them in the woman's room tonight. Already they are working on solutions."

He finished with his task and extended the cup to the older man.

"We must use them for the purpose of survival but we must be on guard to prevent their materially-oriented mentality from influencing our people. The ever-accelerating pursuit of the 'more' ultimately caused this catastrophe. Let us hope that we have not invited the viper into our nest."

Bongen Dadzi welcomed the warm cup into his arthritic hands. It was becoming increasingly difficult to bend the twisted fingers to his will. His good days, those without pain, were less frequent than the bad ones. Winter was coming with its cold winds that stiffened the joints even more. It was his karma and he would have to suffer through it. He blew across the steaming lip of the cup to cool the liquid, then he spoke.

"It is sad to think that Hebrew and Christian teachings are based on pillars like our very own."

His younger companion appeared to be lost in thought; his eyes focused on some middle-distance as he took up the conversation.

"The Western mind knows only 'yes' or 'no' and has no capacity to think in the Yin-Yang complexity. From a practical point of view we must maintain the unique mixture of the Yin-Yang connection between east and west. The world of western civilization has been destroyed by the western mentality and its technology. Now it is time, if there is any time at all, to create a new world fashioned according to eastern values."

"It is the wisdom of the spirit speaking through Bodhisattva," Bongen Dadzi whispered to the quiet room.

Chapter 24

Zero Hour - The Fourth Day

FROM HIS vantage point on a bulging outcrop of rock that overhung the valley, Colonel Woung Lei scrutinized the narrow pass in the distance. It was the gateway to this region from the south. Below on the valley floor, the main highway and the most probable route of any invasion from that direction, remained devoid of traffic. The only movement he discerned through the binoculars was the shimmer of heat waves that bounced off the pavement and seemed to cause the abutting hills to tremble in the afternoon air.

It was irrelevant whether the land they laid claim to was Nepal, China, or Tibet, all that mattered to Woung was that he was now the master of the situation. He congratulated himself on his swift and decisive thrust into this strategically important area.

The memory of a conversation with a fellow officer a few months earlier sprang to mind.

They were sitting in the mess hall after a meal, relaxing over a cigarette, when Shi Rongnu had asked, "You were raised in the old ways, were you not? The ways of our warlord ancestors?"

Woung was surprised by the question. These days it was politically incorrect to mention the warlords. He glanced around to be sure there were no eager ears straining to overhear their conversation.

Shi set his mind at ease. "I ask because I see certain strengths in your leadership that I feel come from our honorable ancestors' values."

They discussed the superiority of the old traditions for a while and then Shi posed an interesting question: What would be the most effective procedures in the event of all-out war with the surrounding nations?

"If the old order has collapsed," Woung replied, "then only the strong will survive. A wise leader would seize food, clothing, medicine, and other supplies in the area, for they will soon be treasures beyond price. Of course, he must also secure the entire district, including any army depots, as his personal domain."

Shi nodded. "Then the circle is complete, and he is now a warlord. Would this wise leader go so far as to exclude from this district any who could not aid in the survival of this new feudal land?"

Woung was shocked at the question; it wasn't something discussed openly. It was not an item in the training manuals of military schools. Was Shi Rongnu a spy, trying to trip him up and report him? He had evaded the question and made his excuses to leave.

Now, however, he was faced with just such a problem. As he saw it, the greatest threat to his kingdom was an uncontrollable influx of people who, like a terrified herd fleeing before a grass fire, would sooner or later appear from the south to seek asylum in this relatively unaffected region.

There were already reports that a group of trekkers had arrived at the monastery. Worse yet, the lamas invited them to stay. The spy told his adjutant, lieutenant Tsong Mei, that the group, four men and a woman, were scientists so Wong felt they posed little threat to the Chinese detachment. Still it was a matter of some concern since the new arrivals were now allied with the Buddhists, and it irked him that they had gotten through his security.

Closing the two main passes from the north had been no great problem. To achieve this end he'd had to disobey his commanders in Sinkiang province, but that didn't bother him in the least. And it had been an easy matter to convince the men under his command that due to the present unusual circumstances, it was in their best interest to remain loyal to him personally, rather than to a distant authority. The promise to soldiers of some vague future power had always been, and remained today, a most alluring enticement. If any of his men had questioned the abrupt change in orders this new direction necessitated, he would have had no qualms in ordering anyone, including his former comrades, to be shot in order to defend his newly acquired kingdom.

His attention was still focused on the shimmering road in the distance when he heard the approach of his personal adjutant, Lieutenant Tsong Mei. The young lieutenant had been re-assigned to him from Colonel Yun-Kei's command at the spy station in Kashgar. Any thoughts of Yun-Kei were accompanied by contempt. The fat fool spent more time worrying about feeding his gut then he did about the real job of soldiering.

Lowering the binoculars, Woung allowed them to swing from their strap around his neck and turned, eager to receive the report he had requested. He was anxious to obtain an accurate calculation of the food supply in the region under his control.

Tsong Mei came to a smart halt in front of his commander and saluted. "Colonel, we have enough food and other supplies in the army's storage depots for at least two and a half months. It may be possible to supplement the supply by requisitioning food from the local population if it's required. The most immediate shortage we can foresee would be rice."

"Yes, rice would be a problem." Woung fingered his lower lip as he mulled over the report. "The population could supplement us with potatoes though. What about water?"

"Water won't be a problem. And the depots have an adequate supply of purification tablets."

"I assume the locals wouldn't be reluctant to take our money in exchange for food?" Woung asked with a slight smirk. The question was more a sneering comment than a legitimate question since he wasn't prepared to pay the locals for the supplies.

Woung was not only a fanatical soldier he was also a true believer in the ways of the beehive. He was convinced that the individual had value only as long as he served the commune, and no individual aspiration or desire was permissible unless it served the interest of the hive as a whole. The present situation had strengthened this conviction to the point of blind fanaticism. Since the total world had shrunk to a few square miles for Woung, he was determined to shape the destiny of that remaining asylum for humanity in accordance with his personal beliefs.

TSONG MEI DID his best to ignore the implication in his superior's tone. Working hard to keep his face neutral, he replied, "I would be surprised if they accepted money for their goods, especially food. The locals don't fully understand what's happened, and they have no idea of the extent of the destruction, but they do sense a disaster is about to happen."

"Then just up the amount we tell them we'll pay."

Tsong Mei shook his head. "They seem to know that money is losing its value. Some might be willing to speculate—in the hope that money will regain its value, but in my opinion the speculators would be in the minority."

"No matter. As long as the population has food or beasts, the army won't go short of anything," Woung replied with obvious satisfaction. With his hands behind his back he rocked back and forth on his feet, a smug look of satisfaction on his face.

Tsong Mei detested the vulgarity and ruthlessness of his leader, and the communists in general, but he held his tongue. He struggled to express his concerns politely.

"Comrade Colonel, it would be a grave mistake to arouse the population's hostility."

The smile slid from the Colonel's face and when he replied his voice had a sharp edge to it.

"Lieutenant, I don't need you to lecture me on how to deal with the situation. I'm well aware that the lamas guide the locals. Further, I intend to rule them by making use of their superstitious and feudalistic ways. This rule will be accomplished under any circumstances, either with the cooperation of the lamas and the people, or without it. I assure you that I will rule! I trust I've made myself clear?"

"With all due respect, sir, may I remind you of how detrimental it was to our own country to enforce our will on the people. Our grandfathers saw what happened when Chairman Mao enforced his doctrine. It set the country back twenty years."

"It wasn't the enforcement of the communist way of life that was the problem there, Lieutenant. It was thousands of years of indoctrination. It was the people's passive acceptance of suffering and exploitation that was the problem. Imperial China's greatest failing was that they taught a way of life in which the lot of the poor is suffering, work, and obedience. We Communists tried to enlighten the people."

"But isn't that exactly what Communism demands of its followers?" countered the lieutenant.

"Perhaps you need a refresher course in Communism, Lieutenant. The Imperial regime, much like a capitalistic society, demanded sacrifice from its subjects as a means of maintaining a suppressive system. Communism accepts the sacrifice of the people as an investment in a better future. But, the collapse of the outside world does not mean the collapse of subordination. Does that make it clearer for you now?"

The young lieutenant remained silent, knowing that any answer would merely widen the gap between himself and the puffed-up fool in front of him.

The Colonel seemed to sense the need for at least some form of conciliatory gesture.

"Look, Lieutenant, whether we like it or not, we're all destined to live, or perhaps to die, together. If the people cooperate, their chances are better than if they oppose us. I need not point out, I trust, that that logic goes for you and I as well. We must make an alliance and act accordingly. Let me warn you however, that when the chips are down, the machine gun will ultimately decide every issue."

Tsong Mei had difficulty with Woung's entire ideology, but he continued to keep his mouth shut. With a stiff salute he left his superior and made his way back to their headquarters in the requisitioned village schoolhouse.

His memories turned to his brother and the massacre at Tiananmen Square.

His older brother, Zen, had acted and spoken like a loyal party member before the Tiananmen Square massacre.

"We have a duty to become a better nation by being better people, unlike those imperialists in Taiwan. People are not stupid. They can distinguish between the party that represents their interest and a dictator's gang that represents its own selfish interest, or worse yet, those of the Americans."

"Perhaps you give too much credit to the people, Zen," Mei said to his brother.

Such had been the discussion between them. In the end they had come to the conclusion that the idea of communism must depend on the conviction of the people, for if it were based on the force of the army it would be no better than the old Imperial rule.

But then Zen had fallen in a hail of bullets in Tiananmen Square.

Tsong Mei had learned a valuable lesson that day. In a society of the hive, an individual whose ideology does not follow the party line can survive only through false pretenses. This realization burned within him but he set his face in a rigid mask of self-control to hide his emotions. He would wait for his opportunity, and then he would have his revenge for his brother's death.

Chapter 25

Zero Time - The Fifth Day
Morning

A GENTLE knock on the chamber door drew Andrew from a troubled sleep. The door opened to admit pale early-morning light, as well as a young novice monk carrying a bowl of water. He placed the bowl on a small table and withdrew as silently as he had entered.

Andrew took the time to arrange the skins on his sleeping pallet into some semblance of order before retrieving his shaving kit from his pack. The water proved to be tepid, far from the steaming bowl he would have preferred, but not unpleasantly cold either. He took up the cake of homemade soap lying along side the bowl and began his regular morning toilet.

"Ludec," he called. "There's plenty of water here for two. A shave will do you good."

The older man had neglected his appearance the last few days. With his shaggy graying hair and unshaven face he was beginning to resemble a hermit.

Ludec ignored the invitation and continued to pace the room, his hands behind his back, muttering what may have been his morning prayers.

"I'm still trying to put myself in the shoes of these lamas. Why the hell are they so friendly? Why are they being so helpful? It would be far more logical to just turn us away since we're only a burden to them."

"Don't give them any ideas. As far as I can see they need our technical knowledge. Then after we fulfill our tasks as they see them, well...to quote Shakespeare, *'The Moor has done his duty, the Moor is expendable'*."

As he uttered the words a wave of futility washed through him. If he weren't such a coward he would have given in to temptation on the trail and turned his gun on himself. Or, he could have slipped over the side of the suspension bridge. He had done neither, so now he would have to live with his decision.

Exasperated with his conflicting thoughts, and with the situation, he turned and threw the bit of cloth he had been using as a towel to the floor. "The whole situation is absurd. We're all absurd! Making plans for future generations—my God! Talk about futile."

The words were barely out of his mouth when Rudi entered the room without benefit of a knock or called greeting. Scooping the cloth from the floor he tossed it back to Andrew and dropped onto a cushion. He joined the conversation.

"I agree. We have to be realistic. I doubt very much whether we have any future." Although his tone was light, as he made his pronouncement Rudi's wan demeanor spoke of the struggles he had gone through to accept the situation.

Andrew nodded in agreement, but hearing the words from someone else's lips made him want to argue that there was always hope until they had drawn their last breaths. Perhaps it was his soul that was arguing with the practicality of his mind.

Rudi continued speaking. "That's where our outlook differs from that of our hosts. They firmly believe in a future. They're determined to build a new world according to their own pattern and we're the tools that will get the job done. And their pattern of society, as we know, is a theocracy—the rule of the Divine through an earthly representative."

Andrew resumed his shave as Rudi rambled on.

"Theocrats have had the most pious, yet the most cruel, forms of government. Remember Iran's Ayatollahs? The Taliban? The Spanish Inquisition? You know, the Aztecs were theocrats and their priests cut out the living hearts of their enemies. No sir, I want no part of that type of society." He cut the air with his hands to emphasize his words. "And I'm certainly not willing to be the sacrificial lamb."

Andrew felt a shiver run up his spine. With a slight shake of his shoulders he dispelled the feeling.

Ludec joined the conversation, exasperation evident in his tone. "Forget about the way things were in the past! Can't you see we're faced with an unprecedented situation here? The experiences of the past don't matter anymore."

"We know that," Andrew countered, "but we're not sure that his Holiness, the Abbot, is of the same opinion. For all we know he may think the situation needs nothing more that a bit of skillful restoration and *abracadabra*," Andrew waved his fingers in the air like a magician, "*Poof!* It's like new."

"I don't think so, Andrew," Rudi said, shaking his head. "He's an educated man. I don't think he has any illusions as to what's going on here."

"I wish I could share your optimism," Andrew replied. He began to pack his toilet articles into his kit bag.

Ludec ceased his pacing of the room and moved to stare out a window. "When I see this stunning beauty around us my entire being cries out that I want to live, no matter the consequences. But, unfortunately for us, our over-complex biological human makeup is extremely vulnerable to the effects of radiation." He rested his arms on the window casing for a moment and shook his head slowly. "Here's a little lesson in biology for the two of you. The simpler the creature, the better its chances of survival in a nuclear disaster. So the cockroach will finally win the day. But if our overextended structure, which is similar to the structure of Uranium 263 by the way, is weakened to a point where the slightest upsetting force dislodges the components, the whole system will fall apart. The simpler the structure..."

In mid-sentence, he twisted away from the window with a shout. "Oh my God! The Yeti!" It was the sound of enlightenment; it was the sound of discovering the obvious hidden behind a veil of blurred images, blurred only because they are too close to come into focus.

"What the hell...? Ludec! Have you totally taken leave of your senses?" Rudi cried as he shot up from his seat.

"The Yeti! The Abominable Snowman! Have you forgotten that we originally came here to track down the Yeti?"

"So what? Have you forgotten that just by chance the whole world has blown up in our faces?"

Ludec grabbed Rudi and shook him lightly as if to shake some sense into him. "Can't you see? In all probability the Yeti is genetically the most stable species of the genus *Homo*. And it lives far above the snow line—the radiation may not reach that high! If there is any chance for the survival of the human race then the Yeti has the best chance."

Andrew seated himself on his *gundri* and watched the small drama unfold before him. Not for the first time he regretted his lack of formal education. His natural curiosity and love of reading could never put him anywhere near the level of their learning. When he'd been asked to join the group he had read as much as he could in the fields of anthropology and archeology. It wasn't enough.

Rudi shook himself free from Ludec's grasp. "What does it matter whether the Yeti survives or not? All the achievements of humanity— the arts, literature, science, and the pillars of logic have gone up in smoke. The Yeti can't pick up the fragments and build a new civilization out of them. Even if the Yeti exists, which is very doubtful, it's only a creature. It hasn't been able to cross over the threshold of self-consciousness, and without self-awareness it isn't human."

Ludec had regained his composure to a certain extent. "And where is the boundary drawn between humanoids and *Homo sapiens* in your opinion, Rudi?" Ludec asked the young German. "After all, there are several theories."

Rudi was not slow to answer. It was obvious that the question was not a new one for him.

"As you say, there are number of opinions. Upright posture and bipedal locomotion that freed the hands for making and using tools is one; stereoscopic vision, which enabled man to judge distances accurately, is another. There's also the inverted thumb, which greatly enhances the dexterity of the human hand."

Ludec turned to address Andrew. "Do you agree with Rudi's explanation?"

"You guys have left me way behind. But I think there would have to be a huge difference in the complexity of the brain." He wasn't prepared to stick his neck out any further than that.

"You're quite right. The enlargement of the neural tube as well as the cortex and the cerebral hemispheres separated *Homo sapiens* from *Homo erectus.*"

"And that was all?" asked Andrew. "But the things that you've been talking about were biological changes. All you've both said is that the tools of thinking or grasping or fighting or seeing were improved by evolution."

Rudi jumped in. "But man couldn't have become a self-conscious being through physical changes alone. Man became man when he was able to act against his instinct. When he could break from the things that held him prisoner to his fears. When did that happen?"

Ludec pounded a fist into his open hand in excitement as he answered, "At that very moment when, for the first time in history, man's brain gave the command to put a dry branch of wood into the flames to keep it burning. Man, like all the other animals up to that point, knew only two reactions when confronted by fire—to flee from it or to extinguish it."

"And that's when he overcame instinct!" Rudi almost shouted.

Ludec nodded. "When, for the first time, he was able to conquer his fear and was ready to maintain fire instead of extinguishing it, he conquered not only fire but also his own instinct-bound nature. That was the moment when *Homo sapiens* came into being."

The grin faded from Rudi's face as Ludec's words sank in. Discouraged, he replied, "Even if you're right, Ludec, there's still no proof that the Yeti exists. And if he does, I don't think he's been able to master fire."

"There is no proof that the Yeti *doesn't* exist. But if he does, in all probability you're right when you say he hasn't conquered fire. If the Yeti does exist, and if he is the most likely to survive this hell that man has perpetrated on himself, then we have a dilemma." He began to pace again and ran his fingers through his hair. "We owe it to any future generations to help the creature take that first step towards a higher form of existence. We have to find him and we have to teach him how to use fire!"

"How? Do you propose to give him a box of matches?" Rudi asked a trifle sarcastically. He jammed his hands into the pockets of his pants and hunched his shoulders. Ludec was so preoccupied he didn't even notice the sarcasm.

"Not matches, no. But a prism, or a glass lens perhaps. Wherever they live, if they exist, there must be some waste material...like manure...Yes, that's an excellent fuel. Hmm, it's far too early to speculate about details, but in principle..." He seemed oblivious to the other two in the room.

Andrew finally lost patience with what he considered a useless conversation. "Man, oh man, you're a dreamer, Ludec. You're obsessing about this Yeti business to avoid dealing with the brutal reality we're facing. To die surrounded by your grandchildren and weeping relatives isn't such a bad death. There's the promise of the future in the surrounding family. The death we're facing now is real annihilation. That's what you're trying to avoid dealing with, Ludec, with all this Yeti talk. Admit it."

"And if it is?" demanded Rudi as he came to Ludec's defense. "So what? We all have the right to dreams; especially dreams that make a bleak situation look a little easier. I'll go along with you, Ludec, even if things do look hopeless."

Andrew was surprised by Rudi's support for the idea. But after all, what harm did it do? "Nothing can be more hopeless than our present predicament, so I'll join the club," he conceded.

"You *are* aware of what happened to the mythical demi-god Prometheus when he stole fire from heaven for mankind," Rudi cautioned them.

"What happened to him?" asked Andrew.

"He was condemned to eternal torture. The Olympian gods had jealously guarded fire and the power it gave them. They weren't about to share it with lower creatures such as man. But Prometheus was a compassionate fellow, and sympathetic to the backward conditions of man. He stole fire from the gods and gave it to man."

"I bet the gods weren't too impressed with that," said Andrew.

"The gods were furious. They captured him, and chained him to the rocks of the Caucasus Mountains. A vulture was sent to eat his liver forever. It was an eternal punishment."

"That's a harsh judgment for providing a bit of comfort to man, isn't it?" Andrew asked.

The tale, however, did give the three something to think about.

Chapter 26

Zero Time - The Fifth Day

NICOLE and Brock had retreated to her room after a brisk walk around the monastery grounds. They now lay relaxed in each other's arms. She watched the last rays of the setting sun as it filtered through the intricately carved shutters of the window and traced dizzy patterns across their bodies.

They had come together the previous night in a passion born of fear and the need to reassure themselves that they were indeed alive. Today their lovemaking was tender; the giving and taking of pleasure rather than fulfilling a need.

Brock's voice was hesitant when he spoke. "I'm sure you expected something far more romantic in a love affair than what I have to offer now."

She twisted a strand of his blond hair through her fingers, marveling at the length of it. Since leaving their base camp they had made do with what they had in their packs as far as personal grooming went. It was Brock's contention that longish hair was easiest to keep if blocked in a short tail at the nape of his neck. Now she gave the strand a gentle tug and allowed it to slide through her fingers.

"I could spare your feelings and deny it I guess, but I won't. Yes, my dream relationship would have involved some romance. You know...dinners out, theatre, and a little sacrifice for the commitment aspect. But, I suppose it could be worse." She did nothing to suppress the small laugh that welled up. It felt good to give in to silliness.

"What do you mean 'worse?'" He twisted out of her arms and raised himself on his elbow in order to read the expression on her face.

"At least there's a physical attraction. My infallible female instinct," she teased, "sensed you were attracted to me early on. Women have this built-in radar that makes it easy to detect a man's interest. And I was right, wasn't I?"

"Yes, you were," he conceded as he settled himself into her arms. "I didn't realize it was that obvious. Still it's a crying shame we were brought together by necessity. If we were meant to be together it should have happened spontaneously. You know—drawn together by mutual attraction."

"Why, Brock Lowden! You're a romantic! A romantic caught in a hopeless race with destiny." The light-hearted banter died. Their situation left little room for frivolous talk. "Do you honestly think we'll have months together? And what if we do? Would we have time to raise a child?"

With one hand he traced the curve of her hip and came to a stop to lightly brush at the edge of her kneecap. The satiny curves of her legs seemed to hold a special fascination for him.

"An honest answer?" he asked. He walked his fingers up the curve of her spine.

"Yes. I'm a practical person and I'm not looking for false encouragement."

"All right. Then I won't lie to you. I have no illusions, but suppose, just suppose you're wrong. What if we have nine more months and after that nine years or more? Do you think we should refuse the opportunity to allow life to continue? Can we accept the responsibility for that refusal?"

"You don't understand my concerns, Brock," she shot back as she pushed him from her arms and moved to sit at the edge of the *gundri*. "I'm worried, not only for my baby's future but also for its health. Radiation can cause birth defects. And one child isn't enough."

"I know that Nicole. But..."

"We would have to have more than one. The whole situation is so hopeless, so...so unreal! Even if I do become some sort of breeding stock, a...brood mare, the outlook is still hopeless."

He drew her down beside him and held her in his arms, the heat of his body gently warming her back. When he spoke she heard the strain in his voice.

"Can you suggest anything better?"

The simple question was sobering, and it washed away her mood of self-pity. She shook her head and relaxed.

Her drifting thoughts settled on the lamas. She was still hurt by the way she had been treated, but she recognized they were restricted by the cultural confines of their society. She was their guest so she'd better get used to it. There was something else that bothered her, and she shared it with Brock.

"Those stone-faced lamas, they're like carved images. How can they be so self-confident? It's as if they're in complete control of the situation and we're their servants. And this is a totally new situation, but have you noticed how calm they are? You'd swear they've been through it before."

"It's not their mood that puzzles me. It's their offer of protection. I can't figure out why they've offered us their hospitality. I wonder if it has anything to do with the Chinese contingent that's near here."

"I'm trying to convince myself it's because of the shared charity and love of Buddhism and Christianity. But when I see their cold eyes and emotionless faces...I can't make myself believe it. I could be wrong, of course," she said as she shrugged. "And anyway, what right do I have to judge anybody as being insensitive? Here I am, enjoying the security of this sanctuary while my family and friends...Oh, Brock!" she gulped, "I feel so guilty that I'm alive! Why me? Why did I live?" Her tears fell silently.

"Please, Nicole. Please, don't even think about it." She felt his arms tighten around her. "And you wouldn't be able to help them even if you were there. Listen to me." He took her chin in his hand and tipped her face up to meet his gaze. "By not appreciating that you're alive you're merely being ungrateful for the life you've been given. And as far as the lamas are concerned? You have to remember that humans suffer only to a certain point and after that our sensitivity sensors shut down. Maybe that's what we're seeing in those lamas."

"Maybe," she agreed as she sniffed and wiped the tears from her face. "I'm just being self-indulgent for the sake of my conscience, and it isn't going to achieve anything anyway—except ingratitude. But you know, sticking your head in the sand to avoid everything once in a while is a wonderful policy."

"At times it may be the best formula to avoid insanity," he agreed as he smoothed the hair away from her flushed face.

"If the best way to preserve our sanity is to shut our eyes to reality then it's criminally irresponsible to give birth to a child. That child will have to face the same dilemma that we're facing today. Brock, I can't agree with the idea of having a child."

"All we have to do is face the present, one day at a time. We're supposed to join the lamas for supper, but we have time for a short nap. It'll do us both good." He planted a light kiss on her forehead.

She was both physically and emotionally exhausted. Accepting his tenderness with a smile, she stretched out on the soft hides and drifted into a fitful sleep.

Brock, however, didn't give in to his exhaustion. His instincts told him that the hospitality offered by the lamas came at a price. What was it?

Chapter 27

Zero Time - The Fifth Day
Evening

ABBOT DZGUN Tse watched closely as his guests entered for the evening meal. Some of the exhaustion evident in their faces at the last meeting had been erased with a few days rest, however the dazed look of shock was still there. To his surprise the interpreter, Loanche, came in with the others. He was sure a messenger had been sent to tell the man his services were no longer needed.

Other than offering them cushions to sit on, he had no intention of making any concessions to the Westerners so the meal was served in the oriental manner—at a low table. Except for the *Tsampa* tea with yak butter mixed into it, they seemed to have no problem with the food.

During the meal conversation was channeled along general lines, touching on the comfort of their rooms and questions about the monastery and surrounding countryside. At the end of the meal he signaled the beginning of the more serious discussion by addressing a remark directly to their leader, Professor Ludec.

"Professor, I am sure you have discussed amongst yourselves our chances of survival and how to best accomplish that end. We would like to know what practical plans you would suggest for the community."

Ludec nodded. "We've done nothing else but talk about survival and our situation here. And yes, we've come up with some ideas." He shifted on his cushion and glanced at his friends. "For one, we feel we should concentrate on keeping the mechanical and electrical machinery in the best possible repair. And, we'll have to concentrate on making sure there is a source of electricity for the radio equipment, since that equipment is our only link with the outside world."

"Well said," agreed Bongen Dadzsi.

Dzgun Tse was glad to see the older man contribute to the conversation. He had been silent though the entire meal.

With a nod of his shaved head, Bongen Dadzsi continued. "I am in charge of the supply and management of the stores, so you must address any questions to me. Our revered Abbot, Dzgun Tse, is recognized by our population as the reincarnation of the famous Bodhisattva Goori, a prominent saint of the Buddhist tradition. It would not befit the dignity of the Bodhisattva to be concerned with earthly matters."

Dzgun Tse didn't allow his face to express his inner smile. In fact, he was perfectly aware of all details concerning not only the monastery but the entire region. Although it would upset his beloved guru, since they were faced with the grave matter of survival, he would have to participate more fully in whatever they needed to do to meet that goal. Reluctantly, he joined the conversation.

"My reverend older brother means that our gasoline supply is very limited. Since there is no hope that we will ever be able to replenish it, the question of how to maintain our source of electricity is indeed pressing."

"It was one of our first concerns as well," Ludec agreed. "But our friend here, Andrew McFairlain, has something worked out." He turned and nodded to the man on his right. "Andrew, you'd better take over and explain your ideas."

Dzgun Tse had been told the man was a mountain climber. He would be resourceful.

"We've thrown the problem back and forth amongst ourselves and come up with a possible solution. Doen in the valley there's a large prayer wheel being driven by the current of the river. We'd like to try and build a wheel like that, but on a much larger scale. We think it could keep the generator going. Rudi's worked out some plans and can explain it better than I can."

Rudi took over the explanation. "I can't see any reason why we couldn't build a larger waterwheel. There are some practical problems, such as the frequency of the wheel turning for the generator, and the regulatory system of the water flow, but those are details that can be taken care of. I'm sure you have some skilled carpenters familiar with the construction of the prayer wheels in the vicinity. All we ask for is their cooperation under our direction. We hope you can assure us of that."

"Yes, of course. The local population will assist you. I have only to request it. Shall we turn to the question of the food supply now? You may have some concerns regarding a shortage so I would like to reassure you that food is not a problem. We have our stores and we also have the support of the people. As our guests, you need have no concerns regarding the food. Your primary concern should be to secure our electricity so that we can maintain our radio communication."

"There's one other thing I would like to talk about," interjected Nicole.

Dzgun Tse heard a faint hiss from Bongen Dadzsi. The older lama's body language made it clear that Nicole should not speak. But Dzgun Tse was prepared to at least hear her contribution.

"I have some training in First Aid. There may be an increase in sickness and I would like to offer whatever assistance I can..."

Dzgun Tse willed his face to a neutral position and dropped his eyes. She stopped speaking. She must have realized that she had ventured into forbidden territory. He avoided eye contact as he replied.

"We appreciate the lady's offer. According to our traditions however, healing is the responsibility of our priesthood. We can accept the lady's offer only in cases of childbirth and infant care. If we have any need for that we will ask for her help."

A faint stain of anger rose on her neck and she opened her mouth to speak again.

If she does, the meeting will be marred with angry words.

From the corner of his eye Dzgun Tse watched as Professor Ludec slid his hand over the table and touched her arm. A signal to accept the refusal without further comment. She seemed to understand the message and her shoulders relaxed, however the anger was still on her brow and around the edges of her mouth.

Ludec's tone was polite when he addressed the lamas.

"Reverend Dzgun Tse, could you bring me up to date on the metal supply in the village?"

With a nod of his head Dzgun Tse acknowledged the question. "As far as the metal supply is concerned, we have skilled smiths and metal casters. As metal objects break and become useless, they will be collected and recast as needed. Most of our mines are outside our present reach. There is only one significant copper mine in our area and unfortunately, that is under Chinese military control. Ah, this reminds me, the commander of the Chinese Forces, Colonel Woung Lei, notified me that he is going to pay us a visit this evening. We can expect him at any time."

WELL, ABOUT TIME, Ludec thought. Nothing more had been said about the Chinese forces in the area. He was anxious to learn all he could about the third party in this high stakes game of survival. He addressed his question to the younger lama.

"Have they laid claim to your territory?"

"Theoretically this is Nepalese territory, but the rules of the past are now void. Woung Lei was swift to disarm our few Nepalese soldiers, so yes, he has control of the territory. But as a Buddhist I will not fight fate. My duty is to serve my people for as long as possible. My advice to you is to seek cooperation with the Chinese."

"It's strange to hear a man who was obviously raised in a western culture being so submissive to fate."

"You, professor, are confusing my western education with my beliefs. My education is only a garment, the exterior shell. Behind that shell is a man who sincerely believes in the teaching of Lord Buddha, which includes pacifism and being submissive to fate."

Andrew, whom Ludec felt was the one member of their group most rooted in reality, challenged the Abbot's words.

"And, in your opinion, Westerners lack these qualities?"

"Surely you see for yourself that the present catastrophe has proven that western competitiveness was fatal to humanity as a whole."

"I'd like to suggest that it was eastern passivity that contributed to famine and suffering, plus a host of other fatal diseases. Just look at the overpopulated countries...India for example..."

"No. I disagree. Death is natural, and the death of the individual is regulated by those calamities in such a way that it enhances the chances of survival of the race as a whole. But what has happened now is total annihilation—a form of suicide decided not by the people but by their representatives." He paused for a moment to formulate his thoughts. "There is a fundamental difference between death and suicide. One is part of the life process; the other is the annihilation of the self by his own will."

The conversation was brought to an abrupt halt by heavy footsteps in the corridor. The Chinese colonel, Woung Lei, had arrived, along with an escort. With an abrupt motion he indicated that the man remain by the doors, then he turned and approached the group. His manner and actions were designed to assert his domination over the gathering.

Ludec rose and the other Westerners followed suit. The two lamas remained seated; the only gesture by which they acknowledged the arrival of the military leader was the pressing of their palms together.

The colonel refused to sit on the cushion he was offered. Instead he walked up and down the length of the room, keeping an eye on everyone present.

"For simplicity I will address everybody as comrades, since I'm accustomed to that. There's no need for formalities and no time to be wasted on them," he began in the local Sherpa dialect. Loanche was finally pressed into service. He began to translate the conversation for those who had difficulty following the colonel's speech. "We are all, like it or not, the privileged few selected by fate to build a new world."

His heavy boots rang loud on the stone floor as he continued to pace. Finally he stopped his pacing directly in front of the lamas and clasped his hands behind his back. When he spoke, it was directed only to the seated Buddhists.

"Our first priority is to work out a general plan, not only for survival but also for the establishment of a new social order. When we draw up this general plan everybody will have his or her own specific duty."

Ludec was stunned. He was treating them as a conquered people.

"We were engaged in a discussion of these matters just as you arrived," the Abbot stated. His face remained set in a mask-like expression, devoid of any emotion. He spoke in English, his only challenge to the Chinese officer.

"Wonderful," Woung Lei replied. He switched from the local Sherpa dialect to heavily accented English. "I am glad to know that you have made some plans. Now," he continued as he vigorously rubbed his hands together, "I detest hypocrisy so I will be brutally frank. I'm not here to engage in time-wasting debate. Time is the key to our survival. The potato harvest and the barley harvest must be supervised. We have to take stock of the available yak herds. We must organize a program to collect metals and to recycle them."

The picture of a dictator rose in Ludec's mind. All the man needed was a riding crop tucked under his arm.

Woung Lei continued to address the Abbot, totally ignoring the Westerners. "These are just a few of the most important and pressing problems. Have you addressed any of these problems?"

"We were discussing plans to build a dam for hydroelectric power as a substitute for gasoline."

"Excellent. When you have completed the project we will divide the energy amongst ourselves according to needs. I hope it's clear to you that I count on you as leaders of the community. The simple people of the area have to be looked after and guided. Remember one thing. Not for one minute should anyone harbor any illusions about acting without my consent. I reserve unquestionable supreme authority for myself. I hope I've made myself clear?"

Ludec could bear it no more and he interrupted. "You certainly have, Colonel, but there is a supreme commander above you."

Woung Lei was forced to acknowledge the rest of the group. But before he could speak, Ludec swiftly added, "You have overlooked nature. We are making our plans without fully understanding the effects of the atmospheric changes. There's the possibility of nuclear winter...even disease."

The colonel's face twisted into a sneer and his voice became steely. "I see that you have fallen into the trap of believing your own propaganda. The scenario of total annihilation. We Chinese have never accepted that paralyzing theory. Even if worse comes to worse, some survivors will remain. It is here that we will start a new world. I hope I have made my intentions plain enough."

The room was silent.

He's just set himself up as king, Ludec thought. Before he could collect his wits Dzgun Tse spoke.

"Yes, most certainly. I would like to make an humble suggestion to the Colonel. The best means of getting good cooperation between the Sherpas and your soldiers would be through us, the temple authorities. Our people are accustomed to obeying the temple. From a practical point of view, working through us would serve the best interests of both parties."

"I have no objection Abbot, as long as you and your organization are ready to execute my commands. That is the sole condition of our coexistence. Otherwise, I'm determined to use whatever force is necessary, no matter how brutal."

He resumed his pacing, although this time he seemed more relaxed when he spoke.

"Our radios have a wider range than yours and we're constantly scanning for outside signals or news. In the Karachi-Ulan-Bator area we have received only fragmented short messages. Rival armed gangs are using force to secure the available food and medical supplies for themselves."

"And the rest of the world?" Andrew asked.

"The rest of the world is a vast armed camp. Survivors are fighting amongst themselves for control. I'm determined to use all the resources at my disposal to preserve our relatively normal conditions here. This decision serves your interests as well."

Nicole spoke for the first time since being chastised by the Abbot. "In that case, we're part of your newly built Paradise, whether we like it or not." From her tone it was obvious that she loathed Woung Lei and everything he stood for.

The colonel sensed the hostility in her voice. He turned and for the first time looked directly into her eyes. The burning coal-black eyes of the Orient met those of the Occident and they waged a silent duel before the Colonel's anger melted into a broad smile.

"Now I understand why Christian tradition says that the harmony of Paradise was upset by the woman," he said smugly.

He left the room with a triumphant smile on his lips. He did not bother with the courtesy of a farewell.

Chapter 28

Zero Time - The Sixth Day

LUDEC RESTED his lanky frame against the balcony that ran along the outer corridor of their wing of the monastery. The adjoining buildings were much lower than the main building and allowed an unobstructed view of the land beyond. In the distance the tiny figures of the locals were just visible as they worked the barley and maize fields. From one corner of this vantage point it was possible to catch a glimpse of the village below and several of the *ghumaune ghar*, or village houses, with their thatched roofs and stone-flagged courtyards.

The villagers seemed to take little notice of the perceptible cooling in the weather. They had limited contact with the outside world so it would not occur to them to attribute the change to an atomic cataclysm. According to their tradition, the weather depended solely on the whim of the mountain gods, and all disasters were accepted as the wrath of those gods. They had no idea that the Geiger counter Colonel Woung Lei had sent Ludec showed a radiation level well above the acceptable limit. It was the beginning of the end.

Ludec's thoughts turned to dying. From the moment of birth the process of dying began. The difference now was that a normal lifespan of several decades was limited to a few months at most. Was it fair to keep Nicole and the others ignorant of the deadly levels of radiation? But was there any merit in killing hope? They were making decisions based on the faint hope that somehow they would survive. What would happen if he removed that hope? Would they sink into despondency?

With a sigh he reminded himself that it was useless to try and reason out what any of them would, or wouldn't, do. Reason didn't prevail anymore. In their present circumstances, the mind transferred reality into a different dimension, and in that new dimension the psyche refused the arguments of the intellect. And perhaps that was called faith.

The sound of solid footsteps on the corridor tile announced Andrew's arrival. His distinct walk was part of the bold self-assured nature that was so typical of the man. Yet for a while on the trail Andrew had panicked. Had he truly come to grips with their circumstances? What would he do if Ludec killed his hope?

Andrew joined him at the railing of the balcony and gazed at the figures in the distance.

Many of the workers in the field were women. Today some of the community's men were busy working on a communal building that was under construction, while others were digging the canal for the hydro mill. Wood smoke and incense, mixed with the aroma of animal dung and pine, reached them on the wings of the breeze.

"They're ignorant of what's going to happen, aren't they?" he observed to Ludec.

"Yes, and ignorance is bliss."

The faint note of sadness in Ludec's voice prompted Andrew to ask, "Have you checked the radiation level with that contraption?"

Ludec made his decision. They had a right to know. "Yes, and it's well above the safety level...about thirty percent."

Andrew gripped the rail so tightly his knuckles turned white. "How right you are then. Only those who are ignorant can be happy."

He contemplated the landscape for a moment longer, then turned his gaze back to Ludec. "What I came to tell you will just pile bad news on top of more bad news. Brock's been into the village and says there are rumors of an outbreak of typhoid. They figure one of the passing caravans brought it in. Some of the villagers have been immunized, but the majority haven't. I guess we're fortunate we were vaccinated for the expedition."

"Is there any vaccine available here?"

"According to Loanche there's some Chinese-made vaccine at their outpost, but he figures they wouldn't be willing to share it. Nicole spoke to the fellow in charge of the monastery infirmary and he says he thinks there's a small supply of Soviet Nation product in glass vials. It's stored in a cold storage room in a cellar. He told her he'd go and check but she'll have to wait until tomorrow to find out how much there is. Of course, there's no way to tell if it's still effective since we don't know how well it was stored—if it's there at all. If it comes in vials with syringes, we know right away that the stuff is old."

"It should still be administered. What do the people have to lose if it's no longer effective? Typhoid...radiation...it's only another variant of the same end."

Andrew nodded. "I get the impression that the locals would consider it just another curse of the mountain gods expressing their displeasure."

"True," Ludec replied. "And in a way I envy their beliefs. For them, disasters are part of human destiny. Earthquakes, avalanches, mudslides...they're all just part of the pattern of life. Their passive acceptance of life gives them strength to endure everything. Look at them," he gestured to the village below. "They go about their daily tasks at a steady pace—harvesting the potato crop, herding the yaks to better pastures, and milking their goats as they have always done."

Andrew turned his back on the scene and propped his elbows on the balcony. "I wonder if our teachers ever considered that one day our knowledge might be a burden to us?"

Ludec chuckled. "Knowledge...a burden. Yes, perhaps it is. The Abbot is an educated man and I sense he's aware of the seriousness of the situation." He batted at a bold fly that settled on the back of his hand. It didn't fly away. The soft blow sent it to the floor where it spun in circles. Finally it righted itself and crawled into a corner. A shiver of cold dread ran down Ludec's spine.

Andrew hadn't noticed the small drama being played out. "If he's worried, why isn't he opening up then? Why isn't he talking about it?"

"You have to remember, the lamas' power over their subjects is based on their divinity. Gods don't discuss the future with mortals. If they descend to the level of mortals, they lose their power."

"Power. It's all about power. Really, when you think of it, the people of the west aren't that much different from the people of the east. We're still driven by the same emotions, but we express those emotions differently."

The sun warmed the stone where its rays hit the building. They stood there, leaning against the railing, enjoying the quiet of the afternoon. In the distance the faint sounds of construction could be heard. Ludec gave himself over to the warmth and peace of the moment. Then Andrew broke the silence and asked in a strained voice. "Are you still going to pursue this business of the Yeti?"

Ludec gave the question some thought before he turned to face the younger man.

"Given what we know about the radiation count, I would have to say yes. Maybe you think it's a useless fixation, something to divert my thoughts to rather than facing reality, but it could also be our best chance for the future of mankind."

He used his hands as a set of scales to demonstrate his idea. "On one hand—annihilation of the human species. On the other hand—survival of that species. I realize it might be one chance in a million, but if we don't try to build a bridge between the hopelessness of the present and a possible future then we're committing the gravest crime against mankind."

"So what are we waiting for? If you're so convinced that we have a shot at it, then it's time we get started, isn't it?"

Ludec turned away to hide his embarrassment. "It sounds ridiculous, even to me but...I'm waiting for..."

"For what?"

"Laugh if you want to, but I am waiting for a sign."

"A sign?" repeated Andrew, incredulous.

"Yes, a sign. Maybe it's the circumstances we're in, or the fact that we're living in a monastery, in almost mystical surroundings, but somehow I feel I have to wait for a sign."

"I hope your sign won't delay us too long. If the radiation levels are as high as you say then it won't be long before we start feeling sick. If the Yeti is above the snowline, we'll probably have to take Nangpa-La pass, near the Cho-Oyu range. It's difficult terrain. The altitude is well over twenty thousand feet so we'll need physical stamina and oxygen tanks. If we wait too long, we won't have the energy or strength to make it."

"I'm aware of all that, but I refuse to rely on my intellect alone. I need something more. I need something to give me a conviction...like those people out there have. They firmly believe there's a continuum to life. That's faith. And I need to feel that faith."

"If that's what you need then I certainly have nothing to offer you," Andrew replied in a low voice.

They became absorbed in watching the unearthly beauty of the Tomache peak as the sun, shining through a faint layer of nuclear dust, painted its pinnacle a bloody red.

Chapter 29

Zero Time - The Seventh Day
Morning

"NO, NO, no...tell him I feel fine. I just want to know if he found the medicine." Nicole did a slow turn around the room while Loanche interpreted her request to the infirmary supervisor.

Roots and dried herbs hung from pegs in the exposed wall studs and dangled from hooks in the ceiling. Several cabinets leaned haphazardly against the far wall and bags of brown grasses, and what appeared to be knots of fungi, were stacked in the corner. She had the sensation that she had somehow been transported back in time several hundred years.

Loanche interrupted her observations. "He says he found some medicine, *Memsahib*. He brought a small bottle to show you but it's in the cold room. He will go and get it."

"Please tell him that I appreciate his help." She hated having to rely on the interpreter but she'd never been a quick study in languages. Both Ludec and Brock seemed to have no problem picking up the local dialect and had told Loanche they didn't need his help. As a result, the man seemed to be at her side every time she turned around. Today she welcomed his help but resented the need for it.

The old lama shuffled off into an arched opening that evidently led to a small cold storage chamber. Within minutes he was back and rattled off a few sentences. Then he held up a glass vial for their inspection.

Loanche translated his words. "He says he found about fifty vials of medicine like this one. But he doesn't think the Abbot will allow them to be used."

"Why on earth not? The people are sick!"

"The Abbot prefers to use traditional medicine, *Memsahib*. It is the way things have always been done."

BACK IN her room, Nicole fought her anger and frustration. From the window she watched smoke rise from many of the houses in the village. To have a fire burning at this time of day was a sign there was sickness within. The people's experience had taught them that fire provided not only heat but it also had a disinfecting power.

On one of her brief forays into the settlement with Brock, a friendly homeowner had told her only the wealthy could afford to build a chimney. The more modest homes made no provision for smoke, which escaped through the thatched roofs and other openings.

She could only imagine what it would be like to live in one of the homes without a chimney when the window openings were closed to preserve precious heat on cold winter nights. There was one benefit to living in a smoke-filled house—the smoke offered a natural preservative for the wood and thatch.

Word had come to the monastery yesterday that the epidemic was spreading with devastating speed among the Sherpa population. At first it was whispered that the Westerners had brought the sickness, but the first case was traced to a porter who recently returned from Tibet.

From her vantage point in the monastery, Nicole had hoped to oversee a vaccination campaign to prevent the spread of the disease. Now, although there was a limited supply of vaccine, she knew her hands were tied.

The infirmary supervisor's words were a real blow to her plans. She'd taken an in-depth First Aid course before her first posting as a war correspondent. She had the skills, and the confidence, to help with the typhoid victims. The only thing standing in the way of saving lives was the withheld authority of the Abbot.

The previous evening they had gathered in Ludec's room where she shared her plans.

"If it's not in pre-loaded pressure vaccinators then there's a chance it could be quite old. And it will have to be administered with syringes. But I could give you a quick course on how to give the injections. The Abbot made it clear he doesn't want me to do any nursing, but maybe he would give us the okay if you guys offered to administer it, rather than me."

The room was small, too small for all of them to sit comfortably. Rudi was perched on the edge of the only table in the room, toying with the oil lamp. He cleared his throat and then directed his comments to the room at large.

"And what if the serum is contaminated? What if we give the people this old medicine and they die from it? He said it was Soviet made. What kind of medicine was the Soviet Nation producing ten years, or even five years ago?"

"As far as the product goes," Nicole replied, "I think we have to take the chance as long as the vials look clear; without any cloudiness in them. The real problem I see is the Abbot's attitude. He said point-blank that he wasn't going to us me as a female doctor. I don't even know if he would welcome foreign men as healers. I'd like to pay him a visit in the morning and make another offer to help. The number of deaths in the village may have changed his mind."

Arms folded over his chest, head down, Ludec thought over her words. "Just in case he gives us the go-ahead, put off your request until after lunch, when we get back from the construction site. Okay?"

Now, from the window of her room, she watched the columns of smoke announce the arrival of sickness and death to people she may have helped. She was angry and her temper grew with each passing hour. What a waste! What narrow-mindedness!

She drew the vial from her pocket and examined it again. The liquid was clear so it had been stored correctly. But it was the label that brought the smile to her tense face. It was clearly marked "Scott-GM". That meant the vaccine was less than five years old. It also meant it could reverse the typhoid symptoms for those in the earlier stages of the disease.

Reason argued that they were going to die anyway. Radiation sickness had just as much destructive power as typhoid. But at least there was a remedy for typhoid.

She jumped as a knock sounded on her door. Had the men come back earlier than expected? To her surprise it was the Abbot who entered.

He bowed his dark head then looked at her directly for the first time. "I have a favor to ask of you, Madam," he said in a calm voice. "The infirmary supervisor has told me of your visit. You offered your help to us in the capacity of a field nurse. My pride caused me to refuse that help. I was wrong and I apologize. Are you still willing to be of assistance?"

Nicole was caught unprepared and it took her longer than she would have liked to reply.

"Yes, certainly. But...I'm surprised."

"You have every right to judge me."

"No, I'm not judging you. It's just...I'm astonished that an idol is human."

"I am human, Madam. When I studied at Santiniketan I mixed with people from around the world. While there I was a student, one of many, and very human. Here I am the incarnation of Bodhisattva, a god. Are you familiar with the story of Thomas Becket?"

"Sure. Priestly vocation has a transforming power. Falling from the altar is the greatest of all falls... oh, I see. So why are you asking me for help? The men are quite willing to help with the vaccinations, and perhaps they would be accepted more readily than a female."

"Not quite. Maybe among the male population, yes, but no Sherpa woman would allow a man to vaccinate her."

"Ah, yes. I'd forgotten that your people are one of the most gender conscious people in world."

He nodded to acknowledge her statement. "The colonel has offered us half of their supply of vaccine since they have more than they need. We should have enough to do our entire population."

A thrill of excitement coursed through her. She was actually having a conversation with a Nepalese monk. She motioned to a chair but he shook his head. It was then that she noticed he had left the door standing open. Obviously he was uncomfortable in her company and it was only the circumstances that had forced him to seek her out. Still, she wanted to share her thoughts with him. Perhaps he could help her sort out the doubts and emotions tearing at her. There was a good chance she was going to die, and he was the closest thing to a priest she had.

"Has it ever occurred to you, Abbot, that everything we're doing here may be just worthless effort? The radiation, or the damage to the atmosphere, could end life, vaccination or no vaccination."

"And you feel that those possibilities absolve us from giving what help we can?" A thick black eyebrow rose to greet his shaved head.

"No, of course not. But I'm wondering which is preferable—to prolong life, or to accept a merciful death?"

"In our religion we are not in a position to fight providence. We must accept fate. After all, the first duty is the preservation of life. As long as we live we have to eat, work, plan, act, and suffer."

"Even make love in order to maintain life?" Would her question shock him? She fingered a button on her shirt and fought the urge to lower her gaze.

He remained unperturbed.

"Yes. We must do all that is necessary for life's continuity. Life as we see it is a force seeking perfection through change. We're not talking about individual life but life in general. The end of life is when perfection has been reached and there is no change possible. We call it Nirvana."

"But there is no such state of the Universe."

"We believe that everything is possible. We can safely say only that certain dimensions are beyond human understanding. For us humans, knowledge is but an island surrounded by a sea of infinite mystery. No matter how much we are able to extend the shoreline of our island, the sea remains infinite."

"Abbot," she replied with candor, "I confess I don't follow your vision or your symbols. All I know at this moment is that Nicole Holden is here, she is alive, and she offers her help in the service of the preservation of life."

"Thank you, Madam. I had no doubt as to your final decision."

For the first time a warm smile opened on his face and he bowed, then departed.

Chapter 30

Zero Time - The Tenth Day
Morning

BROCK TOOK on the construction of the electric plant with the energy and determination of someone trying to lose himself in his work. For once he was glad for the training the Marines had provided.

Andrew and Rudi chose the site, and the locals surveyed the new channel bed for the waterwheel. Then, not content to supervise the digging by the local gang under Loanche's leadership, Brock grabbed a spade and added his efforts. It felt good to do manual labor and to flex his muscles and feel sweat run down his back.

From the warehouse of his memory an old Frank Sinatra tune surfaced. It was a song about a stubborn ant that refused to give up. He hummed a few bars and the name of the tune came back to him. *High Hopes*. That was it! They were a lot like those ants.

Several days of hard work was showing results and the channel that would tame the fast running tributary of the Dudh Kosi was beginning to take shape. The dam and lock to regulate the flow would be built next.

Rudi, who had more mathematical knowledge than Brock, was supervising the construction of the waterwheel and the gears for proper transmission to drive the generator.

"We have to be able to regulate the flow, otherwise the spring floods will wash away everything we've built here," he explained to Brock during a work break. They stood over the skeleton of the wheel that was beginning to take shape. He made a minor adjustment to one of the cogs before he continued speaking. "Here we are, talking like people who have the luxury of making plans for decades to come. Have you felt any effects of the radiation?"

Brock remembered that earlier that morning Rudi had mentioned he'd had loose bowels. Was it something he'd eaten, Brock wondered, or was it something more ominous?

He hesitated before replying. "Maybe yes, maybe no. I had a bit of nausea this morning, some shortage of breath, but that could just be the food, or the altitude. It might have nothing to do with the radiation.

When I work I forget all about it. So I keep working. We can't afford to miss a chance, Rudi, even if that chance is minuscule."

"Maybe we're missing that chance by doing this work here. Ludec's theory about the Yeti might be right. I'm all for getting out there to search for the beast."

"No one's been able to prove the existence of the Yeti," Brock countered as he gave his sweaty forehead a wipe with a rag from his pocket.

"Nobody has been able to disprove it either."

"They could be such primitive creatures that we wouldn't be able to communicate with them even if we found them."

Rudi continued to press his point. "The only thing we need to communicate to them is how to make and control fire. That doesn't need a lot of effort as far as I'm concerned."

"But if we can preserve the civilization already existing here then we're centuries ahead of the game." Brock rose from his seat on a pile of rocks they had excavated from the trench and bent to retrieve his shovel. A wave of nausea swept through him. For a moment the world seemed to tip and slide out from under his feet. It took immense effort to straighten up with the shovel in his hand.

"We'll leave the decision to Ludec, I suppose," Rudi said. "He's the one with the fixation on the Yeti anyway. And if he isn't ready then we shouldn't push him. Hey! Are you all right?"

Damn! Rudi had noticed the near faint.

"I'm all right," Brock replied abruptly as he turned on his heels and returned to the ditch.

RUDI MADE his way farther along the construction sight to where the men were working on the frame for the wheel under the leadership of Ngta Shumbe. The man was a Tibetan refugee who had fled with his family to Nepal several years earlier to escape Chinese domination. The Sherpas didn't receive Tibetans with open arms, often giving them the appellation "Khamba" a word signifying inferior status.

The local carpenters were semi-skilled workers who did seasonal work when needed, but Ngta was a craftsman. He had constructed several prayer wheels in the past and immediately understood the instructions Rudi gave him by means of sketches. Although Rudi felt confident in his decision to have Ngta Shumbe oversee the work, he wasn't entirely successful in controlling the resentment of the local Sherpas who were forced to work under the Tibetan's foremanship.

Fighting back his own rush of nausea, Rudi started to lay out the number of spikes needed to create a cogwheel for the transmission. He had come to realize that in times of need the most elementary solutions were also universal solutions.

While on university breaks as a student, Rudi had often visited the Netherlands where he became fascinated by the construction of old windmills. His admiration had been so great that he visited the master-builders' shops where the ancient skill was preserved. The memories of what he learned there now came back under the pressure of necessity.

By focusing his mind on the needs of the present, Rudi realized, he was, in a sense, allowing his mind to cope and to heal. The present was here. It was real. The anguish of speculation was buried under the pressure of the present, and the specters of the future could not bother him as long as the present was in the foreground.

This logic, in part, seemed to be the source of the local population's serenity. The harvest was here. The yaks had to be looked after. The direction came from the reincarnated Buddha and he could never be wrong. It was not up to the locals to speculate on his decision. Working with them, Rudi had begun to understand the peace of not dwelling on the past or obsessing about the future. The only reality was the here and now.

It was around noon when Rudi noticed a group of women coming from the direction of the scattered houses that formed the center of the village. Their hurried approach, as well as their wild gestures, revealed their agitated states. Ngta, who was working alongside Rudi, straightened from his task when he heard their voices and gaped at the approaching pack.

Rudi was able to understand the local dialect only if it was spoken slowly, so he found it impossible to follow what the excited women were saying. The look on the Tibetan's face told him that this was a serious matter. Fortunately, Loanche was nearby and he explained the situation.

One of the angry women was Ngta's wife and there was a serious quarrel between her and the wife of their landlord, Jangbu.

The story was that the curse of typhoid had reached Jangbu's house, where the miserable lodging on the lower floor was rented to the Tibetan family.

"It's the good-for-nothing Tibetans who have brought the wrath of the mountain spirit down on our family!" Jangbu's wife screamed. "Both my sons are tormented by high fever because my husband, that soft-hearted and soft-headed idler, did not listen to me when I told him not to allow those filthy Khambas into our house."

Hands on her broad hips, Ngta's wife fired back her side of the story. "You make it sound like charity! It is not out of your husband's kindness, or yours, that we live in those miserable quarters. We work like slaves for you. Who does the household chores? Who cuts firewood, fills the water containers, and feeds the goats? And on top of that, we help in the fields and pay a percentage of my husband's carpentry earnings to live in those rooms."

The poor carpenter tried to stem the tide of his wife's frustration, but she refused to stop her tirade. She turned to the rapt audience and continued to give her side of the story.

"They take advantage of our situation. I can accept the chores, but to demand cash as well...when they have more money than they can use? It's too much."

She turned back to the furious wife. "And it was your own stinginess that provoked the wrath of the gods," she shouted. "Just a few days ago you refused to give alms to a wandering lama. And you also offered oil, which you knew had gone bad, to the household deities. Now you have the audacity to put the blame on us!"

Charges and counter-charges continued to fly back and forth. Both parties were on their way to the monastery to seek the decision of the higher authorities, but since they were passing the construction sight, they were willing to explain the case to the two white men who represented a neutral forum.

"What the heck's going on here, Rudi?"

Nicole's voice at his elbow startled him. He hadn't seen her and Ludec join the angry group.

"We were on our way to try and convince a few hold-outs in the village to accept the vaccinations," she explained. "Looks like we might not have to go in search of them. This is quite the group you've collected here."

Rudi filled them in on the verbal battle that continued to be fought in front of them. It became obvious that the tension was likely to provoke actual fighting when laborers in the nearby field joined in the dispute. The poorer workers took the Khamba's side, but the landowners and the race-conscious Sherpas joined the opposition. Loanche climbed a pile of rocks and tried to out shout the racket.

"Listen to me people! The *Memsahib* wants to help you. She has very potent medicine and I tell you she can be trusted. Like the Chinese doctors, she uses a needle to drive out the demon of the malevolent spirit. This quarrel is a waste of time. Take the *Memsahib* to the sick people! Let's go to Jangbu's house."

NICOLE WAS gratified to see that the promise of healing made an impact. The carpenter, who so far had stood in silence, was suddenly overcome by emotion. He grabbed her hand and babbled a few words, offering himself as a lifelong slave to the lady if she could save his family's living arrangement.

Surrounded by excited villagers, they set out with brisk steps toward the village. Brock and Rudi opted to stay behind and supervise the few workers who chose to remain with the job.

On the way, with the help of Loanche to translate, she tried to give a short lecture on hygiene to the crowd of locals.

"All the houses must be whitewashed inside and out, right to the ground. And the sick people's clothes must be burned."

That announcement provoked a murmur of indignation.

"The people protest, *Memsahib*. They say that in this area the people keep their clothes until they are worn beyond repair. To burn a perfectly good garment is an unheard of thing."

When Loanche moved ahead, Ludec came alongside her and whispered in her ear. "He didn't translate everything they said. Some of them still think we're the cause of their problems. If I caught it right, some say that since these strange Westerners came, many unusual things have happened. I can't say that I blame them."

They were now walking among the scattered houses of the village. Nicole noted that most of the homes were two-story buildings. The first floor was generally used as a stable or storage area for tools and implements, although in some cases it was the living quarters for servants, as was the case for the Shumbe family. The lower portions of the houses were washed with red earth while on some of the homes, the upper portions were embellished with patterns. Open spaces between the houses were used as gardens and vegetable patches.

As a war correspondent Nicole had been in countless villages in many countries. She was struck by the neatness here. No mounds of broken and discarded items, no stinking piles of garbage. The areas around the houses had been swept and small blooming bushes stood guard beside the doorways. Some of the tidiness could be accounted for by the fact that there wasn't a lot of packaging waste to deal with. It just didn't make economical sense to transport canned sodas and junk food to this part of the world.

And of course, this wasn't a country at war and she was no longer a war correspondent. She had to keep reminding herself of that fact. The strange topography, the struggle with a foreign language, the fact that she knew what was happening elsewhere, and the presence of the Chinese troops had all combined to give her a feeling of *déjà vu*. All that was missing was the assistant lugging the television camera.

As they approached Jangbu's house, she watched Ngta Shumbe square his shoulders and inhale deeply, as though preparing himself to do battle for his family's lodgings and their honor.

With Loanche in tow, they left the chattering crowd outside and made their way to the family's living quarters on the second floor. Ngta and his wife, joined by his children, crowded together on the upper staircase to watch the strange goings-on.

The group entered a large, relatively well-lit room with glass windows—a sign of wealth. A low partition separated the sleeping quarters from the kitchen area. A cauldron of glowing coals in the sleeping area radiated heat, while a window at the end of the room was open wide to let fresh air into the smoke-filled chamber.

The two semi-delirious youths lay swathed in heavy blankets on a *gundri* covered with yak hides. The floor around the pallet was strewn with images of benevolent deities and healing spirits. The father, merchant Jangbu Shabur, sat next to his sons on a low stool, his face set in a mask of dignity that failed to hide the fear in his eyes.

FOR MOST OF his life Jangbu had solved his problems with money. He imported goods from Namche Bazaar and Tibet, owned large patches of land, and had a right to cut wood in the dwindling state-owned forests. He was now a man of great wealth.

Rumors of the destruction of the outside world were something new to him. He remembered how much excitement there had been during the Chinese takeover of Tibet. But that turmoil soon calmed down and life had gone on as it always had. He thought the same would happen now.

But this sickness that threatened the lives of his two sons who lay shivering under their blankets was a problem he could not solve. The gods ignored his offerings and his prayers. Both of his sons were almost grown, and to lose a male youngster at the age when he was about to become a full-fledged member of the family was the greatest tragedy that could befall a Sherpa father.

A few days earlier he had heard of the woman who gave away medicine to help with the fever, but he had refused to let his family go to her. Now she had come to him. Perhaps the gods had sent the white woman with her strange medicine.

"I'll need some boiling water to sterilize the needle," she

explained to his wife. "I'll give each of the boys one vaccination, then I'll give you and your husband one."

He watched the woman heat the glittering needle and plunge it into his oldest son's arm. The process was repeated for the younger boy, then for his wife and himself. Jangbu watched closely, but nothing happened.

What was she doing now? She had given the sick boys only one dose of the medicine and now she wanted to give some to the Khambas! The filthy foreigners were going to get some of the healing medicine and his sons were still sick. Rage boiled over and Jangbu shot up from his seat.

"No! No! Not for them. Give my sons more medicine. They are still sick! These Khambas are not sick. There is no need to give medicine to them!"

"Everyone in this household must be immunized," the white woman replied. "More medicine will not help your sons become well. They have already received as much as I can give them."

Did she think him a fool? If the medicine could help his sick sons then they should be given more than someone who was not sick. He snatched at the medicine case but the two men who had come in with the woman forced him back into his seat.

There was another way to get what his sons needed. If force didn't work, money would. It had not failed him yet.

Chapter 31

NGTA SHUMBE watched in horror as the scene before him unfolded. He understood that if his family was not vaccinated they might catch the fever and die. And now Jangbu, who held such influence in the community, was demanding that they not get the medicine. All was lost!

Then he witnessed a miracle. The Western woman was firm in her stand that everyone would get the medicine. What impressed him even more was her refusal of the fabulous sum of money offered by the merchant as a bribe for more vaccine. The rejection of two hundred and then five hundred rupees was a very convincing statement about the Westerner's integrity.

He did not resent his master's attitude. Under similar circumstances he would have behaved the same way. Life was harsh and survival went to the fittest. Those who were powerful had the right to use their power to survive. In the Westerners' behavior he saw compassion, something that was completely strange to him, but it was something he could admire.

When the foreigners finished vaccinating the entire household, upstairs where the light was adequate and boiling water was at their disposal, they descended to the lower floor.

Ngta bowed low and said, "My wife insists that you join us in our home. Please, do us that honor." To his surprise, the one called Loanche accepted the invitation as well. He could not summon the rudeness to turn the man away.

Shame flooded through him as he led them into the living area of their quarters. What would they think? He had been saving his hard-earned rupees to buy an abandoned, half-ruined house that he would repair for his family. Their own home would prove their independence, and independence was his greatest dream. In the meantime they must endure these miserable living conditions.

This room was in sharp contrast to that of his master. One opening in the wall, which was covered with a translucent oil canvas, shed murky light into the room. Some planks separated the entire cubicle, which formed the living area, from the stable. He and his wife, as well as their three children, shared the single room with only blankets to separate their sleeping niche from those of the children.

He was acutely aware of the smell of potatoes and onions that hung in the air, and the strong odor of *gundruk*, the fermented product of various greens that was a source of vitamins and the calcium the children needed for their bones.

"Naga," his wife whispered to their oldest daughter, "please boil water. We will offer our guests tea."

Naga went about her task with little enthusiasm. She was of marriageable age, although Ntga despaired of being able to marry off a girl without a dowry, even if she was strong and good-looking.

He offered the guests a seat on a small rug as his wife prepared the tea with yak butter.

"*Shay*," please, she whispered shyly as she passed the cups. To satisfy the local custom she filled each cup three times.

"Ngta," Ludec said as he finished the last of his tea, "I'm very interested in stories of people's travels. Would you tell me how you came to be here in this community?"

Should he tell this man of their struggles to evade the Chinese border patrols as they slipped over the border under the cover of darkness? Of the hidden paths that his father had shown him? No, those were family secrets. He would keep his story simple.

"In Tibet I was a carpenter in the monastery of Inchung, where many Nepalese came to visit. When the Chinese invaded, they stripped the power of the monastery and it became poor. I had no hope of a better life in my homeland. All I knew was the life of a carpenter, and without work my wife and children were going hungry. The land in the valley behind the Nangpa La pass was a prosperous place, so after much thought, we left our homeland. It was a long, hard journey."

"So now you work for the Panchen-Bo monastery and for Jangbu?" Ludec prompted.

"We accepted the first help offered to us, so now we are indentured to Jangbu. But I work hard and save my money. Soon we will be free of this unhappy relationship."

He knew his wife felt the weight of their bondage more than he did. Her anger this afternoon had not come from any feelings of abuse, but she strongly objected to giving their master precious money that they were saving for their new house. He realized it was the insults heaped on her by Jangbu's wife that had finally caused her to explode. Already she had begged for his forgiveness.

He loved his wife, but her rashness may have cost them their living arrangement.

As they listened to the Tibetan's story, Ludec's eyes grew accustomed to the dimness of the room. In one corner he saw the small family shrine where the image of a deity was revered. A yak-butter lamp and some simple food offerings had been placed in front of it to secure the god's benevolence.

A bowl near the dung-burning stove held a large head of cauliflower and some *mula*, the giant radishes grown in the region.

To the left of the family alter, a demonic ceremonial mask, not uncommon in Tibetan households, leaned against the wall. Ludec struggled to pinpoint what was so unusual about the carving. Then it struck him that it was the abnormally long mane of hair attached to the mask. He knew of no animal in the region with such hair. The yak's hair was courser and much shorter.

Suddenly he felt his heart race. Then he warned himself not to jump to conclusions. But what if what they were searching for was so close as to be within their reach?

There was no further need for their services in the house and he didn't want to hold Nicole back from her work. And, as usual, Loanche was sitting nearby, quietly taking in all they said. He wasn't about to share his suspicions until he could confirm them, so he resorted to a small deception to send Nicole on her way.

"Nicole, I'm sure you want to move on to other houses. But I'm still a dedicated anthropologist, despite everything that's happened. This family is an excellent study of the relationship between Tibetans and Sherpas, and I'd like to ask a few more questions. I feel guilty about holding you back. Why don't you leave?"

"All right, Ludec," she agreed readily enough. "But I'd need to take Loanche with me. Are you sure you can manage on your own?"

"I'll do just fine. Please don't worry about me."

She laughed. "You're incorrigible. A scientist is a scientist to the end, I suppose."

With those words she collected her equipment. The carpenter and his wife accompanied her to the door and said thank you and goodbye by bowing with compressed palms.

What if he was wrong? What if it was hair purchased from some bizarre source? But the face! Bestial, yet with distinct human characteristics. He felt perspiration break out on his palms. His dry tongue had difficulty forming the foreign words but he fumbled his way as best he could through his next questions.

"This is a ceremonial mask. Please tell me which deity it honors."

"It represents the mountain gods. I hold it in special esteem because my father...my father found the hair of one of the mountain gods. He was a great hunter."

The hair of a mountain god! His heart hammered in his chest. Yet Ludec sensed that the man was holding something back.

"Please, tell me more. I am very interested in your mountain gods." He fought to keep his voice even, to sound only mildly interested in the answer.

"Tibet is a country of the gods. Before I was given to the monastery as a worker, we lived close to the mountain of Cho-Oyu, which we can see even from here. It is on the border between the two countries. My father chose to live there since there were still plenty of wild mountain goats and sheep. One day my father had a great adventure, which nearly cost him his life. That was the day he found the hair."

"I would like to hear of this adventure." The Tibetan was obviously reluctant to say more. His hands were restless and he glanced around as through searching for something to divert Ludec's interest to another topic. Should he press him? If he decided not to share the story he would just make up something to get rid of the nosy foreigner. So much depended on what he could say.

Finally Ntga pressed his fingertips together and drew a deep breath. After letting it out he continued with his story.

"A little while before the Chinese invasion my father went out to hunt mountain sheep. Sometimes he took me with him, but on this day he went alone. He was away for many days. While he was gone we heard the rumbling of the mountains but that was not unusual. When my father had not returned four days later, my mother sent me to look for him."

He paused in his narration to stare at the mask, as though seeking instructions from the god that it represented. Ludec silently willed the man to continue. The seconds ticked by. Ngta blinked several times and brought his gaze back to Ludec. "I met my father several hours later. He was on his way back with this hair as a trophy. He told me that I should not tell anyone what he had found."

"Did he say why?" Ludec pressed the storyteller.

"Because the mountain gods would be angry."

"Who are these mountain gods? Can you tell me that?"

"They are very big and strong. They have hair to keep them warm. My father found the passage to their valley. That is when the mountain shook. Perhaps the gods were angry that they had been discovered. While the mountains trembled my father lay on the ground covering his head with his arms to protect himself from falling rocks."

Ngta's wife touched his arm gently, as though to stop the story. He bent and whispered something in her ear. She whispered a few words back, then nodded and fell silent. Ngta continued with the tale.

"When the earth ceased its trembling, he found the body of one of the mountain gods crushed by an enormous rock. Only his head was intact. It looked as though he were offering himself to my father, so he took the hair and came home with it."

Ludec was having difficulty concealing his excitement. "Have you ever seen the entrance of that valley?"

"I swore to my father's memory not to talk about it, but to you, *Sahib*, because of the gift of my family's health, I will tell the truth. He once took me to that secret entrance. Nobody can find it because a large wall of snow blocks the way. There is only a very narrow passage and even that is hidden."

"Would you take me there, Ngta?"

The Tibetan's face showed his hesitation. "Already I have told you more than I have ever told anyone, *Sahib*."

"If I told you that there may be a day when the sun will not shine—when it will be possible to stay alive only in the valley of the mountain gods and your family's life as well as our life depends on finding the entrance—would you show it to me?"

"Then I would. But that is impossible. The sun not shine—impossible!"

"Is it not impossible that the mountain should kill the mountain gods?"

"That was different. There is an eternal struggle between the mountains and the mountain gods. Only the mountain gods can live at the top of the mountains. They are keeping the mountains in bondage. The mountains want to free themselves. Sometimes battles are waged between the gods and the mountains. Then the whole world trembles." The expressive gestures and Ngta's face told the story more clearly than his words.

"You say there is also a battle between the clouds and the sun. When the lightning zigzags across the sky and the thunder shakes the trees, then the sun and the clouds are at war. I fear that one day the clouds will defeat the sun. If that happens, will you lead us with your family to the domain of the gods?"

"*Sahib*, I swear by the memory of my ancestors that I will, but it is a long and strenuous way."

"It will happen as I say." Ludec took the carpenter's callused hands in his own and looked with hypnotic force into his eyes as he spoke. "Be prepared for it, Ngta Shumbe. Be prepared for it."

"I am but a speck compared to you, *Sahib*. You are the one who can control the demon of fever, tame the wild river, and force it to work for you."

"That knowledge is not everything, Ngta. Your knowledge about the mountain gods may be more important than all our knowledge combined." Ludec rose from his seat on the swept floor.

When he emerged into the reality of the watery sunshine, he began to doubt his faith in the Tibetan's story. Had he read too much into the tale? Then realization came.

He had been looking for a sign and he had received one. Now he could begin the search for the Yeti.

Chapter 32

Zero Time - The Tenth Day
Late Afternoon

THE VACCINATING of the porters and those villagers willing to submit to her needle complete, Nicole considered her next move. Should she offer her services to the inhabitants of the monastery? It seemed like the logical next step.

Anxious to follow proper channels, she approached the major-domo, an older lama with only limited knowledge of English. He motioned for her to take a seat in a chilly anti-room and wait. He shuffled off, his felt-booted feet barely making a soft brushing sound on the stone floor.

What would it be like to live a lifetime here? To be raised as a child within these walls? There was little laughter or gaiety that she could see. Even the novice monks seemed reserved and controlled. But perhaps the mood of the younger monks lightened when no outsiders were around. She fervently hoped so.

A half-hour later she was led into the Abbot's reception chamber. The younger and the older lamas were once again seated side by side in that rigid posture that was the hallmark of their office.

"Namaste," Nicole greeted the seated men with a bowed head and pressed palms. Her greeting was received with some coldness, as if she was not welcome in the chamber. Her recent conversation with the Abbot had left her with the impression that things had changed. Now she sensed her mistake.

"I've come with a request. If you will allow it, I would like to vaccinate the people of the monastery. I've completed vaccinating the people of the community and there is still vaccine left."

"You ask the impossible, Madam."

It's that damned male thing, she thought in exasperation. *They're not going to accept my offer of help because I'm a woman.* "Perhaps I should have said that one of the gentleman would come to administer the vaccine."

After a moment of contemplation he said, "Many of the Western religions have been shaped with little thought to meet the people's need to live in harmony with nature. As Buddhists, we strive to act in harmony with nature."

"Forgive me, Abbot, but I fail to see any connection between my offer and your answer." Nicole was sure she would regret her remark when she had time to dwell on the possible repercussions. Right now she wanted an answer to her offer, not a pitch for conversion or a theological debate.

"I'm afraid I made the mistake of approaching my answer from afar," the Abbot replied. "I should have said that we are the representatives of the power of nature. The source of that power is spiritual not earthly. We strive to live in the world with the harmony symbolized in the Yin-Yang connection."

"I still don't follow you."

"You seem to us," said the older lama, "to be offering an earthly solution to a spiritual problem."

"Typhoid is not a spiritual affliction. It's a disease!"

"Health in general is spiritual, Madam," continued the Abbot. "It is the inner force of the spirit which creates harmony between body and soul. As long as the balance is maintained, no outside influence can do any harm to the person. Only when the balance falters—and only then—is the body susceptible to sickness."

"Do you really believe that, Abbot?" Nicole was incredulous. "You've had access to some of the best schooling available. How can you say that?"

"It's not my intention to convert you. All I am saying is that I am a believer. Have you heard of the *mandala?*"

"The word is familiar, but I never understood the meaning of it."

"Pity. Here on the wall you can see one of the many *mandala*. At the center there is the unifying force between the male and female characters surrounded by the whirling forces of circulation, which are balanced by the centrifugal and centripetal forces. Everything is in motion. Everything is in balance and the totality is harmony. Here you can see symbolized forces based on total faith. For us to rely on your medicine would be an admission of our imperfect faith. That is the nub of our lengthy explanation."

"Then why did you consent to the vaccination of the population?"

"The common people have not reached the state of inner perfection. They need all the help we can provide, but for us to accept any chemical help would be in direct conflict with all we believe in. Please do not harbor any hard feelings because of our refusal. We still appreciate your generous offer."

Nicole was astonished. As she rose to depart, both lamas stood up and bowed their heads, expressing an unusual courtesy towards her.

She left the chamber with a faint stirring within her, a ripple in her pool of anger. It was envy, envy of a faith that was so strong and so deep.

When the woman departed, Bodgen Dadzsi sighed in relief. He was very happy to have witnessed the strength of the Abbot. The younger lama had been exposed to Western ways and Bodgen Dadzsi had been afraid he might decide in favor of the Western medicine. Now those worries had been allayed.

"MASTER, DESPITE your youth, your wisdom is deep. It is indeed not your wisdom; it is the wisdom of the incarnate spirit of Ringpoche, the Master of masters. Your answer reflected the sutra."

His student bowed to acknowledge the compliment of his teacher.

Bodgen Dadzsi struggled with what he wanted to say next. He loved this young Master and what he was about to say was going to cause pain. But he was tired, ever so tired, and it was time to leave this old body. He bowed his head and spoke.

"A physical body can never elevate to the essential perception of the real Buddha, because all the appearances are just forms without permanent quality and therefore they are beyond comprehension."

"Are you, my teacher, repeating this to me to remind me of the life beyond the physical—because we are now so close to that boundary, or have you some special reason?"

"I have a special reason to speak to you about absolute reality. I am an old man who has outlived his usefulness. Only one purpose remains for me and that is to be a living witness to our teaching. With your blessing I am determined to leave this body behind. I no longer desire to nourish my body. That is the most peaceful way to liberate my spirit and to be an example of our doctrine."

A wave of sadness flooded the younger man's face at these words.

At the sight of the young Lama's pain Bongen Dadzi struggled with his decision. He was more than the Abbot's teacher. Dzgun Tse had come to the monastery as an infant, and Bongen Dadzi had been both the child's companion and father figure for these many years. But to delay the inevitable would do no good. At some point they all would leave this place. His time was now and he would stand by his decision.

"That is the way of those who are followers of Jain," the Abbot replied.

"Jain's way is just one of the many paths. How many paths lead to the summit of a mountain? Many. I have chosen one. Give me your blessing, your holy incarnate." He bowed his bald head in submission to the answer.

"My teacher, father and master, your wish is my wish." The younger man said through his tears.

The glow of the lamp painted mystical shadows around them in the softly scented air.

Chapter 33

**Zero Time - The Fifteenth Day
Morning**

AT THE POINT where the valley of the Bhote Kosi River opened to a wide panorama to the south, Colonel Woung Lei had ordered that a fortified station be set up. From this vantage point he was able to observe all movement through the valley along the former trade route.

Today he surveyed his kingdom with smug satisfaction tinged with a mild sense of foreboding. The surrounding landscape, the air, and the land, all seemed too quiet. As though it were holding its breath in dread of what was to happen sometime soon.

The radio rarely crackled with news from the outside world. It seemed that with the breakdown of organized society, most of the radio stations had either been destroyed or abandoned. From the news they did receive, it appeared as though bands of thugs with the physical means to dominate had occupied many of the stations. Occasionally they would transmit messages. These messages were usually inquiries concerning resources, but few answers ever came back. Each group jealously hid all the resources it could control.

Also among the messages were desperate pleas for help, but there was no longer an organized power left to respond. For all practical purposes the outside world didn't exist for those who had barricaded themselves in the Bhote Kosi region.

Colonel Woung Lei was far more concerned with the possible effects of radiation and with the loyalty of his troops than he was with the situation outside his immediate control. He briefed his men daily, exhorting them with political speeches that stated their only chance of survival was to maintain discipline and unquestioning subordination.

He was thankful that the basic structure of the Chinese society was community oriented. From infancy they had been taught that the family, the commune, or the nation came before the individual. With this background, it was not a difficult task to convince his men of the necessity of his iron rule.

THE LONG balcony that fronted the western wing of the monastery had become a favorite meeting spot for the Westerners. As they waited for the others, Ludec leaned again the balustrade, drew a nail clipper from his pocket and began to trim his nails. Rudi strolled back and forth along the length of the walkway, enjoying the view. It was another pleasant day and Ludec relished the warmth of the sun on his shoulders as he went about his task.

"If Colonel Woung can maintain the loyalty of his troops," he commented to Rudi, "we have no hope of resisting his assumption of control in the area. From our meeting I get the impression he would treat us as nothing more than slaves in the kingdom he hopes to set up for himself."

"He's got the training, and his men are used to being commanded. I don't think there's much we can do about it," Rudi acknowledged.

"Ah, the mysterious oriental mind. They are conditioned to work collectively for a greater potential good. That certainly does give the advantage to the Chinese colonel." He held up his left hand to examine his progress.

"You make it sound as though that type of thinking is unique to the Orientals. It's not you know." Chin in hand Rudi began a slow tour of the small area in front of Ludec. "Take a look at the Germans and you'll see the same blind obedience. My father used to say that French and Italian history was a succession of revolutions and internal city-state fights. But the Germans seemed to have a real need for order, so the nation was unified without too much internal fighting."

Ludec glanced up and Rudi stopped to address his thoughts directly at him. "He thought it was that need for order that allowed the people to follow the controlling governments they've had."

"Mmm-hmm," Ludec responded with a nod then focused his attention on his right hand. "When the people of any nation give up their individuality for the good of the nation as a whole, there is always the potential for unchallenged corrupt leadership. And when that leadership has a fanatic at the helm—well, a Moloch who demands the blood sacrifice of its own sons is created, and the sons meekly consent."

He handed the clipper to Rudi and propped his elbows on the railing, chin in hand. A snow pigeon fluttered up and landed on the balustrade a few feet from them. That was odd. They weren't normally that fearless. It seemed exhausted and lowered itself to rest on its rounded breast.

"Rudi, look at this." A dark mass on the horizon caught his attention. As his mind took in the nature of the sight he felt the blood run cold in his veins and he inhaled sharply.

Rudi followed the direction of his stare then he gasped in shock. At the far end of the lower valley an ominous cloud was visible. The dense, dark formation of dust, almost a solid wall, hung suspended in the narrow cleft of land.

"My God, it's got to be a wall of atomic dust!" Rudi whispered.

"We have reached the end," replied Ludec. "There will be enough radiation in that cloud to kill anyone who is exposed to it." With sweat-slickened hands he grasped at the balustrade for support.

Nicole and Andrew stepped onto the balcony on the heels of this statement. They followed the gaze of the two men and immediately recognized the nature of the vile darkness that covered the southern horizon.

The four of them were still staring in dumb shock when Brock sprinted down the length of the walkway and joined them at the railing.

"What's the wind's direction and velocity?" he demanded to no one in particular. "Do we have any instruments...anything at all...to make a realistic prediction of when it might hit here?"

"No," Ludec replied in a somber voice. "And we're at the mercy of nature, I'm afraid. If the wind is gentle, we may have days. But if it develops into an updraft, we may have only hours."

WITHIN MINUTES of receiving the call from the lookout, Tsong Mei stood with his commanding officer, Colonel Woung, at the headlands overlooking the valley.

Mei now understood the panic in the lookout's voice when he reported a cloud on the horizon. One look at the vile mass was enough to know there was something sinister in its makeup.

Woung brought his binoculars to bear on the entrance of the valley and cursed loudly. Mei swung his own binoculars up. A mass of desperate refugees swarmed along the road leading to higher ground trying to stay ahead of the cloud. They fanned out across the land like locusts, filling the entire width of the valley.

Without hesitation Woung barked an order.

"Battle alert! Use live ammunition! Aim to kill!"

The order sparked a bitter taste in Mei's mouth. It was a callous command. A knee jerk reaction with no consideration of the final outcome. With the arrival of the cloud there was no hope for any of them, so what did it matter if the area was overrun with refugees?

He watched the colonel's ramrod straight figure as he moved back and forth in a near frenzy between the armament placements. What influence would produce a mentality that could issue such an order?

His own parents encouraged him to study the arts, philosophy, and mathematics. When he had applied to the military, his psychological tests stated he was well suited for the Information Service, the intelligence arm of the army. Mei enjoyed the work. Collecting and sorting information into a meaningful picture was rather like solving gigantic puzzles.

When the ISONS expedition became a reality, he had asked to be transferred from his boring position in Kashgar. Colonel Yun-Kai seemed only too eager to place him under Woung's command. His orders were to remain close to the expedition, and to keep contact with them through Loanche, the interpreter. Now, with the destruction of world order, his presence here had become meaningless.

What he hated most in his superior was his simplistic mind, which tried to solve all problems through brute force. Mei's continued obedience was based on his own acceptance of the situation and not on indoctrination or fear.

Down in the valley the instinct for survival drove the fleeing mass of people within reach of the long-range weapons.

"Open fire!" Woung ordered.

So began the opening notes of a bloody death symphony. Rockets and hidden land mines mowed down the front lines of frantic people. In mindless terror the mass continued to advance up the valley. The military orchestra was now in full performance. The rattle of machine-guns played the timpani, which synchronized with the rhythmical base tones of the rocket launchers. The irregular explosions of the land mines and the blasts of the handguns provided under-notes that failed to hide the high keening of those reeling in death. It was a massacre.

The scene disgusted the young lieutenant. *Can this simple-minded fool of a colonel truly believe that by killing these people he can escape the deadly embrace of the cloud?* He wasn't so stupid as to be unaware of the consequences of radiation.

Glancing at his commander's face he noted the indifference of his demeanor, but caught the callousness reflected in the eyes. It was the expression of the power of a subjugating ideology in which the means becomes more important than the end. Surely this would have been the expression on the faces of the men he read about in western history books—those who mowed down their own people in Tiananmen Square in 1989.

When Mei had begun his work in the Intelligence Branch it was with those very events in mind. At least in the Intelligence Branch, he knew his energy would be directed against foreign opponents and not against his own people.

From the advantage of the headlands, Mei surveyed the carnage that continued in the valley. The mass of people below weren't his people, but they weren't foreign opponents either. They were simply desperate refugees looking for a way to survive.

In the cacophony of the battle no soldier heard the sound of Mei's revolver. Sporadic return of fire from the mob increased the fury of the Chinese forces and the confusion was complete. The massacre went on without anyone noticing the colonel's crumpled body.

The blood lust of the troops was at its peak and Mei's command to cease-fire was slow to penetrate the fog of confusion. Section by section the firing subsided. Below in the valley, the decimated mob was too demoralized to continue its advance over the hecatomb of bodies.

Lieutenant Mei took over the command.

"Pack up your weapons and retreat!" He turned to the sergeant standing near him.

"Sergeant Lu, make arrangements to bury the colonel. You are witness to how valiantly our Colonel Woung fought against the invaders." The subaltern advanced and gave a stiff salute. He made no mention of the wound at the back of the colonel's head.

Mei addressed the troops.

"We'll take up a new defensive position to the east of Panchen-Bo monastery. From there we can either destroy or defend the suspension bridge and prevent the mass of people crossing the river."

There was really no reason to mention to the troops that there was little point in defending the territory. If their hope was destroyed, there was every likelihood they would turn into a mob and run berserk themselves. It would be anarchy.

Nature cooperated. An unusually calm, windless afternoon followed the massacre.

IN THE VILLAGE, Ngta Shumba and his family cowered in their cramped quarters. He had no idea what was happening in the valley below, but the sound of the battle was an ominous sign. And there was the cloud. The terrible mass sagged under the weight of its own malevolence and sent shivers through everyone who looked at it.

Around them people were on the verge of panic. He knew some had started to pack their meager belongings and others, mostly the poor who owned no homes or other buildings, had begun to steal out of the village.

Others prepared but waited, knowing full well that beyond the tree line there was nothing—no life at all; the paths to the north led further and further up the mountains. Ngta knew those who went and those who waited were in the same desperate situation, pressed between the black death of the cloud below and the deadly embrace of the white snow above.

Chapter 34

Zero Time - The Sixteenth Day

JANGBU LEFT his warm bed early in the morning to pace the floor. Sleep was impossible when the one who sought that peaceful oblivion was torn with indecision.

His wife wanted to join the others and flee, but it was almost unbearable for him to leave everything he owned behind. He had worked so hard, given up so much time...he had even gone on risky journeys to acquire the riches he possessed. How could he just give it all up? And where could they go? He knew of no place that would be safe from the black cloud.

Perhaps his best bet would be to consult the Chinese and ask them what they felt the future held in store.

As every good businessman must, he had put much effort into maintaining good relations with the rulers of this district, whoever they were at any given time. Before the Chinese there was the Nepalese officials, easy-going fellows one could bribe. The Chinese colonel, who had died yesterday, had not been easy to bribe, but by marked subservience Jangbu had been able to establish a workable relationship with him. Now there was this new lieutenant, Tsong Mei. He would pay the man a visit.

Jangbu had not been certain of how to approach Lieutenant Mei, and decided to try flattery first. Armed with a bag containing small bribes to grease his way, he set off for the community schoolhouse, which was now the Chinese headquarters.

It was not easy to get into the lieutenant's office, for the schoolhouse was closely guarded. Finally, in exchange for some brick tea, the sergeant in charge of security gave Jangbu a pass and he was soon face to face with the lieutenant.

In Jangbu's opinion all Chinese felt superior to other human beings, and especially to the Nepalese. There was nothing in Lieutenant Mei's demeanor to suggest otherwise. He was younger than Jangbu expected, but when he looked into the commander's eyes it was the eyes of an aged man that looked back at him. He appeared unkempt; his uniform rumpled, his hair uncombed. When he ran his hand over his jaw Jangbu heard the rasp of whiskers.

"What do you want?" the lieutenant demanded from his seat behind the old wooden desk. Jangbu had not been offered a chair.

"Lieutenant, I know you are a soldier and an educated man. I also know you have radio communication, so I want to ask you for advice."

"Advice? You want advice?" A mirthless smile turned the corners of the young man's mouth. "Then go and observe what the clever people are doing. Take your advice from them. Perhaps you know of a protected sanctuary where you can escape the cloud of death? If not, find a painless way to die. I've heard that your priests are preparing themselves for just such an end."

"You have nothing...nowhere to...?" Jangbu flustered. Was this true? Did even the Chinese have no way out of what they were facing?

"What were you expecting? A miracle? Go! I don't want to waste any more time on you." With a dismissive wave of his hand Lieutenant Mei stood and turned his back on Jangbu.

Desperate, the merchant pleaded, "If you would provide a military escort for my family, I would..." Jangbu's attempt at a bribe was cut short. The lieutenant turned and slammed his fist down on the desk.

"Get out! There's no place to run to anymore." The shout held a note of hysteria.

Jangbu backed out in horror.

Chapter 35

Zero Time - The Sixteenth Day
Evening

LUDEC'S senses reeled. Any faint hope he had nurtured to this point was extinguished by the darkness of the advancing cloud. The latest Geiger counter reading on the veranda was several notches higher than the previous day's reading. It was time to talk about the Yeti theory in earnest.

He joined the rest of the group who were gathered for the evening in Nicole's room. The electric bulb burned dimly, illuminating only the area where they were seated. The faint light projected grotesque shadows on the walls—shadows that seemed to mock them. The remainder of the room lay swathed in darkness—a cocooning buffer zone between them and the deadly air that lay beyond the room.

"What a wasted effort. We managed to get the waterwheel working, and now what?" Brock asked bitterly.

"I suppose we could consider the lights as our form of an eternal flame," Rudi answered. "You know, that damned wheel could go on turning, producing light for quite a while after we're gone."

"That's a pathetic legacy to leave behind, isn't it?" Nicole asked.

Here was the opportunity Ludec was waiting for. "A legacy for whom, I wonder?" Before he could continue, Rudi turned the conversation down a different path.

"Man's searching thoughts, his probing into the secrets of the infinite, his scientific deductions..." He gestured feebly with his hands. "His art...it'll all be lost. It's going to lie buried in a coffin of a planet circling around the sun. No life. No meaning. What a waste!" His words ended with a muffled sob.

"Perhaps you're painting too dark a picture, my friend. True, this sanctuary has fallen, but there's always the possibility that a group of Eskimo, or Samoans, or Yanomamos in the deep jungle of the Amazon will survive intact." The silence that greeted his words was oppressive. No one believed in that possibility anymore. Worse yet, Ludec himself no longer believed it.

From her seat on the *gundri* beside Brock, Nicole spoke up. Her voice held no reminder of the joking Nicole of the past. "Maybe we deserve what we're getting. We refused to listen to the warning of the scientists, and worse, we refused to listen to our own conscience. One of the first lessons we learn in life is that our actions have consequences."

With a sense of shock Ludec realized that they were resigned to their fate. They no longer struggled against what was perceived as the inevitable. Was this a good thing? Something he should also give in to? Or should he suggest they leave tomorrow, while they still had their strength, and follow his lead on the Yeti?

"We didn't listen because we selfishly wanted to pursue our individual dreams. We didn't want vague warnings of possible doom to stand in our way," Rudi said. He sat on a low stool, his hands dangling between his knees, head drooping. "I remember being told as a child how in his last hours of life the fanatic Fuhrer, Hitler, ordered the extermination of the German race. If he'd had the means he'd probably have tried to exterminate the human race as well. Now look what we've done. We've accomplished what he couldn't."

A gentle knock on the door put an end to their sober conversation. The five looked at each other with a question in their eyes, but no one moved to answer it, or spoke to acknowledge the knock. The door opened slowly and the Abbot entered, giving his bow of greeting.

"Namaste. Please forgive me for disturbing you at this grave time, but it is this inevitable fate which brings me here to speak with you."

"So," said Nicole as she rose from her seat, "now you come, talking like a mortal. When I offered you the vaccine you were as haughty as an immortal."

"Madam, you misunderstood us completely. Sickness is something we think of as a disorder of the body, which we consider an extension of our spiritual entity. Therefore, we believe we can control disease. But nature is above us. Nature engulfs us; we are part of it. If we evoke the wrath of nature then we must accept our destiny. So it is that the lamas of the monastery have started our preparation to meet that destiny."

Ludec was startled by the appearance of the young Abbot. Gone was the cold, immobile face. His features and movements were as animated as any of the others in the room. It was good to see the change in him.

The young man continued. "Dadzsi lama refuses all nourishment, and being an old man, he is already in a state of oblivion. That is his way. By refusing to eat he will allow his life to end without having taken it."

"And you, Abbot? What are you going to do?" Nicole asked solemnly. She stood with her arms wrapped around herself as if to ward off a chill.

"At this time I have come not to speak of myself, but to bring you an unusual offer. As we all know our lives now depend on how long the wind remains calm. Death from radiation is too horrible to suffer if there is a painless alternative. For centuries we monks have had our little secrets, and one is a potion of herbs that enables the one who drinks it to fall asleep never again to wake. This is what I come to offer to you." He bowed in their direction as he concluded his offer.

Silence hung in the room. No, not a silence, Ludec realized, for there was the sharp intake of breath from Nicole and the heavier breathing of the men.

Under the pressure of reality he recognized how unprepared they actually were for death. Death was a final state, irreversible and unchangeable. The intellect knew this, but the *ego* was reluctant to accept it. Somehow the '*I*' wanted desperately to survive. Or perhaps it was instinct that took over.

"I accept your offer!" said Nicole.

HORROR WELLED up in Brock. Their relationship, as young as it was, gave him hope that there could be a future. With her four words she killed any desire he had to fight to the end.

"Nicole!" he cried as he reached for her. His despair vanished when he looked into her tear-filled eyes.

"What am I suppose to do, Brock? Tell me! Do you really expect me to drag on to the end, vomiting, bleeding and losing my hair? Is that what you want?" she sobbed, the tears falling freely.

"No. I want you...I want us..." He drew her into a hard embrace and buried his face in her hair. She clung tightly to him.

"Remember our conversation that day when we crossed the swinging bridge?" she asked, her voice thick with emotion.

He nodded but couldn't speak. Sobs deep in his gut threatened to overwhelm him.

"I said then that some day I might want to choose my death. I'm doing that now. Don't hold me here, Brock. Please. I'm going to die and I'd rather do it this way."

Visions of the ghastly aftermath of Hiroshima and Nagasaki replayed in his mind; grainy black and white shots from the television history shows. He didn't want that for either of them. He released her and turned to the monk.

"I'll accept as well."

He turned to his three friends. Andrew, Rudi, and Ludec stood side by side with thin compressed lips as though holding back the words that threatened to leap from their mouths. Their determination to remain alive held, and Brock nodded his understanding. He tightened his grip on Nicole's hand and turned back to the Abbot.

When the young man spoke there was compassion in his voice. "I'll send two vessels with the potion." He then turned to leave the room.

As he reached the door Ludec stopped him, saying with sincerity, "Abbot, it has been an honor to meet you. You are the most Christ-like man I have ever met."

The Abbot replied, softly, "You flatter me...but I fear I am only a man."

With the Abbot's departure, an uneasy silence filled the room, broken by Nicole's soft sobs. This was the first time a serious division had developed within the group. Now there were those who were ready to give up and those who were willing to go on to whatever end awaited them. Each had selected his or her own fate. Brock didn't regret his choice.

Ludec addressed the group. "There is still the possibility of finding the—"

"No Ludec," Nicole broke in. "No more words. I've made up my mind. Please—don't make it any harder. I've resigned myself. I don't want to go through the process again. Please."

The older man nodded, then turned to Rudi and Andrew. "Perhaps we should go to my room. There are probably things that Nicole and Brock want to discuss alone."

Nicole's gratitude showed in her tear-filled eyes as she kissed him lightly.

Brock silently shook each man's hand as he filed past. It was a final farewell.

Chapter 36

Zero Time - The Sixteenth Day

LUDEC pushed open the door to his room and let the others enter first. They sat for a time in silence, each lost in their own thoughts.

The dim light of the single bulb intensified the eerie feeling; the presence of the unknown, the nearness of the unimaginable, and the closeness of death. Ludec remembered a sentence he had read somewhere that said, 'No philosophy would exist if man were not aware of his own inevitable end.'

Yes, life has never been so important, so desirable as now. We must find some answer, some meaning for our existence.

The time for abstract concepts and words was behind them. It was time for something concrete. Something that would be a consolation in all this insanity.

Damn, Ludec thought, as he realized, almost with anger, that he needed to urinate. At the very time when he was absorbed in a search for something spiritual, permanent, beyond the physical, his perishable, material body was dragging him down to the basics of reality. Eschewing the chamber pot, he half-apologized to the others as he excused himself.

Making his way carefully without the aid of a lamp, he descended the wooden stairway to the ground level and groped his way to the far end of the yard. There, in a walled corner, the people in the compound used a pit as a latrine. Surprisingly, it wasn't as noisome as some of the wayside toilets he'd used in Europe. The secret seemed to lie in the bucket of ashes that was kept in a barrel beside the pit. An occasional sprinkle did the trick.

When he returned to the staircase he sensed the presence of someone standing under the stairs. He stopped cold in his tracks, then the individual greeted him softly and he recognized the voice of Ngta Shumbe, the Tibetan.

"*Sahib*, I want to talk to you. I have been waiting for you, just for you."

"For me? But why?"

"I am going away, *Sahib*. Everyone is leaving. The cloud of Kali, the god of Destruction, is hovering over the valley. It is as you said;

soon the sun will not rise. I am going to the valley of the mountain gods. The valley you were so interested in. I am taking my family there. Do you want to join us, *Sahib?*"

His shock was so great he had to clutch at the banister for support. Here it was! The meaning for his existence. He would follow through with his decision to bring fire to the Yeti. Perhaps, just perhaps, it would be this action that would ensure the continuation of mankind. He made the decision for the others as well.

"You're a good man, Ngta. I accept. There are three of us that want to join your family. You know them from the construction, *Sahib* Rudi and *Sahib* Andrew."

"They, too, are good people," Ngta agreed with a nod. "But the way is hard. And we must start early tomorrow."

"We can be ready."

"It is a long way to the Cho-Oyu. The gods defend their home by not allowing enough air in the valley. Breathing is painful there. I remember the way, even though I was there only once as a young man. No one can find it except those to whom the gods choose to reveal the way. My father was such a man. I see the same goodness in you *Sahib*, and in *Sahib* Rudi and *Sahib* Andrew."

"Ngta Shumbe, I thank you for your words. We will be at your house at dawn tomorrow."

"No *Sahib*, not to my house. There will be others who would wish to follow us if the white man is also leaving with us."

Of course. I should have thought of that. He gave a silent thanks for the Tibetan's keen mind.

"Please join us on the path that leads north from the village, the one where the spirit of the dead tree stands guard beside it." With these words the Tibetan left. As he made his way up the stairs Ludec noticed how noiselessly the carpenter crossed the courtyard in his soft-soled boots. He was quickly swallowed up by the darkness.

At the top of the stairway Ludec turned to cast a glance in the direction of the cloud. In the pale light of the moon it spread across the lower valley like a gigantic antediluvian reptile. It had advanced somewhat, not far, but enough to be noticeable.

As he reentered the room, Rudi was speaking. "...likely that this cloud is the forerunner of the nuclear winter. I would think most of the earth is covered by it now. Can you just imagine! An inky blackness spread over the surface of the Earth with only the highest peaks protruding." He shook his head at the thought.

Andrew was sprawled on a beautiful carpet that covered a portion of the floor. With one finger he absently traced the pattern as he spoke. "Even if the wind shifts and goes back down the valley, at this altitude we have a big problem. I would think the ozone layer has been destroyed. Without that, we're in for a real dose of ultraviolet radiation."

"But the natives are already acclimatized to the higher ultraviolet level, aren't they?" Rudi asked.

"And so are the Yeties!" interrupted Ludec.

"There you go again with your Yeti fixation," Andrew said, not unkindly.

"Mock me if you wish. Up to this point I was my own severest critic. I questioned my own judgment and didn't want to create any empty hopes. But now all that has changed." He rubbed his hands together briskly. He felt like a new man. He had a mission and with it came renewed energy.

"And your magic sign that you were waiting for? Did it suddenly appear somewhere between here and the latrine in the compound?"

"Yes, as a matter of fact it did." He took a moment to savor the surprise on their faces. "I made a discovery a few days ago. I didn't share it with anyone because I wasn't sure what I would do about it. Now I think it is time to act. The carpenter, Ngta, has a Yeti scalp."

He saw the incredulous look on their faces and spoke to reassure them. "I saw it with my own eyes and even examined it at close range. He told me how his father, a mountaineer, obtained it."

Andrew shook his head. "Even so. How will we ever find the creature?"

"Just now, when I was outside he approached me to say he would be leaving for the Yeti valley in the morning with his family and he's offered to take us along. That valley, I feel, is the last asylum on this godforsaken planet. Our final chance and last hope."

Still reeling from this news Rudi asked, "Are you saying that the legend of the Yeti has some basis in fact?"

"Most legends do, Rudi. Schliemann was laughed at for his fixation on Troy until he started digging gold out of the ground. The panda was a legend for nearly sixty years until it was actually found."

"But this...this is...who would ever believe..." Rudi held his hands up in a hopeless gesture and shrugged his shoulders.

Ludec smiled. "Sometimes it is only the thin line of imagination that separates legends from reality. Now, the question, my friends, is whether you are ready to put your skepticism to rest and launch out on this last venture."

"What do we have to lose?" Rudi asked. "At the most maybe our lives, but we'll lose our lives anyhow. So I'll join you. And you, Andrew, what do you choose?"

"I'm in," he replied. "If nothing else, I guess I'll have one last climb. When do we start?" Slapping his hands on his knees, he rose to his feet.

"Tomorrow, before the sun rises."

"Even if we're only legend-hunters, a bit of planning for high altitude climbing is in order. We'll need our oxygen tanks, ropes, ice axes, ice clamps... I'll get that together tonight." Andrew made his way to the door.

"Not too much equipment. Keep in mind this is a one-way journey."

Despite the bitter note in Ludec's voice, he chuckled. The paralyzing indecision of earlier in the evening was gone. They now had a purpose.

As Andrew went to collect the equipment Rudi could not resist asking, "Tell me, do you still plan to teach the Yeti, if there is indeed such a creature, to use fire?"

"If there is such a creature I will try to take him up to the next step on the evolutionary scale. That means using fire."

"There's another danger we should consider, Ludec. I think an assault on the asylum by a large number of people might destroy the Yeti's valley. We need to keep our departure a secret."

Ludec nodded. "Ngta made it clear he doesn't want anyone else to come with us. I have had my suspicions about Loanche for quite some time. I wouldn't put it past him to be working with the Chinese."

"I'm glad I'm not the only one who suspects the guy. We'd better be careful when we leave. I'm going to help Andrew with the equipment. Why don't you get a bit of sleep? We'll be needing all our strength in the next few days."

As the door closed behind Rudi, Ludec moved to his *gundri* but stopped midway to the platform. Nicole and Brock. Should he tell them about Ngta's offer? A vision of Nicole's tear-stained face came to mind.

Her decision hadn't been made lightly and the group's chance of success in finding the valley was very slim. Torn in his decision, he took a step toward the door, and then halted. Perhaps it was better the couple go in peace, rather than fight another battle with fate. No one knew what awaited them beyond the snow line.

Chapter 37

Zero Time - The Seventeenth Day
Pre-Dawn

THE DARK hours of deep night plodded by and still Naga, the oldest daughter of Ngta Shumbe, lay wide-awake, eyes staring into the darkness. Her world teetered on the brink of destruction and to make things worse, she was certain she was going to have a baby.

Her affair with Tsering, Jangbu Shabur's oldest son, had begun several months earlier. Last week had been an agony. When the hot fever struck the house she was not sure whether her lover would survive. Thanks to the Western woman, both Tsering and his brother were now on the road to recovery.

She should be celebrating but instead she found herself angry and afraid. The entire village was in an uproar, caught up in the sudden desire to run from the invisible menace. The troubles of yesterday paled in comparison with the uncertainty of the future.

It was the uncertain future that kept her awake. She was worried about her pregnancy. To be sexually active at an early age was not unusual in mountain society. She even suspected that her parents knew very well what was happening between herself and Tsering. After all, the wooden stairway was far too creaky not to reveal their nightly excursions.

Once Tsering was well on his way to recovery she had hoped to continue their relationship. If a child, especially a baby boy, were born of their union there was a chance that Tsering would take her as his wife. That would be unbelievably good fortune for a poor Khamba girl like herself.

She suspected her father was secretly hoping for this miracle to happen. Even if Tsering's mother would not allow her son to take a foreigner as his first wife, she would have a good chance of being his second wife. That was still an acceptable status and would provide a secure future for herself and the child. But the events of the past few days were ruining her hopes.

It's not fair! I'm so close to a better life and now this happens! Why? Why now?

She wasn't sure what it was that was happening, but the frantic running around, the packing, the shouting—and on top of it all—the total silence from the lamas in the monastery were depressing signs. From the direction of the *gompa*, or bell-tower, the deep booming sound of the ceremonial gong could be heard. The bell's ringing signified sorrow.

Naga's heart was heavy with distress and full of fear. When her father ordered the family to be prepared for a long journey into the mountains she sensed that some unknown catastrophe was drawing close. She did not want to be separated from the father of her child.

Yesterday, when Tsering's father, Jangbu, left the house on a secret mission, Naga had sought out Tsering. She found him resting in the garden swathed in a cocoon of blankets. With a shy smile she made certain they would not be overheard, then she took his hand in hers.

"Tsering. Feel here." She placed his hand on her belly. "Perhaps you can't feel it now, but there is a new life there, your baby and mine." Her smile turned into a grin. "Are you happy?"

Tsering's eyes opened wide with surprise as his hand roamed across the flat planes of her stomach.

"A baby? Naga are you sure?" His voice held a hint of pride and his round face beamed with pleasure.

Naga's heart swelled in happiness, but seconds later her joy evaporated.

Tsering shoved the blankets off. He rose shakily to his feet and puffed up his chest. "I'm a man now, that's for sure."

His reaction centered solely on himself. There was no excitement for the fact that they were going to have a baby together, only for the fact that he had proven his manhood. A sense of unease crept through her.

"We could be a family together, Tsering. My father is not wealthy, as you know, but there is an old house he plans to fix when he has the money saved. If your father..."

Tsering's hand cut the air to stop her words. "Let's not speak of this now. I'm...I'm very tired. The illness...Tomorrow we'll talk more." He had turned and left her standing there.

That was yesterday. Today everything was different. Now she knew her father had reached a decision no daughter had the power to change. She was determined, however, not to lose Tsering and her chance at a secure future. Rising from her pallet on the floor she silently climbed the ladder in the pre-dawn darkness.

TSERING WOKE to someone shaking his arm. It was Naga. He wasn't happy to see her for he knew what she wanted to discuss. His mother would skin him alive if she knew he had been carrying on with 'the filthy Khamba girl downstairs.' There was little choice other than to follow her outside or she would surely wake the entire household.

To his surprise she didn't want to discuss setting up house in the village. The family was leaving. Leaving the village to travel into the mountains.

"Now you have to decide, Tsering. Early this morning we're going into the mountains. Are you coming with me?"

"Where are you going?" He needed to stall so he could think. His father had come home yesterday in a state of shock and refused to speak. Everything that used to be solid was now slipping away. Many of the people in the village were leaving. No one knew where they were going, but they knew they had to flee.

"To a hiding place. To the place where the mountain gods live."

"And you want me to go with your family?" His mouth felt dry and he licked his lips to moisten them.

"It's your family now, too. The child in my belly is yours. If you don't come with us, you may never see your child. My father says the place where we're going is safe."

This was intriguing news to Tsering. His father might be very impressed with a son who could provide such information. "That's hard to believe, Naga. How does he know it's a safe place? Where is it?"

"A hidden valley up on the Cho-Oyu. I don't know where. Only my father knows."

"He must have lost his mind! Either that or you are lying to me," Tsering hissed. *Does she think I'm a fool?* "There's nothing up there. There's nothing there at all but snow. My father will find us a safe place. He knows the Chinese. He'll ask them to help us."

"There must be more than snow. There must be something to live on, Tsering, the Snowman lives there." He could hear the note of desperation in her voice as she tried to convince him of her story. She would grow up to be a whiny wife.

"Superstitious old wives' tales. Nothing lives up there." He'd heard enough. She'd dragged him from his warm bed to listen to nonsense. He turned to go back to the house but she grabbed his arm.

"That's what you think! But the white men think differently. They're coming with us. The white men are not stupid. They have the medicine that cured you."

She was angry now. In the soft light of the moon he could make out her figure as she stood, feet firmly planted, hands clutched into fists. He amended his prediction about her. She would grow up to be a strong woman, much like his mother.

"How do you know they're joining you?" he countered.

"I overheard father whispering to mother, that's how."

"You're trying to blackmail me. I belong to my father's clan," he replied stubbornly.

"And the child in my belly? Where does he belong?"

"You're trying to force me. Do you think you're the first girl that has ever been pregnant? There are many, and they don't try to bend their men to their wishes. No, I won't let myself become the puppet of a stupid girl."

He spoke the words with as much force as he could muster, then turned and walked away. He was glad to see she didn't follow, although he heard her call out:

"We leave in a few hours, Tsering. Please come with us."

Chapter 38

Zero Time - The Seventeenth Day
Dawn

BROCK LAY beside Nicole on the yak-hide-covered *gundri*, his arm cradling her head. His gaze was drawn to the small table beside the bed.

Just as a ticking time bomb drowns out other noises for those who are aware of its significance, so it was with the two beautiful cups on the table. They beckoned, reminding him of his date with destiny.

Their impending exit seem unprecedented and unique, more horrible than anything that had ever happened in the past to any hero, martyr, or altruist. The others had died for some purpose, even if that purpose was for future generations. Their deaths weren't a jump into the mass grave of mankind. When Brock spoke his voice was both sad and reflective.

"In the past, at least dying held some promise of a future. There was a burial...a speech or two. There were a few tears and survivors. Somehow the knowledge that others were left behind gave a sense of fulfillment. What do we leave behind now? A gigantic sarcophagus revolving in space for eternity."

Nicole remained silent; her breathing calm. She seemed resigned to her decision.

"It's so damned hard to accept that the highest form of life on this planet finally reached a stage where they self-destructed. We deluded ourselves into believing that the life of the *'me'*, this little speck in the universe, would last forever. I was convinced there was plenty of time for me to get married and have children."

"I thank God I didn't have children. What would you, or I, say to those children now? *'I'm sorry, but by some miscalculation we took away your future'?*"

"I envy my grandfather. He was a simple farmer. He died at the age of seventy-eight while he was out plowing his cornfields. There was so much dignity in his death. He spent his life working for a future that he would pass on to the next generation. It was a simple life, an honorable life. A life well spent returning something to the earth."

The unknown mixture that would ease their passage continued to beckon while both fought their reluctance to accept the final action. Finally Nicole's low voice came from his side. "Brock, please give me one of the goblets."

He didn't argue. Picking up the two vessels, he handed one to Nicole. With ceremonial slowness they drank the deadly brew. He had no idea of what to expect and was pleased when a wonderful tingling blush spread through his body. A feeling of languidness followed.

Nicole curled herself into a comfortable sleeping position and Brock fit himself into the curve of her back. He held her tightly in his arms. The last thing he saw before drifting off was the intricate wood carving of the mystical demons of Buddhist mythology hanging on the wall beside the *gundri*.

IN THE monastery's lower-level storage rooms, Andrew helped Rudi collect the pile of equipment he had assembled earlier in the evening. Despite the fact that he was simply retrieving their personal property, he felt guilty for taking it, like a thief in the night.

He gathered up the backpacks and carried them into the courtyard where Ludec kept watch for prying eyes. The older man seemed convinced that Loanche could be nearby, watching.

Beyond the monastery walls the usual gentle night sounds were replaced with harsh whispers of men under stress; complaints of tired, fretful children; and the sound of burdened pack animals moving on the rocky trails leading from the village.

Where are they going? Is there really a sanctuary anywhere?

Rudi came out of the storeroom lugging the last of the climbing gear. He too stopped and listened to the sounds of activity of the fleeing population. "Why don't we tell the lamas where we're going?" he asked.

Andrew's nerves were on edge. He knew it would be a hard climb ahead and their energy levels were very low. "Do you know where this place is, Rudi?" he snapped.

"No," came the reply.

"Then how do you figure you can tell them about something you know nothing about? And the Tibetan told Ludec he doesn't want us to share it with anyone." The harsh words were greeted with silence.

I should have kept my mouth shut. He didn't deserve that.

He began passing out the supplies so their loads would be even. The silence stretched on.

Ludec settled his pack comfortably on his shoulders. He cleared his throat and broke the tension with his words.

"It's probably a wise decision," he stated. "I can just imagine the stampede that would result if everyone knew about the sanctuary. And from what I've seen, the Chinese would finish off all the survivors to secure it for themselves."

They had dressed with care. Since they were too weak to carry heavy loads, Andrew had packed a minimal amount of food, selecting the most compact and nourishing variety from the expedition supplies. The heaviest items they would have to carry were the oxygen tanks.

After ensuring their loads were securely settled on their shoulders, they moved out of the courtyard into the main area of the compound.

The gateway of the monastery was no longer guarded. That meant the servants had scattered. The eerie silence within the monastery announced that the lamas had either died or were dying. Andrew gave one last look at the window of Nicole's apartment and silently walked out of the compound.

"Have we really found our connection to the Yeti?" Ludec mused. His question wasn't directed to anyone in particular. "I confess I am still skeptical even though I've seen that scalp with my own eyes. It sounds so fantastic." He moved aside to allow a small family, yak in tow, to pass him on the path. The wife cried softly as she led a small child by the hand.

It was Rudi who replied to Ludec's question. "Marco Polo was considered a liar when he talked about his adventures. We all have a tendency to equate the improbable with the impossible. And remember when they found those fish fossils that were supposed to be sixty million years old? Then just a few years ago, the same fish was found alive and well at the bottom of the Indian Ocean. To my way of thinking, our skepticism has gone too far."

Andrew chuckled. "Isn't this ironic? We came here to put an end to the legend, and now, if we actually find the creature, what do we do with our proof?" Their conversation ceased. Walking was difficult enough without wasting breath on talking. They didn't bother to look back at the dark massive outline of Panchen-Bo. There was nothing there for them anymore.

DZUNG TSE, the Buddha incarnate, the monk with Western as well as Eastern education, watched the three trekkers slip out of the compound. Were the other two still in the woman's room? He felt a need to know that they no longer needed his attention. Once he was free of all obligations within the monastery he would leave this world and meet his fate.

The hallways of the monastery were quiet. No one stirred, no light burned. Even the echo of his footsteps seemed muted, as though his own presence was already diminishing. At the door to the woman's room he knocked softly. No answer. He pushed the door open and saw them together on the *gundri*.

She was lying in the fetal position, a position symbolic of the unity of the beginning and the end. Next to her, the bronzed body of the man completed the Yin-Yang symbol of totality. Death had not yet destroyed the pinkness of her skin or the silkiness of her hair, and she still radiated the desirability of life over the repulsiveness of decay.

He felt no attraction to her in any sexual sense, but rather by the spiritual reverence due to the life-producing potential embodied in the female and the male. He settled onto the rug at the foot of the *gundri* and allowed his thoughts to drift back....

He had only a very faint memory of himself as a small boy in his father's smoke-filled farmhouse. Equally vague was the picture of several lamas entering their hut and his father prostrating himself before them. The lamas placed various objects in front of him to tempt his childish curiosity, then they prayed together.

He was attracted to a set of wooden prayer beads of various colors. Without hesitation he reached out, claimed it and began to play with it. The lamas ceased their praying and bowed very low to him. Now he knew the significance of that day. Of all the objects placed before him, it was the prayer beads that had belonged to the lama who had been, until his death, head of the famous Panchen-Bo monastery.

This accident of choice, if indeed it had been an accident, had been the turning point in his life. He was still puzzled by the unanswerable question—was it only a coincidence, or the real attraction of an indefinable force that had directed his child's hands at that critical moment? Were these forces of attraction expressions of a spiritual current which, like an underground river, flows undetected, then surfaces at the most unexpected times to create the crucial moments in an individual's destiny?

Now, sitting at the feet of the couple on the gundri, he took stock of his life. Was he the real embodiment of the spirit of Buddha, the Budhawitsa? Or was he just a fake? Gazing at the couple before him he sought his inner voice. It was the voice of his guru that he heard.

"You cannot know your strength if you have never been presented with an obstacle." With these words, Bongen Dadzi had gone against all orthodox rules and insisted that the young man be sent to Santiniketan for schooling. There he had been exposed to another culture and had learned to appreciate his own; had learned about love and had learned to appreciate his strength when he resisted.

Yes, he had been faithful to his vocation. He had been tested and he had won.

Here before me is the eternal Yin-Yang, the eternal duality of male-female existence. But I am the representative of the encompassing circle, which embraces the two—the self-perpetuating spirit of the circle, which is eternal unity.

He rose and made his way to his own chamber where he lay down on the hide-covered gundri. He would not rise again in this body.

O lions amongst men,
Buddhas past, present, and future,
To as many of you as exist in the ten directions
I bow down with my body, speech, and mind.

Chapter 39

Zero Time - The Seventeenth Day

LUDEC was relieved to see Ngta Shumbe waiting with his family on the outskirts of the village, their meager belongings tied on the back of a yak.

They set out at a brisk pace that took no notice of the need to conserve their strength. Ludec was surprised. His surprise turned to concern when he noticed the Tibetan repeatedly cast worried glances back at the village.

"Are you concerned someone is following us, Ngta?"

"Yes. The place we go to is sacred. I promised my father's spirit not to profane it. Only the unusual happenings in the sky are forcing me to seek the gods' protection—but only for us. Not for those who have no sense of its sanctity. You are good people, but not Jangbu, not the Chinese. No!"

"I understand. Can you tell me our route?" It seemed important to know where they were heading. What if some of them didn't make it? The others should know how to reach the valley. But speaking was becoming difficult for him and he realized he was fighting fatigue. Was it due to his recent inactivity or was it the effect of radiation?

"We go to the far slope of the Cho-Oyu. The last time I was there was a long time ago, when I was just a child. It may be hard for me to find the entrance. It is hidden under a great sheet of ice—a glacier. But when we enter the valley the air will be warm and the grass will be green. It will be very pleasant."

"But that doesn't make any sense." Rudi had been listening to the conversation and he now broke in. "We'll be well above the snowline by that time!"

Ngta nodded his head, as though to reassure them that he was indeed telling the truth. "There is a big hole where the bowels of the earth are showing. Warm air breathes out into the valley. That is where the gods live."

"Geothermal heat," Andrew offered. "I've seen it before on a few of my climbs. Are there bushes around, too, Ngta? I suppose there would have to be, if the creatures are surviving there."

"Yes, there are. Not big trees but bushes and grass."

All conversation came to an end. The brisk pace and the shortage of oxygen discouraged long discussions.

The carpenter led the way at the head of the little caravan, followed by his wife, tending to the yak. Then came the three younger children. The children were full of youthful energy, running ahead of their parents, flinging stones at imaginary beasts and generally enjoying the outing. The older girl, Naga, lagged behind the family, obviously very dejected. The three Westerners brought up the rear, some distance behind the Tibetan family.

They climbed steadily for several hours and finally broke out of the "V" shaped valley of the Bhoe Kosi to reach the top of the ridge. From there the view opened up to a wide panorama of surrounding peaks. The extent of the formidable black cloud was visible below. It had buried the flat lands but had not yet affected the magnificent protruding uplands where a chance for life would still remain.

For the earth to survive as a viable planet, Ludec mused, a lot depended on the cloud never reaching the highest peaks, or at least to the height of the Yeti sanctuary. The creatures might survive if the enclave was self-sustaining and remained above the radiation line.

The Cho-Oyu was a gigantic tower glittering like a mound of diamonds, sparkling so brightly they had to shield their eyes from the glare in the early afternoon light. It beckoned, and they followed the siren promise of a safe haven.

"There," said Ngta to the Westerners, pointing to the peak. "Follow the direction of the narrow edge of the pinkish hue. Then there is that rugged edge at the left of which is a greenish gap. Somewhere there we will find the entrance."

Ludec squinted and followed the line of the carpenter's finger. "Do you mean that gorge next to the...one...two...three...fourth peak down, where that deep shadow is?" he asked.

"Yes. And as you see, that is well above the snowline."

After a short break they continued their climb, the natives setting the pace. Although they no longer moved fast, they moved at a steady rate that the Westerners had a hard time matching.

Late in the afternoon their path took them around a large boulder.

From his position several yards behind the Tibetans, Ludec was surprised when Naga climbed the gentler slope of the obstruction to look back along the road from where they had come.

Shading her eyes, she watched the path, longing written all over her face. *She's looking for someone*, Ludec thought. Then her shoulders slumped and she hung her head.

Ahead of them on the trail, Ngta happened to glance back and saw his daughter's actions. Ludec read curiosity, then surprise in the Tibetan's expression before it turned to a look of horror.

He rushed back and grabbed the girl by her legs to drag her from the boulder. A short but loud argument ensued which ended with the father slapping the girl's face. When Ngta's wife tried to intervene, he pushed her aside. Naga was still standing on the trail, motionless yet defiant, when Ludec caught up to the group.

"What's happened?" he queried as he took in the scene. The mark of Ngta's handprint stained the girl's cheek.

The Tibetan spoke slowly for the sake of the Westerners, although he still shook with rage.

"Look at this fool!" he indicated his daughter with an accusing stab of his blunt finger. "She told her lover, Jangbu's son, where we were going! That is the same as telling the Chinese commander. I know how anxious Jangbu is to please the Chinese, and if they learn that we are looking for a sanctuary, they will lose no time in trying to find out where it is!"

The words were like a physical blow to Ludec. He steadied himself against the boulder as he let the news sink in. Naga read the despair in their faces and began to weep as she cowered in her mother's arms.

"Shit!" Rudi yelled. He picked up a sizeable stone from the trail and hurled it into the valley below. "That means there'll be a brigade of soldiers moving up the trail behind us."

Andrew nodded, then added. "Soldiers armed to the teeth and ready to kill. The only advantage we have is a head start."

"Then we'd better move on so as not to lose it," concluded Ludec with a deep sigh. What's done is done, Ngta. Do not berate the child anymore, please."

The small caravan set off on the road again, but the atmosphere had changed. Before the altercation they had merely climbed steadily. Now Ntga pushed them to the limit. Ludec realized the trek had become a race for life.

Chapter 40

IN THE village, the morning light found the inhabitants in total confusion. Some wanted to take all their belongings with them and others wanted to flee without anything, just to save their lives. Jangbu belonged to the former group. With his two sons assisting him, the contents of the house had been carried into the courtyard and were being packed into a wagon and onto the patient yaks. His younger son, Dzong, worked with diligence, but the older, Tsering, worked with a distracted air.

"What's the matter with you? Are you still sick or are you just idling?" demanded Jangbu, as he shouted at his son. "Go over to Anghir's house and bring me two extra pack saddles for the yaks. Get moving!"

To his father's surprise, Tsering refused to leave. According to Mingma, Jangbu's wife, the boy had been acting strangely for the past few days. As far as Jangbu was concerned, the woman should deal with the boy's problems, he already had enough on his mind.

"Off with you! What are you waiting for?" The tormented man raised his hand to deliver a swift cuff to the side of the idler's head.

Tsering flinched, but stood his ground. "Father, you are taking us in the wrong direction."

"How do you suddenly know so much? Have you had a vision in the night that you can tell your father what he is doing is not right?"

Undaunted, the young man continued. "Because I was invited by the Khamba girl to go with them. You want to go northwest, Father, but they went northeast."

"What is the difference? We have to flee this terrible cloud. What difference does it make where we go? Nobody knows where the cloud is heading."

"The carpenter knows a safe place, or at least that is what the girl said. She said that the Snowmen, as the Khambas call the mountain gods, live there."

Jangbu had never had any doubts as to the existence of the Yeti. Like most of the natives, he believed the creatures had a hiding place and that was why they were so seldom seen. Only on rare occasions did they wander beyond the safety of their own territory. Jangbu was angry that the simplistic Khamba had more wits than he had given him credit for. He stood, speechless.

Tsering licked his dry lips and shifted from foot to foot. "If you don't believe me, believe the white men. They have gone with the Khambas. You know that the white people are smart."

"When did they leave?" demanded the stunned Jangbu. He grabbed the young man and shook him violently. "Why did you not tell me this as soon as you knew?"

With some effort the hapless Tsering managed to make his reply known, "E-e-early this m-m-orning Father, before the sun rose."

Disgusted, Jangbu released the boy and did a swift calculation. The group had several hours start and he had not finished packing his caravan. There was no way he could overtake them now and still salvage his goods. He could think of only one solution to his problem. He would have to inform the Chinese.

A squad of men, unencumbered by children and animals would surely be able to overtake the fleeing group.

He turned to his worried wife. "If what the boy says is true, I have to tell the Chinese commander. Only he has the power to overtake these fugitives and force them to reveal their secret. I'm sure that for important information such as this, they will allow our family into the sanctuary as well."

After giving terse orders on the packing of the household, Jangbu hurried to the Chinese headquarters in the schoolhouse.

"Halt," the sentry commanded as the merchant approached the school door. "What business do you have here?"

Jangbu was suddenly uneasy, unsure of what to say. Would this foreigner understand about the Yeti? Would he believe it to be a fable and once again he, Jangbu, a wealthy merchant, would be treated with derision? Surely the lieutenant would believe his story if only he would be allowed to explain about the westerners.

"I must see the commandant," he shouted at the top of his voice in the hope that the lieutenant would hear. "Please let me talk to the commandant. It's a matter of great importance. I have some very valuable information to share with him."

MEI, WHO had now attained the self-appointed rank of colonel, recognized the squealing voice of the hapless Nepalese and stepped out of the schoolhouse.

"Ah, I see the merchant has not yet found his hiding place. Are you so stupid, my merchant friend, that you've come yet again to bribe me for a safe place?"

Even as the words slid from his lips Mei loathed himself for speaking them. So much had changed within him since he'd turned the gun on Woung. He'd despised everything the man stood for, yet the very act of pulling the trigger had changed him into the man Woung was. He hated what he had become, and he hated the world and everyone in it.

The fawning merchant before him epitomized what it was that he hated most—the inability to stand tall in the face of defeat.

"Perhaps I have found a sanctuary, Commandant."

The desperate merchant was almost groveling at Mei's feet in his attempt to convince him of the veracity of his statement.

"The Tibetan carpenter who lived in my house knows of a hidden valley where the Snowman lives. They are on their way there as we speak."

"You stupid, stupid merchant!" Mei heard the blood roar in his ears as shouted at the man. "Do you expect me to believe your superstitious Nepalese legends? They're a pack of old wives' tales. Get out of here!"

"The white men believe the Khamba, Commandant. They went with him."

The words seemed to come to Mei from a great distance. He felt another sarcastic remark building on his tongue when Loanche appeared from the direction of the monastery. "They're gone...They're all gone!"

Mei felt himself come to his senses. Here was something he could deal with. "Who are gone? Speak, man!"

"The white people. They even took their bottled air with them. A lot of the equipment in the storage room has been taken and they've left!"

If the white men had indeed gone with the Tibetans, there might be some truth to what the merchant was saying. Ignoring both the merchant and his former agent he turned and entered the schoolhouse, calling for his staff sergeant. Both Jangbu and Loanche followed hard on his heels.

"Prepare a high altitude patrol immediately," he instructed his assistant. "Take the soldiers in the best physical condition. Take only light weapons but be prepared for armed resistance. You're to overtake a party of fugitives. A Tibetan with his family, accompanied by a group of white people. I want them back, if possible alive, but if they won't surrender, kill them all except the Tibetan carpenter. He's to be brought back alive. Understand?"

The man saluted. "Yes, Colonel."

As the sergeant turned to leave the room, Mei shouted after him. "Proceed at forced march speed. They have approximately five hours head start."

"Don't worry, Colonel. We'll find them."

After the sergeant's departure Colonel Mei turned to Jangbu and Loanche. "You two are going to stay here with me. After all, you're responsible for this search. If it turns out to be nothing...well..."

The keening wail of the merchant's protest rang in Mei's ears long after he entered the schoolhouse.

Chapter 41

Zero Time - The Nineteenth Day
Afternoon

FROM A distance, the Cho-Oyu peak had appeared formidable to Ludec. As the days passed and they came nearer, it looked even more so. They had to cross steep, sharp ridges, between which lay thousands of years of accumulated snow. The terrain highlighted man's insignificant and brief existence. Gigantic rifts bridged over with fresh snow cracked the surface of the glacier, creating invisible traps for the intruders. Andrew had ordered them to rope together—the thin umbilical line offering some hope of rescue should one of them fall.

The total effort of the group was concentrated on their final objective, that particular cliff with the overhanging snow crest as pointed out by Ngta.

"See that snow wall under the overhanging cliff? That is where we must go," the carpenter repeated at each rest stop as though fearing that he himself might not live to reach the spot.

They were all extremely tired, and the thin air was another factor that worked against them. Sleeping in less than optimum conditions, coupled with minimal food, had taken its toll. Still they maintained that stubborn stamina needed for survival. Ludec felt severe pain in his head with every step he took. By sheer willpower he forced his limbs to obey him, each step an effort. Every move was made on command. He remembered now the tales of an uncle who had been an underground fighter for the Czech resistance in the Carpathian Mountains.

Starving, and with only one pack animal to carry their remaining heavy machine gun, the unit of men moved on. Even when the horse died, the men picked up the gun and continued. "*Man can endure far more than any beast,*" he heard his uncle's voice ringing from a great distance. "*Man knows what the beast cannot—the aim of his efforts.*"

Naga had given up trying to force the yak to continue climbing. Shortly after crossing the snow line they left the animal behind, along with a good portion of the food.

By mid-afternoon shortness of breath forced the Westerners to start using the oxygen. Filling their lungs with oxygen gave them not only relief from breathing problems, but also, more importantly, it gave them a psychological lift.

They were rapidly approaching their destination when a wall of rock blocked their path. Ngta sheltered his eyes from the blinding light as he searched for a break in the wall. As he waited, Ludec looked back to mark the path of the dark cloud. *We're caught between the gates of heaven and hell.*

He was snapped from his musings by the whine of a ricocheting bullet. Below, on the surface of the glacier, he could make out little specks moving in their direction.

"Soldiers!" screamed the girl and her mother with one voice. They both turned as though to run but the carpenter restrained them.

"You fools!" he yelled. "You know that to run here is equal to death? You will have the children running in panic over the edge!" He turned to Ludec and grabbed his arm. "Along this wall somewhere is an opening. It may be covered with snow, or even ice, but it is here somewhere, I am sure of it."

They continued to climb, guided by the sure-footed Tibetan. He moved fast, but his movements were deliberate. Bullets flew about them with greater frequency, thudding into ice and snow and ringing off the rock face. Suddenly a new sound underlined the determination of the Chinese.

Ludec clawed at his oxygen mask and moved it aside. "They're insane," he said in desperation, looking at the tons of overhanging snow. "Those are rockets. Can't they see the snow wall hanging over our heads?"

Andrew nodded, then replied. "Of course they do." His voice was muffled but Ludec could still hear the contempt in his words. "It's part of their plan. I think they know they can't catch us, so they're trying to stop us any way they can." He tore off his oxygen mask and let it hang from the canister.

A tremendous explosion split the air.

Several yards to the right of Ludec the carpenter's wife collapsed and the younger children disappeared along with a portion of the narrow trail. Naga screamed in horror, transfixed by the sight of the children as they disappeared into the depths. Still screaming she ran to her mother and tried to get her to her feet.

With Andrew's help Ngta and his daughter managed to drag the injured woman into the shelter of a dark recess. The remaining survivors crowded into the shallow cave-like cleft.

The spirit of the remaining family members was broken by the deaths. Naga cradled her mother in her arms as she rocked back and forth sobbing. Ngta stood at her feet his arms hanging limply at his sides. Ludec turned away from the sad scene to allow what remained of the family a bit of privacy.

It was then that he spotted the greenish translucence in the snow wall. It was an odd phenomenon that reminded him of the glass blocks popular several years earlier for building walls. Light could pass through the blocks but it was impossible to observe what was on the other side. He ran a hand over the wall. It was snow that had partially solidified into ice.

"Andrew," he called over his shoulder. "Look at this. Have you ever seen anything like it before?"

Ngta joined the men as they stared at the wall. He too ran his hand over the surface and then said, "Here we are my friends. This is the entrance. But we will have to dig through this wall to get to the other side."

"That we should be able to do," said Andrew grimly. "But the bigger problem is the Chinese. They're not going to give up on us just because we've dropped out of sight. Anyone have any suggestions?"

Ludec shook his head. "We've managed to lead them straight to the gates of Shangri-La, and I can assure you they have no intention of sharing it with us."

The Tibetan returned to his wife and daughter. "You go on," he said in an even, flat tone as he took his wife in his arms. It was obvious that the woman would not survive much longer. "But you must dig fast. Take Naga with you. I will stay here with my wife."

"No! Father..." the girl gulped through her sobs.

Ngta raised his hand to stop the flow of her words. "I will stay with your mother. She has been a good wife to me but now our lives have come to an end. You are with child. There may be a future for you." His decision was final and the girl nodded.

Ludec pressed his back against the narrow entrance to the cave and peered around the corner. It was obvious the Chinese were gaining ground on the small party, and bullets continued to smack into the snow around the opening. "There must be a way to stop them. If not, they'll kill not only us, but the entire Yeti colony as well. They have no—"

"Stop philosophizing and start digging!" Andrew yelled. He unburdened himself of the air canister and his pack and began to attack the wall with a slim ice axe.

Rudi dug through his pack for his gun and took up a position at the opening of their shelter. "I'll take sentry duty. At least I can secure our backs while you're digging the tunnel."

The small group attacked the snow-wall with a determination bred of fury and desperation. The Tibetan sat immobile, his wife now dead in his arms. For him, the struggle was over.

A shot slammed into the ice wall over Ludec's head. He glanced over his shoulder and watched Rudi line up the three oxygen canisters across the mouth of the cave opening. Grim faced, Rudi took up a position to the side of the canisters and braced his gun against the snow wall. The thought crossed Ludec's mind that a direct hit on any of the canisters would cause it to explode, like a miniature bomb.

Like three mad badgers they continued their onslaught against the ice wall with anything they had at hand. Axes, feet, hands and climbing sticks became weapons directed at the obstacle to freedom. Finally a small hole appeared in the wall and Ludec felt a gush of mild air caress his face. But before he could cry out in triumphant joy, an enormous explosion blew out the candle of his consciousness.

Chapter 42

Zero Time - The Twentieth Day

LUDEC floated, light as a feather. He felt no pain, no weight, no anxiety, and no despair. Time ran backwards.

HE WAS IN Moravia, sitting in the living room where the lazy cat lay beside the fireplace. His niece, Marica, was busy decorating the Christmas tree with her mother.

"Why do you refuse to get married?" scolded her mother. It was an old theme, one she returned to time and time again. She was getting old and it was clear to Ludec she was painfully eager to have grandchildren. "Soon you'll be qualified as a spinster. Nobody who's interested in marriage is good enough for you."

"Mother, that's none of your business," replied Marica. Her tone fell just short of sounding nonchalant.

He knew Marica enjoyed breaking with convention. She'd had several affairs and had not cared that the family was scandalized.

Desiring to stay out of the conversation, he sat in silence. Since Marica's rebellion was concerned only with sexual liberation, she wasn't in danger. It was so much wiser to let her express her frustration in this form of rebellion than to channel it against a social order rigidly enforced by the government.

Lujza, Ludec's sister, was not easily deterred from the theme of matrimony.

"As a single person you'll never qualify for a suite. Living alone is far more expensive than it is for two. You'll never be able to afford a car, you know. Living expenses will swallow up your income."

Marica abandoned her attempt at decorating the tree and turned to her mother. "You want me to sell myself to someone for financial advantages? For material gain! I know another word for that, Mother, and it isn't wife." Her temper cooled somewhat with her outburst and she continued speaking in a more controlled fashion. "I don't want to bring a child into this world. Your horizon is limited to the narrow streets of Prague. You can't see the powder keg that Europe has become. We've no guarantee that the world isn't going to be blown to pieces one day."

Lujza appeared stunned at the fury of her daughter's attack and searched for a safer direction in which to turn the discussion. "If everyone had refused to bring children into this world because of uncertainty, mankind would be extinct by now, Marica. Your grandfather died of typhoid in a Russian prison camp after the World War but my mother managed to bring us up. And we managed somehow, even after your father's death."

"Stop it, Mother. Just stop it. We're supposed to be talking the same language. I'm not saying that individual hardship should be a reason for remaining childless, but the prospect of total destruction is another story."

Lujza looked at Ludec in despair, hoping for some support. "Why in heaven's name do you just sit there, Ludec? Have you nothing to say? As the only surviving male you're supposed to be the head of the family."

"No he isn't," her daughter shot back. "We all have equal rights now. The times when girls were in an inferior position just because they were girls are long gone. No, Mother, there's no male superiority anymore."

"Male superiority, as you call it, is based on biblical principals young lady!"

"Oh, it's the Bible now is it? That's nothing but a nice collection of fairy tales!"

"You, Marica, are afraid of the wrath of the atom," said her mother solemnly. "I am afraid of the wrath of God."

A blast of cold air blew away the image of home. Ludec was peering into his friend's refrigerator. Professor Thomas Schuller was also an internationally recognized scientist. His field of genetics interested Ludec, who also had a good grasp on the laws of inheritance.

"As you know," Schuller was saying, "under refrigeration all metabolism either slows down or comes to a stand still. At this stage it's much easier to observe the changes in the cell caused by nuclear radiation."

"What dose of radiation are you using in your experiment?"

"About the same as what a person would absorb if he were four or five kilometers from the center of an atomic explosion. Higher doses are impracticable since eighty-five percent of those closer to the center would be incinerated immediately."

"And what was the result? Were there any surprises?"

"No, not really. All the findings support the theory that the more primitive the cells the more radiation they can absorb. More complex and developed cells are affected by smaller doses."

"That sounds fair enough to me."

"Fair? Why do you say that, my friend?"

"Because the creatures that are most likely to produce atomic explosions, namely human beings, are going to be affected by it the most. That's fair."

"That's logical, but whether it's fair or not I leave to the moralists."

"Thomas, you're a man whose interest is in the parts. You examine the particles, the components and their governing laws closely. I'm an anthropologist whose aim is to reconstruct reality out of the scattered parts that have been hidden for ages. Morality is a value known only to man. In that sense I feel that it is fair that man take most of the punishment for his actions."

"Ludec, I would never dare argue with you about values. That's an area I want to stay away from."

"But you have no choice. Every man has a value system whether he likes it or not. Only the animal is blessed with the happy innocence that man once knew in Paradise. We're all fallen angels now so we must choose and bear the responsibility of our choice."

"Now that is unfair!" countered his friend, throwing his hands into the air. "Why am I, a man who never had anything to do with aggression, or chauvinistic nationalism, or racism, or any other form of ideology for that matter, condemned to live under the shadow of an atomic war? Do you call that fair?"

"Yes, I do. Look around you. We, and I mean 'we' collectively, are using more fuel, food, electricity, wood, and other resources than is our generation's fair share. Our struggle and rivalry that seeks more is the primary source of conflict. We, therefore, have to share the collective responsibility."

"Are you implying that I must share the responsibility for someone else's greed?"

"Individually you may not be responsible, but collectively you are. If we all changed individually, we would also change collectively, but that's just as unlikely to happen as our cells changing individually for the sake of our body as a whole."

Just as he finished that sentence he became aware of how white the pebbles were on the promenade. A Lutheran minister was walking on his left, his hands clasped behind his back. In the distance he could *see the needle sharp towers of the cathedral. Cologne was a beautiful city.*

"The song of a bird is so heartwarming. No matter how long the winter lasts, our feathered companions herald the promise of spring. And then at the first cool breeze, they instinctively sense that the time for departure is near."

They strolled along the promenade, heads bared to the sunshine.

"And the direction of their flight is instinctively guided by biological radar," Ludec added. He kicked at the occasional pebble for the pleasure of watching it roll along and then disappear into the mass on the walkway.

With a nod that acknowledged Ludec's input, the minister continued. "We human beings also have this built-in radar. You, Professor, used it when you fled to the west. You felt that a wider horizon and freedom of movement would give you a better future than that offered by the restrictive life here."

"But freedom has a price, Minister. Only a society where freedom is balanced with responsibility can survive, and that balance must be maintained voluntarily."

"Mmm-hmm," the Minister agreed, once again nodding. "Collective freedom versus individual freedom. We were saturated with the subject during my seminary years. You, as a young professor, uphold your end of that responsibility if, by example, you influence as many young people's lives as possible. They will then be your spiritual successors."

"Maybe, but in many areas the influence has to begin at a much earlier stage than the university level. Imprints, as they're labeled in scientific jargon, are indestructible. By the time a student reaches university age, the example set by a teacher is effective only if the teacher is compelling enough. If not, he probably does more harm than good."

"I agree. The hunger for values in youth is so strong that the preaching of a hollow, but compelling religion, can recruit a lot of disciples. When disillusionment finally comes, and it will, it leaves behind the charred souls of idealists who have turned into cynics."

Ludec didn't know when or where an air force general joined them, but he became aware of his presence when he addressed them in a voice heavy with sarcasm.

"Hysterical warnings, like those of your minister's here, are serving our enemies' best interest. When our youth become convinced that our democratic way of life is corrupt, and not worth defending,

they will fall into the enemies' lap like rotten fruit. Only strong nations are destined to survive."

"Forgive me, General," Ludec broke in to what promised to be a diatribe, "but I've come to realize that strong nations are here to dictate, and weak nations only to obey. As Czechs that's the lesson of history we've had to learn."

"Essentially you're right professor," agreed the General. "The Darwinian principle is based on strength. Nature respects only strength!"

"Your concept of strength is misleading," interrupted the minister. "You equate strength with physical force. The cunning of the salamander or the chameleon represents an advantage in the battle for survival not associated with force. Intelligence and moral steadfastness are just as much tools for survival as muscle and claws. Today's spiritual strength is also an asset for survival."

Now he was back in the drawing room of the family apartment in Bratislava and Marica continued her argument by completing the minister's thought.

"...and that spiritual strength, which is not necessarily based on religion, can be acquired only through education. That's why I want to be a teacher and not a mother. As a mother I could influence only one or two children, but as a teacher I can leave my mark on hundreds. If all the teachers in a country cooperate with the information..."

"Therefore, Mr. Kabela," the FBI agent said to Ludec who was suddenly back at his first briefing after his defection, "you must understand why we need to gather information from all the sources we can. The cooperation of all those who defect to us is an important source of our intelligence. So, please cooperate. There's no need for any feelings of guilt."

Ludec was disgusted that he was expected to answer questions concerning the political convictions of those who a few days ago had opened up to him in confidence. The disgust was not because the convictions were anti-western, but rather because he considered the conversations to have been confidential.

"Do not believe that pig!" someone shouted.

Ludec looked up and saw a dark-skinned man brandishing a hand grenade. "I am a member of the Puerto Rican Liberation Army. The worst type of traitor is the type that betrays his or her own people. We must fight to the end!"

"Even if the end means the total destruction of the planet, you fool?" asked Marica with a hysterical note in her voice.

Another distraught female voice continued,

"Don't listen to terrorists—any terrorists. I lost my husband in a terrorist attack. He was the most gentle of men."

"To hell with your sympathy. We want our land."

With these words the Puerto Rican threw the hand grenade. There was no explosion, only a rumbling sound as the grenade broke into pieces.

Slowly the rumbling sound drew Ludec to another world.

For a brief moment he clung to the sad expression on Marica's face as she said "Nobody listens to Cassandras," and then he returned to reality.

AS LUDEC regained consciousness he realized he was laying on the floor of a cave surrounded by debris. From deeper in the dark recesses came a rumbling, murmuring sound of geothermal origin, which accounted for the warmth of the soil beneath his body. As his eyes grew accustomed to the dim light, he became aware of human-like creatures squatting around him, watching him closely. They were gigantic. A surge of adrenalin wiped the confusion from his mind—he had discovered the Yeti!

Cautiously, he forced his battered body into a seated position and searched for signs of the others. He found none. Heartsick, he realized that the blast had thrown him through the snow wall, but had either thrown the others outward, or had buried them beneath the rubble of the collapsing cave. The opening was now sealed beneath tons of rock. The valley was safe once again from an invasion of men but he was alone with the Yeti.

Turning his attention to the beasts, he examined them from his subservient position on the floor. They didn't appear to be aggressive. In the dim light of the cave their hairy bodies showed only a slight difference between males and females and Ludec thought that difference was indicated mostly in their size. That designation, however, might prove to be misleading he thought, since the size difference could also be accounted for by the fact that older juveniles could be among the group. Some were easily identified as females for they held hairy infants close to sagging breasts. A gray sky backlit the cave entrance and the creatures huddling near the entry stood out as huge black silhouettes.

How large was the group? He began to count them but lost his train of thought when the grunting began. They seemed to be conversing but the sounds they made were incomprehensible to him.

Some high-pitched squeals came from a few more excitable creatures. An extremely powerful male standing next to him watched silently with piercing, dark eyes.

He had solved the mystery, yet the solution was meaningless now. Or was it? Quickly he searched his pockets for the camera lens. To his great satisfaction he found it there, undamaged. An indescribable peace engulfed him, as his exhausted body demanded dreamless sleep.

Chapter 43

Zero Time - Six Weeks Later

IT WAS difficult to measure time. For a while he marked the days by scratching lines with a rock on a stone wall, but it occurred to him that he had no idea how long he had been either asleep or semi-conscious. In the end he gave up on marking the wall. What did it matter? He would rely on his instinct. His sense of time told him that he had been in the Yeti valley for about a month. That one month separated him from his past by light years.

He realized he would have to adjust to the Yeti way of life. The tyranny of need conquered his repulsion, and soon he was able to eat the small mammals and rodents that were the Yetis' main source of nutrition. He also became accustomed to urinating and defecating in front of the creatures without shame. It had not been too difficult to do so, for the Yeti paid no attention to such natural functions. Their only habitual hygienic action was burying their excrement. Ludec imitated them in all respects.

His only departure from their ways was an occasional bath in a warm creek when his skin began to feel too crawly. The Yeti used water only for drinking and at first seemed greatly amazed by Ludec's habit. They soon became used to his odd behavior, although none chose to follow his example. They had their own habits.

They groomed and scratched each other while carrying on what he assumed was a conversation of soft grunts. Sometimes the big male would scratch Ludec's back, too, and he submitted to that sign of friendliness with some fear. He could find no reason for the fear, other than the sheer size of the creature, as the Yeti had now accepted him as a member of the tribe. They ate and copulated in front of him as instinct dictated.

Ludec was surprised at how fast he was able to adapt to their primitive way of life, which, a few months ago, would have been totally unacceptable to him.

The one thing he missed most was the absence of another human voice. After several weeks he resorted to talking to himself for the comfort of the sound.

"I suppose when I start answering myself then I'll know I am in big trouble." His guffaw at this huge understatement caused several nearby creatures to cock their heads, as though trying to decipher what the strange sound was.

"If I teach you to use fire, can I also teach you how to speak? But of course! You do know how to speak. It's presumptuous of me to think you can't speak just because I don't understand your language." A small youngster ran up to him and hooted loudly before running away in mock terror.

He sensed that his acceptance by the Yeti was due to the great attention the dominant male paid him. He was obviously the leader, for the others never challenged him and he was offered food first. Ludec's actions seemed to fascinate the large male, who showed signs of far more intelligence than the rest of the group.

As the weeks passed his clothes, damaged in the explosion, began to fall apart. This forced him to take an action he had theretofore avoided. Reluctantly he returned to the scene of the blast and began to dig, using only his bare hands. Some of the ice had melted in the warmer environment, but the debris also included rocks. It was slow going, but after several days he found first one, then another body.

The first corpse was that of the Tibetan woman. Her clothes were in excellent condition. He also managed to salvage a pair of the carpenter's mittens and Andrew's leather jacket. He buried his face in the leather, hoping to detect the lingering scent of his friend.

"Oh, Andrew. You came so very, very close. What whim of fate decreed that I should make it and not you?"

Evidence of the others came to light over the next few days; only of Rudi was there no trace. From this he concluded that either he had been completely blown to pieces, or the explosive force of the blast had taken the route of least resistance, sucking Rudi out of the small cave and over the precipice.

Throughout the days of the search the huge male dogged his every move. He watched as Ludec exchanged his worn-out climbing boots for Tibetan woman's soft wrap-around type of moccasin. Then to Ludec's surprise, the Yeti tried to get his big feet into the boots he had cast off. "Now here is a marvelous achievement. So, my new friend, you are not only bold and curious, you are also intelligent. But don't be in too much of a rush to stuff those feet into a pair of shoes. You have much more important things to learn." The creature's curiosity and willingness to try new things was an encouraging sign for his plan to introduce the control of fire.

The most important step in that direction was to make the Yeti understand the advantages of fire. The occasion presented itself one day when the leader gave him a raw mass of meat that had been part of a mountain goat. He accepted the meat, but instead of biting into it, he gathered some dry branches, some dry grass and a few of the discarded bones of previous feasts. All the while he watched the Yetis' reaction, especially that of his big friend.

"Gather around, one and all. Something wonderful is about to happen." He clapped his hands to get their attention.

Sensing something unusual was indeed going to happen, they drifted over. The dominant male moved in very close. Ludec brought out the lens with such an air of importance that its significance became obvious not only to the leader but also to the less intelligent members of the clan.

Raising his hands and face to the sky he cried. "You see Rudi, Andrew, Brock, and Nicole! I did it! I did it. Can you see?

"And you, my rapt audience, I give you a great gift. I, the new Prometheus, will now give you, the new man, fire! But it comes with a solemn charge. Use it wisely. More wisely than those that came before you."

With great care he focused the sun's rays on the dry leaves. The assembled audience emitted sounds of excitement when they saw the concentrated light beam, but when the rays of the sun started to coax a meandering pillar of smoke from the grass, their excitement quickly became mingled with fear. When the first flames appeared that fear became uncontrollable.

As one the Yeti, including the leader, retreated, grunting and howling in terror. Ludec was prepared for it. Quickly he lifted a piece of ragged blanket and covered the flames. Soon the fire was reduced to smoke. The spectators' relief was audible.

Ludec repeated the performance again, with the same results. The Yeti seemed to be familiar with the phenomenon of fire, but it was associated with danger and disaster. He was working against a deep-seated fear. Perhaps some long ago volcanic activity.

"No need for fear. You are safe. You are safe. Come, come and see," he soothed as he beckoned them back.

After demonstrating the production and extinction of fire at least six or seven times, he saw a change in the attitude of some of the creatures. When the flames erupted they moved a bit but with no signs of the panic they had during the previous occasions. Some of the younger ones even advanced, grunting and posturing, as though challenging the flames. Obviously they were waiting for Ludec to deal with the danger.

The last time he produced the fire Ludec did not cover the flames. Instead he took the meat and held it over the flames with a damp stick. Here was a new surprise for the Yeti, but since Ludec remained squatted in front of those dangerous flames, they too stayed near although ready to flee at any moment if the fire got out of hand. It did not. Soon an appetizing aroma filled the air. When Ludec thought the meat was roasted he took a bite.

"Oh, so good." He smacked in lips loudly in a great display that was only partly feigned. The cooked meat was like ambrosia after the raw food he had eaten. "Can I interest you in a bite?"

He tore off a piece and extended the tidbit to the chief. "Take it, go ahead," he encouraged the suspicious male. He hesitated at first, but then took the warm morsel. He rotated it in front of his eyes then sniffed it and flicked at it with his tongue before taking a tentative bite.

From the look on the leader's face it was obvious that he found the cooked meat appealing. Then he gave a sound of definite joy. It took much less persuasion to make the others accept the roasted meat, and soon young and old were anxious to have a taste.

The male offered a second chunk of meat to Ludec and indicated he'd like it roasted. Fire had made its first conquest. His moment of triumph was overshadowed by the realization that he had no one with whom to share his feelings of exhilaration.

The next day, and the next, Ludec practiced his magic. In a short time it became a daily event. *If they survive the radiation I have indeed become the new Prometheus. If Zeus is kind, I will have ensured the future of a creature with free will.*

Chapter 44

Zero Time - The Second Month

HE WAS now caught in the stream of time, a swift stream that rushed forward, carrying his life towards a welcome end. His skin was like parchment; his thin hair was a tangled dirty mane. He was in constant pain and had lost most of the teeth from his softened gums. He no longer had an appetite and was somewhat nauseated by the primitive food, although cooked and offered to him by the leader. He now passed his days in the most protected corner of the cave on a heap of dried shrubs and hides.

The approach of death did not alarm him. It was as though he had already died under the avalanche with his friends, and the present was just an unrealistic, but satisfying extension.

His feeling of satisfaction came from watching the rapid progress of the Yeti now that they had fire. At the entrance of the cave, the female population constantly maintained a fire. The lens, the mystical symbol of superior power was held in reverence. Only the leader was allowed to touch it. When not in use, it was kept in a little niche in the cave wall, jealously guarded by the chief.

It was astonishing to watch how their brain reacted to the infinite possibilities opened up by fire. Cooking meat was the least of it. The new invention had inspired cooperation in the tribe. Now the women were organized in groups, one to keep the fire alive, another to gather dry wood and shrubs and another to heat up the stones that they carried away to heat the corners of the cave where the geothermal heat did not penetrate.

The males had become more interested in hunting mountain goats and didn't rely so much on rodents and small animals, which had formerly been their food staple. Big chunks of meat were now digestible. They experimented in coordinating their activities to make a more successful hunt.

Ludec, with his fading strength, submitted to his fate with a feeling of great accomplishment. On the whole he felt satisfied. From his pallet he murmured, "All has restarted. The process is under way. I have fulfilled my purpose."

A dreadful howl burst from the leader's broad chest and drew Ludec from his semi-conscious state. It was a new cry that he had not heard from the beasts before. With horror, his wavering consciousness registered the sound of hate in the cry. Through his weakened eyes he watched as a nightmare unfolded.

A young male, one whom Ludec had recognized as the rival of the chief, had grabbed the lens and was about to flee the cave. It was clear from the way he held the lens close to his chest that he was trying to transmit its magical force into his own body. He proved to be no match for the more powerful chief.

With a swift movement, the dominant male grabbed a large bone that smoldered in the fire and pushed it into the rebel's face. His thrust directed the weapon directly at the thief's eyes. The young male shrieked in agony as the bone found its mark. Not satisfied with disabling his challenger, the chief seized the lens from his rival's hands, then, using the burning bone, he showered a succession of furious blows on the victim, rendering him a bloody heap on the cave floor.

Ludec, mustering his failing strength, tried to intervene, but in his rage the hairy giant ignored the restraining hand of his benefactor. With a single sweep of his arm he smashed Ludec against the wall of the cave.

Blackness crowded out the murder scene. With his failing breath, he murmured, "Forgive me, great Zeus, only now do I realize that fire is power, power means competition, and competition means war. Forgive me."

The new Prometheus began his descent into the Underworld, where the waters of the Lethe washed out the torment of awareness.

Epilogue

Zero Time – Ninety Thousand Years Later

THE SKYLINE of the city is that of a lofty volcano. Large skyscrapers stand on the perimeter, while the buildings in the inner city are not as high. The community center is in the middle of the inner plateau. Nobody knows why, but this city structure is traditional and no questions are ever asked about its origins. The school building is a circular structure.

Three teenagers exit the school and gather on the sidewalk. Their fresh complexions range from light brown to deep chocolate, but they show little awareness of the difference.

"The conceit of our teachers is disgusting," one mutters as he bangs his chest with a sturdy fist.

"It's not only the teachers," another huffs. "Most of the grown-ups are the same."

"They certainly consider us morons, and themselves all-knowing superiors. Why does the teacher use those stupid legends as arguments to try to prove his point?"

"We can't be so sure that he's wrong," the third tries to caution the other two. His remark is only fuel for their anger.

"You've always been a teacher's pet. Do you believe there were times in the distant past when men could fly?"

"And I bet you believe that other ridiculous theory the teacher uses," the other comes to his friend's aid, "the theory that early man was even capable of going into space. What a load of rubbish. We've only now managed to put the first man-made object into orbit."

"Well..." Embarrassed, the boy scuffs a wide foot along the edge of the sidewalk. "There's reason to believe that our ancestors did know how to release the energy in matter."

"What a stupid supposition!" a challenger hoots. "Our science has just started to experiment with the enormous energy locked inside matter. If it could be harvested, it would solve all of our energy needs. Now if that legendary ancestor of ours had mastered the use of that energy, by now he would be Lord of the Universe! So where is he, wise guy?"

"I don't know. Maybe something went wrong. I read a book about the oceans that cover the Northern Hemisphere. Deep-sea divers have found buildings and other things on the ocean floor that aren't natural formations. They say the oceans weren't always there."

"Look at him. He reads all kinds of garbage. I bet you even agree with our teacher's assumption that behind all legends there is a trace of reality."

"Why not? Some of the greatest discoveries were made on that assumption. Some old ruins were excavated because the explorer had enough tenacity to stick to his guns."

"You're nuts, that's what you are! Maybe they were just lucky. I bet you even believe that absurd legend that claims we learned the use of fire from a kind of God. Now that's just plain stupid."

The one who stood alone gives up. Seeing his hesitation, the other two laugh. There is a trace of a grunt, the sound of the ancient Yeti language, in the laughter.

The End

Alexander (Sandor) Domokos

Alexander (Sandor) Domokos was born in Szabadaka, Yugoslavia in 1921. The family fled to Hungary as refugees that same year.

The only child of an upper-middle class family, as a young man he attended military college then transferred to the Gendarmery after being commissioned. After the onset of World War Two he was called to front line duty. During the siege of Buda in February, 1945, Mr. Domokos was captured and held as a prisoner of war in Russia for six years, then endured a further four years under deportation and police surveillance in Hungary. He fled Hungary in 1956 and, with the assistance of the United Nations, settled in Winnipeg.

Mr. Domokos is a versatile author of short stories, plays, novels, essays and poems, as well as an accomplished sculptor. He currently has five books in publication in his native Hungary and two electronically published novels. His autobiography, *The Price of Freedom,* has won a Clara Award and an EPPIE Award. His works have been part of several Anthologies of Canadian-Hungarian authors and have been published in the Purdue University Calumet fine arts annual "Skylark," The Douglas College Review, Lethbridge Magazine and Canadian Fiction Magazine.

He retired from the University of Manitoba in 1986, and lives with his wife and daughter in Winnipeg, Manitoba.

Rita Y. Toews

Rita Y. Toews is a Canadian writer who took up the challenge to write at the age of 50.

She has assisted with the writing of three novels, *The Price of Freedom, Shades of Gray and Prometheus. The Price of Freedom* has won a Clara Award and an EPPIE Award.

Rita has been published in numerous magazines, including "Western People," "Mysterical-E," the Knights of Columbus magazine "Columbia" and "Green Prints."

Rita is currently working on a mystery novel set in her hometown of Winnipeg, Manitoba, with Hungarian author, Alex Domokos.

Reviews are listed on our website at:
www.domokos.com/Promreviews.html